MISHAP MARRIAGE

Helen Dickson

Published in Great Britain 2014
by Mills & Boon, an imprint of Harlequin (UK)
Eton House, 18-24 Paradise Road, Richmond, S

ROM
Pbk

© 2014 Helen Dickson

ISBN: 978 0 263 90945 6

Printed and bound in Spain
by Blackprint CPI, Barcelona

Helen Dickson was born and lives in South Yorkshire, with her retired farm manager husband. Having moved out of the busy farmhouse where she raised their two sons, she has more time to indulge in her favourite pastimes. She enjoys being outdoors, travelling, reading and music. An incurable romantic, she writes for pleasure. It was a love of history that drove her to writing historical fiction.

Previous novels by Helen Dickson:

THE DEFIANT DEBUTANTE
ROGUE'S WIDOW, GENTLEMAN'S WIFE
TRAITOR OR TEMPTRESS
WICKED PLEASURES
  (part of *Christmas By Candlelight*)
A SCOUNDREL OF CONSEQUENCE
FORBIDDEN LORD
SCANDALOUS SECRET, DEFIANT BRIDE
FROM GOVERNESS TO SOCIETY BRIDE
MISTRESS BELOW DECK
THE BRIDE WORE SCANDAL
DESTITUTE ON HIS DOORSTEP
SEDUCING MISS LOCKWOOD
MARRYING MISS MONKTON
DIAMONDS, DECEPTION AND THE DEBUTANTE
BEAUTY IN BREECHES
MISS CAMERON'S FALL FROM GRACE
THE HOUSEMAID'S SCANDALOUS SECRET*
WHEN MARRYING A DUKE…
THE DEVIL CLAIMS A WIFE
THE MASTER OF STONEGRAVE HALL

*Castonbury Park Regency mini-series

And in Mills & Boon® Historical *Undone!* eBooks:

ONE RECKLESS NIGHT

Did you know that some of these novels are also available as eBooks? Visit www.millsandboon.co.uk

Chapter One

1800

There were few on the tiny island of Santamaria who did not raise their heads to the dull boom of the signal gun announcing the arrival of a vessel approaching its shores. The ship came out of the clouds, her sun-bleached sails gleaming white in the brightness of the day. The sound of the gun stirred the sailors and islanders out of their lethargy in the smoky whitewashed taverns and brothels of the small town to come to the quay-side and watch as the immense merchant brig, studded with thirty-two cannon, was guided into the arms of the verdant cove to her goal.

The number of curious onlookers increased as the ship sailed closer and waited as the sails were dropped and the vessel coasted to an easy berth at the pier in the deep harbour. Above the noise of the gulls cavorting overhead, the quartermaster could be heard barking orders to the men on deck as they played out ropes as thick as a sailor's biceps and the gangplank thudded into place between ship and shore. The crowd of onlookers were quiet, and all focused on the captain, who was the first man to step ashore.

'Dear Lord!' John Singleton, the trusty first mate, remarked, squinting his eyes against the sun as they swept the crowd. 'The reception committee is impressive, I'll say that for Santamaria. After weeks of ship's biscuit and salt meat, my stomach craves roast beef and obliging young beauties.' He doffed his hat and grinned at a delicious creature at the forefront of the crowd, with caramel skin and a veil of smooth black hair that hung to her waist.

The captain sent his first mate, who had the reputation of an incorrigible seducer of women, a wry, assessing glance. 'In that order, I trust, John.'

'In that order,' John affirmed, the wench's provocative smile having turned his blood to honey.

The third man was dressed in black frock coat, grey wig and black shoes, which were quite old, and his grey stockings sagged. His black breeches were wrinkled and shiny with age, as was the frock coat. The man, known as the Reverend Cornelius Clay, looked like a huge, disgruntled bear that had just come out of hibernation. He noted where Singleton's eyes lingered and scowled. 'Have a care, Singleton. That one has a married look about her.'

'Aye, that she does. Ah well, it'll make the chase all the merrier.'

'We'll take a look around,' the captain said. 'Santamaria belongs to a man named McKenzie. He's a man of some education and the son of Colin McKenzie—the man who made Santamaria what it is today. Apparently there's a cruel streak to young McKenzie and his harsh treatment to anyone who dares threaten his authority has made him a man to be feared. His word is law on the island, but he has the reputation of being refined and accommodating. It will be interesting finding out just how accommodating he can be for the time we have to spend on the island.'

The reverend looked with interest at the ale houses. 'Thanks to that damned hurricane we have repairs to make—and stores to replenish. How long before we can be under way, Captain?'

'Not too long. At a stretch we can afford two weeks, no more. We're already delayed. We've got a schedule to keep.'

* * *

Just past the hour of siesta, Shona McKenzie rode her horse over the hills and through the cane fields, happy to be away from the house and Carmelita, her sharp-tongued sister-in-law, and she intended to stay away until it was time to prepare for the evening meal. Several sailing ships swayed at anchor in the cove and closer to shore small boats skimmed the water. Antony, her brother, often invited officers from the visiting ships to dine at the house, giving Shona and Carmelita the opportunity to gown themselves appropriately and entertain them.

Looking ahead of her, from that vantage she had a good view of the shimmering island. All around her was a luminous expanse of jewel-blue sea, shading to lighter green as it met the reefs on the Atlantic side. Wave after wave of rich green vegetation mounted to tree-covered heights, which stood out against a sky of cloudless blue. The land ran down over two promontories that, like embracing arms, almost encircled the island's one deep beach of almost-white sand stretching for about half a mile.

Leaving the cool of the high ground behind, she headed towards the large cluster of buildings that hugged the cove. Having seen the brig sail into the harbour, she was as curious as everyone else to know who it belonged to.

Ships plying the islands of the Caribbean, trading fancy silks, baubles and other produce of Europe for the raw material of the islands, put in at Santamaria on a regular basis, but a merchant vessel of this size had not been seen in months, so its appearance was a remarkable event indeed. Not until she was close enough to read its name emblazoned on its prow—*Ocean Pearl*—did she realise who it belonged to.

It was the shipping magnate, Captain Zachariah Fitzgerald, the merchant-adventurer worth thousands, one of the most powerful men in the Caribbean. It was said he owned large tracts of land in Virginia and had a fleet of ships, with warehouses in every port. There were rumours that he had shadowed dealings with pirates and others, that he had been a pirate himself, but, fact or legend, Shona had no way of knowing.

Caribbean society had been abuzz with stories of the enigmatic adventurer ever since he first docked in the colonies some years ago, but despite his reputation as a hard-headed businessman, the local society complained that he rarely made appearances at their genteel gatherings. The second son of an earl, on the eventual demise of his father, his elder brother, Viscount Fitzgerald, would inherit the vast estate in Kent, so Zachariah Fitzgerald had left England to wrest his fortune from the untamed sea.

The quayside was an animated scene, alive in a chaos of sight and smell and the laughter of ragged children. Idle sailors loafed about and drab strumpets quite boldly hawked their wares for a shilling or two. Shona shuddered at the squalid scene. At least she had an existence above this. What did it matter that she was neither loved nor wanted as a member of her own family.

As was always the case when Shona McKenzie rode into town—or entered any company—she became the focus of everyone's scrutiny, male or female. Accustomed to it, she ignored it, and after a moment everyone turned away. Shona was able to observe the activity on board the ship above the heads of the crowd. A man appeared, followed by two others, and by his manner Shona assumed him to be the captain of the vessel.

Tall and full of flare, from his large hat with a quivering white plume in its brim, long scarlet frock coat and roll-top boots, with the easy, sprightly stride of a seasoned seaman and his companions in his wake, Captain Zachariah Fitzgerald strode along the pier to the shore, his long coat flaring about his legs.

The crowd melted a pathway before him as he marched through them. From her place in his path, Shona had a clear, uninterrupted view of him. Her heart fluttered and an indescribable awe—or fascination—came over her as she stared at him. His face under the wide brim of his hat was strong, striking, disciplined and exceptionally attractive. In fact, he was the most handsome man she had ever seen. His expression was cool and guarded. Perhaps thirty years old, he was tall and powerfully built, exuding virility and a casual, lazy confidence. The dusty white trousers he wore that disappeared into his boots seemed to emphasise the muscular length of his legs.

Shona knew full well that a lady ought not to be seen in the town alone, knowing also what was expected of her as the sister of the most prominent man on Santamaria, but today she disregarded the conventions of society and the rules laid down by her brother and her father before him in favour of her own wishes. She hardly noticed anyone else. Her attention was entirely focused on the man walking in her direction.

As he walked he surveyed the onlookers with a lazy interest, his attention suddenly arrested by the stunning young woman astride a white horse. His gaze settled heavily on hers. Shona forgot her manners and stared back. Something communicated from their eye contact and the chaos about them seemed to recede in the strangeness of that first moment of meeting.

The message conveyed from one to the other had a warmth, a recognition, and Shona was conscious of a feeling of disorientation, which surely was not usual in the circumstances.

A slow smile of lazy interest curved Zack's lips. She was a vision he struggled to grasp as reality and it was all too much for his first mate, who was smitten. Behind Zack, Singleton flushed with pleasure and stumbled in a parody of a bow. Amused by Singleton's weakness and telling him to pull himself together, then coming to a halt directly in front of her, Zack surveyed the young woman's fine figure, lovely heart-shaped face and big green eyes. Her long golden mane tumbled down her back, exotic, full of life, and Zack noted how the fair tendrils twined over her delicate shoulders. She wore a light blue dress, which covered her horse's flanks and revealed more of her shapely sun-kissed shins than was considered decent—not that Zack was complaining. He never had been able to resist a beautiful woman.

For her part, Shona was beginning to feel a little foolish, knowing full well that riding astride, dishevelled and showing a fair amount of bare leg, was hardly how young ladies in England behaved. But then, the four years she had spent in one of the best schools in that country, which had dealt with tedious niceties and courtly manners, had bored her to distraction.

And here she was being stared at by a thoroughly magnetic and compelling man, a man whose direct and confident gaze made her heart beat faster—though that, in small part, might have been due to the hot tropical sun having addlcd hcr wits.

As she held his stare, unable to look away, she marvelled at what fascinating eyes he had. They were lively and a piercing silver-grey—eyes that seemed to trap and hold the light. She detected a sparkle of amusement in their depths as he perused her, not quite successful in masking his roguish astonishment.

'My dear young lady.' Stepping back, he swept her a negligent bow—which Shona thought a tad mocking. 'Zachariah Fitzgerald at your service.'

One brow arched, his eyes remained on hers. 'May I say you are a sight for sore eyes.'

Shona stared at him. His voice was deep and throaty, like thick honey, a seductive voice that made her think of bodies and those erotic engravings in the French books she and her friends had loved to pore over at school, and all kinds of highly improper things. It seemed to caress each word as it came out, she thought, and there couldn't be many women who could resist a voice like that. If it met her mood, she could enchant and charm any man, but instinct told her this man was not one of the insincere young *roués* seeking to extend their reputation at her expense.

'I am?' she said warily, tilting her head. 'And how is that, pray?'

Zack frowned. Her self-possessed response surprised him. Her face was perfect, so stirringly beautiful and young. Her eyes were clear green, brilliant against the thick fringe of jet-black lashes. They stared back at him, open, yet as unfathomable as any sea he had ever gazed into. To find herself confronted by a group of ogling sailors who hadn't laid eyes on a woman in weeks—and certainly not one who looked like she did, which brought home to him the starvation of his own long and forced celibacy—he'd expected her to blush and lower her gaze at the very least. She did neither.

'By the Holy Blood, young lady,' he murmured, moving close to her horse and giving it a friendly stroke, his hand suggestively brushing the bare flesh of her leg, 'you're a handsome enough piece to tempt any man. I'm mighty flattered to have made your acquaintance. Had I known Santamaria was inhabited by such beauty, I would have made a point of sailing into its harbour sooner. I would like to invite you on board my ship so that we might become better acquainted.'

Amused in spite of herself by his high spirits, yet disliking his attempt at flirtation, Shona raised a full, arching brow at him. 'That would be highly improper, I'm afraid, Captain. I also think that you should remove your hand from my leg before I find yet another use for my whip.'

The roguish glint that must surely be what had charmed half the females in the Caribbean made his eyes dance with silver lights. 'I am disappointed that you are so unaccommodating. What can I do to make myself more agreeable to you?'

'I told you. Take your hand off my leg.'

Reluctantly he slid his hand away, but he continued to stand there, appraising her.

Shona's flesh burned from his hand's caress. Suddenly, his direct masculine assurance disconcerted her. She was vividly conscious that all eyes were upon her and of his close proximity to her. She felt the mad, unfamiliar rush of blood singing through her veins, which she had never experienced before, not even with Henry Bellamy, the handsome son of a duke back in England whom the whole school had been in love with. Instantly she felt resentful towards this captain. He had made too much of an impact on her and she was afraid that, if he looked at her much longer, he would read her thoughts with those brilliant, clever eyes of his.

'You have a smooth tongue, Captain, but save your breath. I am not so easily won over. Santamaria belongs to my brother, Antony McKenzie,' she said, giving him a haughty look. 'I am Shona McKenzie, his sister.'

'Then I am pleased to make your acquaintance, Miss McKenzie.' Zack was familiar with the name and this young lady's fabled beauty. Her father had been known in most circles. In that of young men, Shona McKenzie was often the topic of heated debate. She was the ice maiden, unattainable, the heartbreak of many a youth and the professed goal of many more.

He was unfazed by her identity and his smile widened across his beautifully chiselled lips, his white teeth flashing against the bronze skin. His dark eyes gleamed with devilish amusement as he contemplated her as if seeing her anew. Shona could only mark the resemblance he bore to a swarthy pirate.

'Your island is most beautiful and extremely fertile, I hear. Your brother seems to have made the most of it.'

'The credit is down to my father—Colin McKenzie. He made it what it is today. When he died my brother carried on his work.'

As if on cue, at that moment the crowd separated to make way for an elegant barouche occupied by Antony McKenzie and his Spanish wife, Carmelita, her face shaded by a dainty parasol. Carmelita was the only daughter of a wealthy Spanish merchant. Spoilt and overindulged all her life, while Shona was in Europe Carmelita had met Antony when she had visited Santamaria with her father. After a brief courtship they had married—which Shona considered was Antony's undoing.

The carriage halted beside Shona's horse and

Antony, wearing a conspicuously well-cut coat and immaculate linen, climbed out, his expression as he glanced at his sister one of severe disapproval. Finding her on the quay without a chaperon, with tarts and men who had rolled out of the taverns, her hair and dress in disarray, he considered her behaviour unworthy of her birth and breeding and with total disregard to his position on the island.

At thirty-five years of age, Antony was tall and fair-haired, distinguished-looking rather than handsome. He was shrewd and calculating and unbending, a man who would do anything to wrest what he wanted from life. In four months' time Carmelita was to be delivered of their first child—a boy, Antony hoped, to carry on after him.

Antony's stern features were set in an unsmiling expression of severe disapproval as he regarded his sister.

'Might I suggest you go home, Shona. It is unbecoming for you to be in town unattended.'

Meeting his exacting eyes, Shona felt her face burn at his public censure. 'I was about to do just that, Antony, until I saw the ship. I simply had to be here when it docked.'

Antony turned from her and faced the newcomers, his disagreeable scowl quickly replaced by a smile of welcome.

With sharp, cold eyes Carmelita surveyed Shona's flushed face, taking in her unbound hair and dishevelled appearance at a glance. She leaned over the side of the carriage to speak to her with her eyes narrowed like a cobra about to strike. 'Just look at you, Shona—you are inappropriately dressed and your hair is all over the place,' she said with quiet reproach, her voice heavily accented with Spanish and her eyes as dark and cold as a Scottish loch.

'That's because I've been riding, Carmelita.'

'Madam,' Captain Fitzgerald said coolly, 'the young lady is not deserving of criticism. She is by far the comeliest maid I've ever had the pleasure of meeting.'

Carmelita opened her mouth to utter a harsh rejoinder, but seeing the hard look in the captain's clear eyes, she closed it quickly. She smiled a bitter smile, tempted to inform him that Shona McKenzie was the Devil's own child, but thought better of it. Shielding her face from him with her parasol, she continued scolding her sister-in-law. 'You're growing quite impossible, Shona!'

'I'll try to be better,' she promised in a matter-of-fact way.

Carmelita's cold stare stabbed Shona with deadly equality. 'Are you mocking me?'

'Of course not, Carmelita. I wouldn't dream of it.' The best way to deal with her sister-in-law, Shona found, was to ignore her when possible and treat her with cool civility when not.

Carmelita gave her one of her dangerous looks. 'You seem to have a predilection for mixing with seamen and the common folk. It is not how a well-brought-up young lady should behave—how your brother wants you to behave. You are nothing but a liability. How dare you embarrass Antony in this manner. You really should know better.'

Shona tossed her head, her chin thrust out with defiance. Certainly she owed it to Antony to treat Carmelita with polite deference, but filial duty only went so far. Antony said his wife was headstrong, which, Shona thought with asperity, was too nice a word for the woman. Grasping, shrewish and on occasion even vicious was how she would best describe her.

'Please leave it, Carmelita,' she replied with chilling politeness, returning her attention to Antony, who was introducing himself to Captain Fitzgerald. 'I hardly need you to remind me how to behave. I answer to my brother, not you.'

'Don't be impertinent, Shona. You'll get your-self talked about.'

'Is that so? No more than I am already.'

Carmelita seemed to recognise her limit, for she said nothing else on the matter, but the toss of her head with haughty Latin arrogance told Shona that it was not forgotten.

Antony introduced himself and his wife to Captain Fitzgerald and welcomed him to the is-land. The captain did likewise, presenting his first mate and the reverend—slightly stressing the word *reverend*.

'Aye,' Singleton explained with a merry twin-kle in his eye as the reverend sidled off to the nearest waterfront tavern. 'The captain considers it necessary to have the crew's spiritual needs taken care of on a long sea voyage.'

Antony nodded, not having noticed that there was anything untoward in the first mate's words. 'And does he keep their spirits up?'

'Oh, aye—when there's enough faith aboard.' *And enough rum aboard,* he almost added, but thought better of it.

'When I was informed of your ship entering the cove,' Antony said, addressing himself to the captain, 'I thought I would come and greet you myself. I have heard of you, of course. Your name is well known throughout this part of the world.'

The captain raised an eyebrow. 'Indeed? You flatter me, Mr McKenzie.'

'Your ship looks as if it has taken a battering.'

'A few days out of Virginia a storm blew—by ill luck the severity of which was quite exceptional in those latitudes for this time of year. We were blown over two hundred miles off course and lost the convoy we were with. The damage you see is minor and can soon be mended.'

'Where are you bound?'

'Martinique—and then London. Rather than delay for another month or even two, awaiting the gathering of another convoy, I will take my chance on being able to catch up with the one I was parted from.'

'Very wise,' Antony agreed. A merchant vessel as large as the *Ocean Pearl,* weighted down with cargo, would be lucky not to attract the attention of privateers of all nations. Not by the score, but by the hundred they swarmed in both European and American waters. In consequence, except for especially fast ships, a system of convoys had long been organised.

'We've put in for a general replenishing— to take on supplies and fresh water—and then we'll be on our way. I am indebted to you, Mr McKenzie.'

'You are most welcome, Captain Fitzgerald, and still more so if you will accept my invitation to dine with us tonight—while you give me news of what is happening in the colonies. I do have newspapers delivered from Virginia and London—old news is better than no news at all—but there's nothing like hearing it first-hand. I shall send a carriage for you and Mr Singleton later.'

Captain Fitzgerald turned away, his gaze again falling on Shona still in the same spot. His eyes narrowed, half-shaded by his lids as he coolly stared at her. Something nagged at the back of his mind, telling him that she represented the worst kind of danger to a freedom-loving bachelor, warning him that there might be repercussions should he accept McKenzie's offer to dine at his house, but she was so damned lovely he ignored the warnings.

Shona straightened her back, her chin moving slightly upwards in an effort to break the spell he wove about her with his eyes.

He threw her a salute, bowing ever so slightly, then headed off towards the town.

Without waiting for Antony to order her to be

gone, Shona turned her horse about and headed in the direction of the house.

The evening was gentle and warm, with a soft quality known only on the Caribbean islands. Overlooking the bay stood Melrose Hill, the McKenzie residence, the long curved drive lined with huge coconut palms. Melrose Hill was a two-storeyed, sprawling white mansion. It was sheltered by the rise of the land and by the trees surrounding the house. Swathed in native flowers, a wide veranda ran the whole of its length, riotous colours of frangipani and bougainvillaea clambering in profusion over trellising. The sun had already gone down behind the hills so the house was now in shadow, but a number of large lanterns had been lit along the veranda.

On entering a wide, airy hall, Zack was impressed. A long, crystal chandelier was suspended from the lofty ceiling, the shimmering prisms setting the hall aglow with myriad dancing rainbows.

The house smelled of resin and wax polish. Through the door into the dining room, finishing touches were being put to the large oval table by two dark-skinned footmen under the supervision of a mulatto major-domo.

The French-style furniture and gilt-framed paintings were elegant, and throughout the house rich Aubusson carpets, rugs from Persia, marble from Italy, lacquers, jade and ivory from the Orient and other treasures from around the world embellished the rooms. Floor-to-ceiling French doors opened on to the flower-laden terrace and the gardens at the back of the house, and filmy curtains wafted in the night breeze, cooling the stately dining room. In fact, the setting was as civilised and luxurious as any Zack had seen in the houses of noblemen who owned great estates in the sugar islands.

As she prepared for the evening, Shona sat at her dressing table as Morag painstakingly arranged her hair in an elegant *coiffure*. For some reason she wanted to look her best—could it be the extra guest Antony had invited? Her corset had been clinched tightly over the shift, pushing her bosom upwards until its fullness strained against the gossamer fabric. Everything was in readiness and equally blended portions of tension and excitement grew in Shona's breast as she donned her gown.

The satin bodice was covered with lace, the scallops of which overlapped on to the bosom.

The low sleeves were full, ending just below the elbow, and were attached to the bodice beneath the arms to leave the shoulders bare. A wide deep blue sash was tied about the waist and trailed in streamers down the back of the ivory lace and satin skirt.

'You look grand,' Morag remarked as Shona studied her reflection with a critical eye in the long mirror, giving a slight adjustment to the neckline. Miss Shona's was that rare beauty which was almost never at a loss. If she could find herself a husband, she would stir his heart to burgeoning pride, if not open lust. 'A sight for sore eyes you are.'

Shona smiled at the maid who seemed to have been with her family for ever. Born in Glasgow, Morag had come to the island as a young girl as maid to her mother. On her death she had transferred her devotion to Shona, and since returning to the island she attended to all her personal needs. 'It's funny you should say that, Morag. Someone else said the same thing to me earlier.'

'Well now! Anyone I know?' she asked, fluffing up the lace on the sleeves.

Shona lowered her head to hide the sudden flush that sprang to her cheeks, which the mere thought of Captain Fitzgerald brought about.

Knowing she would be in his presence in just a short while caused her pulse to leap and a thrill to rush through her. Morag's question summoned her back from her lovely reverie.

'I'm afraid not—but we are expecting him to dine with us tonight. He's the captain of the *Ocean Pearl*—Captain Fitzgerald.'

'And is he handsome, this Captain Fitzgerald?' Morag thought that he must be if the glow in Shona's eyes was anything to go by.

Raising her head, Shona flashed a brilliant smile. 'Oh, yes, Morag, he is very handsome. Very handsome indeed.'

'Then it's a good thing you're looking your best.'

Morag was fastening the tiny buttons down the back of her dress and they failed to note Carmelita's entry into the chamber.

'Are you finished, Shona?' Carmelita enquired sharply, concealing her envy as she glanced at her sister-in-law in her stunning gown.

Morag quickly fastened the last button, then stepped away and quietly disappeared from the room.

Carmelita was petite and sultry, with long black hair and deep brown eyes. Ever since Shona had returned from England to find Carmelita married to her brother, they had never got along. When they had first set eyes on each other, Carmelita's back had stiffened, her shoulders arched and her hair had seemed to bristle. Like a cat, Shona had thought. A suspicious, angry, threatened cat.

'You made quite a spectacle of yourself this afternoon,' Carmelita reproached, giving her an accusing stare. 'Really, Shona, your want of conduct is embarrassing your brother dreadfully. He was most displeased.'

Shona stiffened at the rebuke, but she said nothing, knowing any argument would only make Carmelita more determined to be unpleasant. Carmelita resented the responsibility Shona represented and Shona resented her tyranny, but open hostility between them was rare. Much easier to endure, ignore and count the days until she could return to England.

'If you insist on behaving so disgracefully,' Carmelita continued, 'I'm afraid Antony will have to ask you to refrain from visiting the town. Were you not his sister, you would *never* be welcomed in polite circles. It's high time you put your mind to settling down instead of gallivanting about the island at every opportunity.'

The months of schooling her features into a

polite mask around her sister-in-law were forgotten—the anger Shona was feeling showed clearly on her face. When she didn't speak, Carmelita took a step towards her, her sultry eyes narrowing. 'We cannot both run this house,' she said, her voice holding a quiet, dangerous threat and resentment. 'You must see that. I intend to be mistress in every sense and I will not let you stand in my way.'

While Carmelita was obviously willing to fight, Shona did not intend to make it easy for her. 'You may rest assured, Carmelita, that I have no intention of marrying just to please you. Melrose Hill is still my home.'

'Perhaps it is, but *I* am mistress here now. If you dispute that, then you know what you can do.' She turned to the door. 'The house is large, but not large enough for both of us. So don't push me, you wretched girl, or you'll find yourself without a home in short order. Much good your stubborn pride will do you then!' In a swirl of light blue chenille, she marched across the room. 'Here is Antony now.' She gave her husband an exasperated look. '*You* speak to your sister, Antony. She won't listen to me. The sooner she is wed with a husband and children to occupy her time, the better we shall all be.'

On that note Carmelita went out, determined to have her way in this. She meant what she had said. There was no room for two mistresses at Melrose Hill and, while ever the servants deferred to Shona, Melrose Hill would never truly be hers.

When Carmelita had left, Shona finally allowed her defences to crumble. Her shoulders slumped.

It was at times like this that she missed her father. The suddenness of his death had stunned her—even now she found it difficult to accept. He had seemed so full of life for a man of sixty-five. Yet however much she wished otherwise, he was dead and buried, for ever gone from her sight and company. She had sailed from England to Santamaria only to find on arrival that Melrose Hill was no long her home, her one sure haven. Having loved the time she had spent in England and missing the friends she had made, she was desperate to return and would do almost anything to bring that about. But she was honest enough to admit that her life on Santamaria could not be described as unpleasant.

Alone with her brother, she looked at him and decided to ask him directly. She looked into his eyes and said, 'Are you as desperate as

Carmelita would have me believe for me to marry, Antony?'

He hesitated. Shona saw regret in his face for a moment. Then his expression hardened and he said firmly, 'Yes, yes, I am.'

His words nipped Shona's pride and she stared at him, feeling tears prick the backs of her eyes. He held her look. She saw that he meant what he said and she was deeply disappointed.

Sensitive to his wife's condition and determined not to have her upset in any way at this time, heedless of Shona's distress, Antony said, 'It must be settled soon. You know what Carmelita is like. There will never be peace between the two of you, so I am of the opinion that it would be best if you were to leave. Ever since you came home you've been living a sense of reproach to Carmelita. Listen, Shona—'

'No, *you* listen, Antony. You wouldn't be talking about reproach if you hadn't wed Carmelita. She called me a liability earlier. So I deduce that means she wants rid of me.'

'Rid?'

'Yes, rid of me, disable me, pack me off somewhere, anywhere, as long as it's far away from Santamaria.'

Antony's face became flushed with anger.

'Stop this, Shona. There is very little I can do about your disagreements, is there?'

'Except take her side.'

'I don't want to take her side. I don't need to. I have a high regard for both of you. But Carmelita does have a point. Damn it all, Shona! Are you set to be a spinster who rejects every man that comes courting? You have the looks and the wealth to choose among the finest families in Europe and the Caribbean, but you dally like some dreamy-eyed girl waiting for her knight on a white charger who will never arrive.'

'I am not a silly girl, Antony, and nor am I fanciful,' she retorted sharply.

'Be that as it may, the subject can no longer be put off indefinitely. John Filligrew is an un-attached, wealthy young man who is smitten by you. He won't wait for ever.'

Shona gave him a look of disdain. 'Me and John Filligrew? He is personable, I grant you, and having known him all my life I am very fond of him and we are good friends, but I really would rather die a spinster than attach myself to him for the rest of my life. Let me go back to England, Antony. I would like that and I would be far enough away from Carmelita not to trouble her.'

'Absolutely not! Father stipulated that you were not to return to England until you have a husband to take care of you. I intend to abide by that. I know what you are like, don't forget. Away from my protection and without a husband to guide you, I shudder to think what you might get up to.'

'Thank you for the vote of confidence,' Shona said drily. 'But I will not give up on this. I *will* go back—even if I have to wait until I am of an age when you no longer have any control over me. You could write to Aunt Augusta or Thomas and ask them to keep an eye on me,' she suggested bravely. Thomas was their cousin, at twenty-nine he was six years younger than Antony and a minister of the church. As a boy and then a youth, he had visited them on Santamaria on two occasions with his parents, Aunt Augusta and Uncle James. Shona adored him and missed him terribly. She had so enjoyed seeing him when she had been in England.

'As far as I am aware Thomas is having time off from his work, and, since coming out of mourning, Aunt Augusta is too involved with her social life to take charge of an unattached female. He gave her a hard look. 'Before you go down to meet our guests, I must ask you not to anger Carmelita further.'

That look made Shona shrink. 'I'll try not to.'

Antony nodded as if there was no doubt about it.

Having had her fill of reprimands for one day, Shona brushed by him and proceeded along the long corridor to the stairs. She needed to reflect on her options before she took any further steps to resolve her future. One thing was certain. Things could not go on as they were. She had no illusions about her brother. Her greatest fear was that if she failed to find a husband of her own choosing to marry, he would find one for her.

Yes, she longed to return to London. She wanted to dance in ballrooms where gliding, beautifully attired couples waltzed about the floor. She wanted to shop in all the fashionable shops, to promenade in Hyde Park and have handsome bucks falling over each other when they turned to look at her. But, she reasoned with the hard-headed practicality that usually balanced out her dreamy side, she could not have any of that without a husband by her side.

Being in England with time spent in London had given her a taste for an independent life, but like most young women she was a romantic at heart and had long since accepted that she would have to marry eventually. She had no objection to this. Indeed, she welcomed it, providing she could marry a man of her choosing—a man she loved.

Chapter Two

Most wary of the extra guest, Shona made her way down the wide curved staircase with as much stealth as she could manage. At the entrance to the great hall, she halted, suddenly aware of the pounding of her heart. When her eyes focused on Captain Fitzgerald standing near the door, staring out on to the veranda, everyone else faded into the background. An odd, melting sensation came over her, a sensation that somehow made breathing difficult and made her heart race as if she had been running.

Attired in elegant evening dress and buckled shoes, with his height and sun-bronzed complexion, Captain Fitzgerald appeared highly conspicuous, standing there breathing vigour and vitality. He affected the company like a fresh wind. His curling hair, drawn back and held at his nape by a thin black ribbon, gleamed a deep burnished brown above a pristine white neck-cloth and ivory brocade waistcoat, while his powerful shoulders filled his olive-green coat to perfection.

A rugged pirate in gentleman's garb, Shona reflected.

His chiselled profile was touched by the warm light of the candles and the growing ache in her breast attested to the degree of his handsome-ness. She observed him reach up to tug at his neckcloth as if it might be too confining and wondered if he might feel ill at ease in his formal attire. But he must have known how to conduct himself at social functions—or at least how to charm the female sex. As soon as they began to gather, he was surrounded by half a dozen ladies who were eager to make his acquaintance. Captain Fitzgerald greeted them all with an ease that could not fail to set their feminine hearts aflutter.

In an attempt to regain her serenity, Shona let out a slow steadying breath and entered the hall, bringing him about to face her as the heels of her blue slippers tapped against the oak floor. He wore an expression of utter boredom on his face, an expression that altered dramatically when his eyes met hers.

Excusing himself, a smile tugging at his lips, he moved across the hall with the grace and speed of a jungle cat. She could not take her eyes off the way he moved—his easy grace, the suppleness of his limbs and the oiled machinery of his body.

The way he carried himself made it easy to believe that all that was said about him was true. Power, danger and bold vitality emanated from every line of his towering physique. When he halted before her he bowed with a grand sweeping gesture. Then Shona met his eyes. At that precise moment she became convinced that there were no eyes in all the world that shone brighter than those which now smiled at her. As she stared into those translucent depths, it was easy for her to imagine a woman being swept away by admiration for him without a single word being uttered.

What the devil was the matter with her? What was it about this man that he should have this effect on her, she who had held in scorn all the gentlemen who had done their best to ingratiate themselves into her good graces?

Mentally casting off the spell he unwittingly cast, she scolded herself for acting as addled as a dazzled schoolgirl.

Smiling, he looked down at her while his eyes plumbed the depths of her beauty.

'Welcome to Melrose Hill, Captain Fitzgerald. I hope you enjoy your evening.'

'I am enjoying it already,' he murmured for her ears alone.

Shona was used to the admiration of young men and though she liked it well enough—what girl wouldn't?—Captain Fitzgerald was the first to stir her senses and capture her imagination. 'What is your opinion of Santamaria? Is it to your liking?'

'Very much so—from what I've seen of it.'

'And how does it compare with Virginia?'

'Very well. I do have some basic common knowledge of the colonies, but I'm from England, not Virginia, as you seem to have surmised.'

'Yes,' she said. 'I know, but you do have connections there.'

Zack folded his hands behind his back and appeared to look thoughtful. 'I do have a shipyard and warehouses in Virginia—indeed, it would be difficult for me to conduct my business without them, but my home is in London.'

'And after Martinique, London is your next port of call?'

He nodded, having suddenly become fascinated with the advantage his height gave him. Standing a full head above Miss McKenzie, he had a very pleasurable view of what lay beneath her demure bodice whenever he chanced to look that way, which was rather often. The high swell of her creamy breasts was a tantalising sight for any man and Zack most certainly enjoyed this treat.

While he was speaking, other guests began to arrive—thirty all told, some officers of the vessels in the harbour and merchants who had made their home on Santamaria. One of the footmen announced dinner.

Carmelita turned to her husband. 'We'd better go in. Captain Fitzgerald, will you bring my sister-in-law along?' she urged as she took her husband's arm and moved towards the dining room.

'It will be my pleasure.' Zack gallantly presented his arm to the golden-haired beauty, at the same time catching her hand and pulling it through the crook of his elbow, not giving her a chance to deny him.

Shona yielded rather than make a scene, but behind Carmelita's back she glared up at him and hissed, 'You are quite outrageous, Captain.'

'Has anyone told you,' he breathed, blithely

ignoring her irritation as he bent his head near hers, 'how beautiful you are?'

She lifted her slim nose to a higher elevation, avoiding any reply. Still, she could not quell the stirring of pleasure his words aroused. At the table, he held her chair as she slipped into it. Thoughtfully she watched him walk around the table to take a place opposite her. That was the moment she realised a solution to her future course of action might be staring her in the face, a solution that would enable her to cast off the shackles her brother had placed on her that bound her to the island. But could she bolster the courage to carry out the wild plan she had suddenly conceived?

With eyes cold and unrevealing, Carmelita observed the pair and the looks that passed between them. She was suddenly inspired. Of course, Captain Fitzgerald was the critical factor. If the two of them should form an attachment, the combination could be explosive. Her mind was racing. An expression of calculating scheming was pasted on her face and she was feeling a little breathless with excitement.

The dinner was a relaxed affair and extremely civilised, and at times seemed quite unreal. On the one hand the table appointments were elegant, the English fare Zack favoured excellent, the service of the footmen everything that could be desired—and the delectable Miss Shona McKenzie in his line of vision at all times.

Reflecting on her proposal that she intended to put to Captain Fitzgerald, Shona glanced at him. The decision made, her resolution seemed a fantasy, dreamed up by someone other than herself. But he was magnificent, exuding the kind of strength and masculinity that women found extremely appealing. He didn't appear to be entirely at ease with Antony. His manner towards him was civil, but stiff, wary. However, he looked as if he had perfected the knack of making a woman feel special—he was bending close to Mrs Frobisher seated next to him, listening attentively and watching the elderly lady with those silver-grey eyes. The same eyes that had looked her over appreciatively earlier.

The conversation was about what was happening in Europe and America, combined with the usual supper-party trivia, leisurely and varied and well marked with ship owners' diverse opinions on the interests of their profession, while the ladies discussed the various society magazines and fripperies that had been brought on one of the vessels. Shona was in animated conversation with the foppish John Filligrew, a boyishly handsome youth of twenty-one with high colour in his smooth cheeks and a tangle of coppery curls. But every now and then she could feel a pair of silver-grey eyes watching her with a predatory stare and her head would turn and her eyes would meet those of Captain Fitzgerald.

'In a domain such as this,' Antony said in answer to a question Captain Fitzgerald had just posed about the early days of the island, 'my father established a great many duties. Bringing slaves and bondsmen to the island, he supervised the clearing of the forests, sold the timber and prepared the fields for cultivation. We now have cane fields and our own vessels to transport the commodities. There is also the rearing and tending of our livestock. In fact, we grow and rear everything we require.'

'I understand you have land and properties in Virginia. With all there is to do on the island, do you find the time to go there?' Zack enquired, his long fingers toying with the stem of his wine glass.

'I go whenever I am able, but on the whole, like my father before me, I employ reliable people to oversee and run things for me.'

'Antony,' Carmelita said from the opposite end of the table to her husband. 'I'm sure Captain Fitzgerald doesn't want to hear all this.' She smiled at Zack. 'I'm sorry, Captain Fitzgerald. My husband does tend to talk business all the time.'

'Please don't apologise. I'm overwhelmed by the abundance on such a small island.' His eyes flicked to Shona and a slight smile curved his lips. 'In fact, I find it so appealing that I am tempted to reside here myself.'

'And you would be welcome to do so, Captain,' Antony said. 'If you can find the time before you leave, I would enjoy showing you the island.'

'Thank you. I would like to take you up on that. Are you not troubled by buccaneers, Mr McKenzie? The number of outlaws and castaways infesting the Caribbean has increased considerably of late. I marvel that you have not been driven out.'

'We should have been on several occasions had we not taken precautions against being caught off our guard.'

'Such as?'

'In several places along the shore, I have men

living who would give me warning of the approach of any hostile body.'

'And you can count on their loyalty?'

'It is not a case of counting on their loyalty, but their greed. I pay each of them a wage for doing nothing, which of course would cease if I were driven out, and any of them who brings me a timely warning knows that he will receive enough money to keep him in idleness for years. Santamaria also has its own defence. As you will have seen for yourself, the leeward side of the island is sheltered from the full force of the trade winds, so that the waves of the Caribbean lap easily on the shore—unlike the rest of the island and the high cliffs, which have no defence against the wind-driven rollers of the Atlantic. I have men stationed to defend the island at all times. It's a brave pirate who will attempt to sail his ship into the cove.'

The conversation was interrupted when a footman poured more wine. Zack looked across at the delectable Miss McKenzie still in conversation with John Filligrew, his head bent close to hers as he whispered some confidence in her ear. Zack experienced a flash of completely unfounded and unexpected emotion, a white-hot surge of jealousy unlike anything he'd ever felt for any lover he'd ever had. He wanted to rush over and pull the man away, to tell him he had no business leaning in so close, no right to get so near to her—this woman he had never met before today.

She was talkative and vivacious, with a lilting voice that was like music to his ears after six weeks at sea without female companionship. Her expression was endlessly fascinating as she smiled, frowned and wrinkled her slightly freckled nose and rolled her eyes. Looking up, she caught his eye and he had the odd feeling that she knew what he was thinking.

'Have you always lived on the island, Miss McKenzie?' he asked.

'Yes, except for the time my father sent me to England to be educated.'

Zack looked at her, musing as he stared. He was wrong in his initial assumption. Despite being raised in this place, so far from the corrupting influences of civilisation, she had been exposed to them after all.

Shona noticed how incredibly light his eyes were in the flare of the candles. It was impossible not to respond to this man as his masculine magnetism dominated the scene. A curious sharp thrill ran through her as the force between them seemed to explode wordlessly. He watched her, his eyes alert above the faintly smiling mouth, and she promptly forgot John Filligrew.

Faceless numbers of suitors whom Shona had cast away loomed upwards before her consideration. Not one of them had stirred a spark in her blood, yet Captain Fitzgerald was able to make her heart beat with a sweet wildness that stirred her very soul. All the while his gaze was upon her she grew flustered and cast about her as she swallowed a glass of wine and dabbed at her mouth with her napkin. Captain Fitzgerald's incendiary eyes scorched her over the flower arrangement.

Finally Antony slid his chair back. 'I shall look forward to hearing more about Virginia, Captain Fitzgerald. May we at least have the pleasure of your company until you leave the island?'

'Indeed you will.'

With the signal that the dinner was at an end, the ladies reconvened to the drawing room, where coffee was served, while the gentlemen remained to drink the port imported from Spain that had been Shona's father's drink of choice. In search of clearer air, her mood listless and dreamy, Shona went out on to the flower-laden terrace and walked along its length. The delicate tropical fragrances filled the warm air.

Glancing to the trees beyond the garden brought back memories of those distant days she would walk there with her father, when the trilling of birds filled the air and the soft flutter of moss dripping from the trees would brush against her face. She could even imagine the whiff of his spicy cologne and the smell of leather and horses on his clothes. However brief those recollections were, she was pierced by a longing so profound that it was all she could do not to cry out in anguish.

Now the evening was laden with the sound of chirping crickets, of blended voices drifting from the house. A languid breeze gently swayed the branches of the trees, rustling their leaves and sweeping the fragrance of sweet shrubs on to the terrace. Her mind occupied with her musings, she stared out across the shadow-mottled lawn and sighed. Suddenly a footfall sounded behind her. A dark shadow moved close to her and she was engulfed in a cloud of fragrant smoke. Her heart fluttered in her throat. 'Oh,' she uttered softly. 'I thought I was alone.'

'Your pardon, Miss McKenzie.' The deep, rich voice of Captain Fitzgerald sounded concerned.

'I did not mean to startle you. I was merely taking my pipe in the open air before I return to my ship—but be assured—to discourse with a beautiful woman on a moonlit night on a tropical isle is a pleasure beyond compare. Does the smoke bother you?'

Feeling her heartbeat quicken alarmingly, Shona was amazed by the effect his sudden presence was having on her pulse rate, but she was resolved not to let it show. She stared, trying to penetrate the dark shadows that hid his face. 'Not at all. Enjoy your pipe at your leisure. I rather like the smell of tobacco. It brings back poignant memories of my father. He used to enjoy a pipe on occasion.'

'A natural enough habit. They grow tobacco in Virginia. The Indians taught us how to smoke it.'

'So I understand.'

'If I am intruding, I will leave you.'

'No,' she said quickly, 'please—you don't have to go.'

He nodded. 'Very well. I will stay.'

'How long do you intend being on the island, Captain?'

Stepping out of the shadows, he looked at her through the wreath of smoke that curled from his pipe. 'One week at the most.' His hand cradling the bowl of his pipe came out and in a brief span the long stem swept the moonlight to encompass the rolling hills beyond the trees. 'And then I must leave all this and return to London.'

Tilting her head on one side, she met his eyes. 'You sound regretful. But you will return, will you not?'

'At some point. Would you care to talk?' he invited, propping his shoulder against the wall of the house and holding her gaze with his own.

Shona leaned against the trellising. 'About what, Captain?'

The answer was slow in coming. 'Anything.' He shrugged his broad shoulders. 'Whatever would please you. Why don't you begin by telling me something about this charming island you call home? I know that originally the Spanish claimed it for the Spanish crown and christened it Santamaria.'

'That was so. They formed a small settlement and the islanders earned a living by hunting the wild cattle and hogs that overran the island and selling the smoked meat to passing ships. But eventually they vacated the island in favour of the larger islands in the Caribbean. It became a haunt for pirates until it was seized by the British and my father acquired it from the Crown.'

'He was English?'

Shona shook her head. 'He came from Scotland. When he was a small boy his father, who was a cattle rustler, was hanged for his crimes from the great tree in Inverary. Orphaned and determined to make a better life for himself and those who came after him, he moved south. With an agile mind and being quick-witted, he soon grasped the way of money, borrowing money for ventures and succeeding where others failed. Soon those he'd borrowed from came to him— merchants and aristocrats alike.'

'That was some achievement—the actions of a man driven by his ambition.'

'Yes, he was, but he was also a man of principle and nobody's fool. From an early age he was determined to succeed.' She remembered her father telling her how he'd acquired stately properties, country estates and huge tracts of land both in Britain and in the colonies. 'His success earned him respect, but much as he yearned to be accepted into the higher ranks of society, he was rejected. He was thirty-five years old when he married my mother—the daughter of a country gentleman—and secured Santamaria from the Crown.'

'And they decided to make it their home.'

'On their first visit to the island they fell in love with it. They were so taken with it, and found that the climate suited them perfectly, that they decided to settle here. Soon, with every reasonable amenity available, and forming a cultured and charming small society of merchants on the island, my father built a house to outshine any of their friends who lived in London. Sadly, my mother didn't live long enough to enjoy it. She died of a tropical fever shortly after giving birth to me.'

'That must have been hard for you—being deprived of your mother at such a young age.'

'It was, although I was too young to remember her.'

'And you were close to your father?'

'Yes,' she said in a quiet voice. 'I adored him. When I went to England he visited me there. When he left and came back to the island he became ill. I never saw him again.'

'I'm sorry. Your life must be pretty limited on the island—your social life stilted, hidden away from the world.'

'I'm not, not really. I love the island and the

life here—but sometimes I feel like a bird in a cage unable to fly free,' she said on a note of regret. 'I loved England and the time I spent there. I made lots of friends, girls I went to school with. One day I will go back—soon, I hope. But you are right. Visitors to Santamaria are few and far between.'

'Then it's a crime, living here without connecting to the outside world.' His stare tracked her with an intensity that she could feel from the short distance that separated them. 'You should be in Virginia or London, being worshipped by wealthy young planters or noblemen and dancing till dawn.'

She stared at him in the gloom, flattered and quietly thrilled to think he thought enough about her to voice his opinion on what he thought was best for her, even though she hated the idea of leaving Santamaria for good. She was wildly encouraged all of a sudden to think that if he liked her so well, then surely he would help her. He was clearly a gentleman, no matter what the rumours said about him having dealings with pirates.

She would ask him now. Her excellent instincts told her that she could trust this man.

'What would you say,' she began slowly, 'if I asked you for a favour?'

'A favour?' His eyes narrowed in sudden wariness. 'What sort of favour, exactly?'

Her eyes held his and her confidence did not waver, though her heart was in her throat. Squaring her shoulders, she said, 'Tell me—are you married, Captain Fitzgerald?'

'No. Why do you ask?'

'Would you take me to England?'

Zack sighed heavily, knowing he could not. As lovely and womanly as she was, he knew he'd find it difficult to conduct himself with the sort of gallantry his mother might expect of him. Shona McKenzie was very much a lady and the consequences of dallying with sweet innocents ensconced on his ship could affect his life in a most permanent fashion.

'The *Ocean Pearl* is a merchant ship, Miss McKenzie. I'm sorry. There are no suitable accommodations for passengers.'

'I'm not talking about being a passenger, Captain Fitzgerald. Would—would you consider marrying me?'

'Good God' was all he said, otherwise he simply stared at her, into her hope-filled emerald eyes.

Somewhat heartened that she hadn't been refused outright, Shona went on, 'Before you give me your answer, perhaps I should mention that my father left me a substantial inheritance and—'

'Please don't go on,' he interrupted, raising a hand to stop her. 'I believe I understand. Forgive me if under the circumstances I don't know the appropriate response—perhaps I am expected to say that I am honoured—you see, it's the first time in my life that I've been proposed to. Is that why you asked me to stay, Miss McKenzie?' he asked crisply. 'To soften me so you could ask me this?'

She lowered her head at the question and nodded. 'Yes, it was.'

He cursed softly, shoving himself away from the wall. How dare she presume to know what kind of man he was, to take advantage of his feelings and his desire for her, which he had not bothered to hide. With his thumb, he tamped the coals into the bowl of his pipe. His hands were large and, though they appeared to have the strength to break anything they had a mind to, they were amazingly gentle—the slim clay pipe seemed like a fragile bird between them. Taking a leather pouch from his pocket, he shoved the pipe inside and placed it back in his pocket.

'My name is Shona,' she said, trying to drag him into a familiarity that he did not desire.

Zack took a deep breath, praying he would wake up and discover this was part of some strange dream. Too late, he knew he should never have accepted Antony McKenzie's invitation to dinner. The danger had been too great. He should have stayed away and tried to forget he had ever met the lovely young woman on the quayside. He didn't need this kind of trouble. He could have availed himself of the company of any of the women on the seafront, but, oddly, he hadn't quite felt in the mood for the full-blown temptresses he usually favoured. Somehow Shona McKenzie had wheedled her way under his skin. He should have stayed with his ship and sailed with the tide for the next island, as his instincts had warned.

'Why are you so intent on marrying me? There must be enough unattached wealthy males on the island you could marry.'

'No, not one,' she replied.

'Then do you see me as a ticket off the island? Is that it?'

Uncomfortable with both the question and

the penetrating look in his eyes, Shona averted her gaze, fixing it on the dark perimeter of the garden. Captain Fitzgerald was a stranger and she found it difficult to discuss her present circumstances with him. How could she tell him how unhappy she was at Melrose Hill, that she missed her father desperately and the house in which she had been born and raised was no longer the home she knew—and that the only way she could escape Carmelita's acid tongue was to marry and leave the island for good?

'Yes,' she admitted fiercely. 'I want to leave the island. Antony is fiendishly protective of me and will not allow me to leave unless I have someone else—a husband to take care of me.'

Zack put his hands on his lean hips and regarded her coldly. 'If your options are limited, then you will have to keep looking, Miss McKenzie. It will not be me. Absolutely not!'

Shona moved closer to him, not really knowing what she intended, but she wasn't ready to give up yet. Turning her face up to his, she licked her lower lip, a softness entering her eyes. 'I... can't persuade you to change your mind, Captain?'

He gave her a hard look, his mouth tightening as he stared at her softly heaving bosom and the tantalising mouth that was full and soft and trembling, trying to ignore the mute appeal in those large, luminescent eyes, seeking refuge in his anger. She might look fragile, but he was beginning to suspect she was as strong as steel inside.

'Devil take it, I will not be persuaded or manipulated into marriage, not even to a woman as lovely and bewitching as you, Miss McKenzie,' he said, refusing to be moved. Normally he steered clear of entanglements with females of marriageable age or any females who might place demands on him, preferring instead the more honest and uncomplicated relationships with women of lower class and of lower expectations. It was the easiest way, he had learned from experience. A brief encounter back in England with a woman who had attracted him for a short time had left him shackled by bonds that could never be broken. He was not about to repeat the mistake.

'I am a man who has made his own choices for most of my life. As much as I would like to appease my manly appetites with you, I will not, like some lapdog, blandly accept your proposal of marriage. Next time you decide to throw yourself at an experienced man of the world, tread lightly or you will not survive. I'm not termed a pleasant sort. I have a foul temper which can snap up naïve young ladies like you without a second's notice. So be warned, Miss McKenzie. Do not tempt it. When and if I decide to marry, I prefer to do the asking myself.'

'I...thought that...'

'What?' he jeered, ignoring the way the colour drained out of her soft cheeks as he continued with deliberate brutality. 'That if you let me take advantage of you—I might be swayed.'

He seemed enormous and very close. His powerful body emanated heat, matching the heat that was rising in her cheeks. 'I—I don't know.'

'Life isn't like that. I have kissed many women I have been attracted to, but that doesn't mean to say that I wanted to marry any of them.'

Shona was conscious of a sudden surge of anger, realising just how stupid and naïve she had been. 'You may be used to kissing ladies all over the place, but I do not have your experience,' she told him with simple honesty, giving Zack further insight into just how truly innocent she was.

'Nevertheless, you were misguided to think I would marry you.'

'I should tell you that my dowry is quite substantial.'

Zack's entire face instantly became hard, shuttered and aloof. He looked her over carefully, as if to judge her for her worth, and appeared dubious as his brows snapped together and a feral gleam appeared in his narrowed eyes as they locked on hers with angry disgust.

'Now you do insult me,' he said, his voice so controlled that Shona felt an icy chill sweep down her spine. 'I cannot be bought, either. I have no need of your money. I have plenty of my own. However large your dowry, Miss McKenzie, what makes you think you are worth it?'

Shona gasped, her humiliation complete. 'Now it is you who insults me,' she flared, a fresh surge of anger rising up inside her like flames licking round a dry log, furious with herself for being stupid enough to think he might help her.

'If you have so much money, then what you do should not be a problem. You've had life handed to you on a silver platter. What more could you possibly want?'

'Liberty,' she cried passionately. 'Freedom to do as I choose. Creature comforts are not all that matters to me.'

'If you imagine that marriage will give you freedom, then think again. You will find yourself bound by shackles of a different kind. But if that's what you want, then go ahead. You can live where you choose or buy yourself another husband—which shouldn't be too difficult. You have other assets to your credit besides your substantial dowry,' he ground out with suave brutality, his insolent, contemptuous gaze raking over her. 'Another ship bound for England will drop her anchor in the cove before too long with some other fool on it for you to marry.'

Captain Fitzgerald's jibe, savage and taunting, flicked over Shona like a whiplash. Stung to anger by his harsh words, hot colour flooded her cheeks and her soft lips tightened as she exerted every ounce of her control to keep her temper and her emotions in check. Stiffening her spine and lifting her small chin, she looked at him directly. Zack saw her put up a valiant fight for control—a fight she won—and she looked as regally erect as a proud young queen. Her eyes frosted over.

'I understand you perfectly, Captain Fitzgerald. You are a devil—a barbarian, a callous barbarian—and I am sorry I approached you. We will say no more on the matter. I will trouble you no further and I thank you for your time.'

When she tried to sweep past him, his strong hand spun her around. 'Barbarian? Believe me, Miss McKenzie, you have no idea how much of a barbarian I can be. You don't want to be my wife, I assure you,' he said, his voice rumbling soft above her like distant thunder.

His hold on her arm tightened. Slowly, with menacing deliberation, he backed her against the balustrade. His grip wasn't overly painful, but the casual strength exerted in his fingers startled her. His other hand rose to grasp her chin, but Shona turned her face away, eluding capture. When his hard fingers at last closed over her jaw, she gasped in alarm.

'Let go of me. You are hurting my arm. I can't fight you. You are much stronger than I.'

Zack stared down at her. He hadn't missed the flare of temper in her eyes, or the fear. He clenched his teeth in frustration. Impatiently he released his hold on her arm, his hand unintentionally brushing her breast. He was instantly aware of the contact, and so was she. He could tell by the furious blush that flooded her cheeks.

Shona tried to ignore the effect of his touch.

'I asked you to let go of me,' she uttered icily. 'Remove your hands from my person.'

It was a supremely correct response, just the kind Zack would expect from a woman of her social standing. Perhaps he could turn her reticence to his own advantage.

'I will do precisely that,' he said, deliberately running his fingers along the side of her breast, 'when I have made you realise your mistake in thinking you could manipulate me into marriage.' Releasing his hold on her chin, with grim satisfaction he saw her flinch. He bent closer, his face dark and threatening and like granite in the moonlight. 'As my wife you would be at my beck and call and I could take you any time I pleased. I would take my pleasure of you whenever I wanted. Shall I show you how I would assert my husbandly rights?'

Dimly, Shona saw his mouth slowly descending to hers. He put an arm about her waist and pulled her to him, moulding her body against his. Her legs felt weak, the back of her knees aching. As she gazed into his hard face, some lambent protective instinct cried a warning that she was getting in too deep. Panicked, she turned her face away a scant instant before his lips touched hers, her breath coming in rapid gasps as if she was running. Undaunted, Zack tipped her face back to his and lowered his mouth to hers. He assaulted her lips with a controlled expertise that left her gasping, engulfing her in a heady scent of brandy and tobacco. She was too surprised to resist and hung limp in his embrace. With no protest forthcoming he asserted pressure, his kiss growing more dedicated to strengthening her response and nearly devouring her lips in a tantalising frenzy.

His plundering, devouring kiss sent Shona spiralling off into a hot darkness where nothing mattered except his seductive, urgent mouth and knowledgeable hands. Overwhelmed by his raw, potent sexuality, she fed his hunger, her parted lips welcoming the thrusting invasion of his tongue, the sensations inside her mouth like tight buds that burst into blossom, filling her with splendour. She felt as if her whole being would melt, but her heart began to drum a faster rhythm as his fingers continued to stroke the side of her breast in a leisurely, erotic caress. From a low level of consciousness there grew a vague feeling of pleasure and, had the circumstances been different, she might have enjoyed the hard, wickedly masculine feel of his body against hers. But she reminded herself that he was doing this to abuse her, to demonstrate his power over her, to subdue her into a quivering wreck.

Trailing his warm lips over her cheek, Zack felt himself weakening in response. Devil take it, he couldn't keep his hands off her. This wasn't working. He was losing the battle for control.

Shona sensed his struggle. Through the haze in her mind, she heard him groan softly and, with an abruptness that left her swaying, he tore himself away. He stood there, staring down at her in silence as if seeing her for the first time, his look a mixture of pain and pleasure and anger. She was glad for the support of the balustrade against her back. Otherwise she might have fallen, her legs were so weak.

'Why did you do that?' she whispered. Her emotions seemed to be all over the place and a rogue tear trickled from the corner of her eye.

Zack hardly knew why himself as he looked at her standing there, teary-eyed and vulnerable. And lovely. By God, she was so lovely. He wanted her with a fierceness that stole his breath. His mouth tightened as he stared at her softly heaving bosom and the tantalising mouth that was still full and hot from his angry kisses. Lifting his hand to wipe away the tear, he drew back when she wrapped her arms around her waist, as if trying to protect herself from him. His jaw hardened, trying not to feel as if he were abusing a stray dog.

'Don't be concerned, Miss McKenzie,' he rasped, his voice low and harsh in the silence, 'that my *barbaric* display will be repeated. I won't touch you again. I have enough troubles on my plate just now without adding to them by taking a wife. I bid you goodnight.'

Striding into the house in search of his first mate, intending to leave right away, he raked his fingers through his hair in frustration. The vexing tide of anger which had consumed him began to subside. Only the ragged pulse that had leapt to life in his throat attested to his disquiet as he looked ahead with feelings of regret. Miss McKenzie's proposition pounded inside his head, combining with the torment of his own harsh rejection, and he wondered how she had managed to make him feel such a cad for refusing her.

Dear Lord, she was a magnificent creature, but heaven help the poor devil who got landed with her as a wife. He liked his women quick-tempered, spirited and with fire in their veins. It made for a satisfying and exciting relationship, but Shona McKenzie with her bullheaded stubbornness would not only need a husband as strong-willed as herself, but with the patience of a saint.

Shona stood looking out over the garden, shaken by what had just happened and the trend of her own thoughts. Nothing in all her twenty years could have prepared her for Zack Fitzgerald. His kiss had sent an explosive thrill crashing through her body. Her heart had raced with guilty pleasure. And this, heaven help her, was exactly what she had wanted from the man she chose to marry. Often she had dreamed of such a kiss, but this, her first, made those insubstantial dreams seem the shadows they were, the reality of flesh on flesh causing a delirium of delight. His lips had been warm and moist, caressing her own, pressing, probing, firm, growing more and more insistent, demanding the response she instinctively gave.

Her large green eyes swam with unaccountable tears, which she instantly dabbed away as earlier she had dabbed red wine from her lips—perhaps she had drunk too much wine. To say that she was aghast by her behaviour was an understatement. When she had fired her maiden salvo over the bow of convention and picked up

her battle flag for liberty, she had not imagined
Captain Fitzgerald's fierce reaction to her proposal. It seemed impossible to her now not only
had she proposed marriage to him, but had practically demanded that he do so.

She was still musing on what had occurred
when she realised the shadows surrounding her
were empty. Without a word or a stir of air, he
was gone. Only the lingering smell of tobacco
smoke was left to remind her that he had been
here.

She wasn't sure whether her anger and fierce
disappointment was due more to his rejection of
her proposal or because she was still left with
the dilemma of her future. But whatever it was,
it would be an evening etched in memory and
emblazoned in her heart for all time.

One thing she was certain of—Captain Zachariah Fitzgerald was the last man in the world
she would ever marry.

Carmelita had seen Shona go out on to the
terrace. When she did not return, curious as
to what was keeping her, she went to find her.
Another survey of the gentlemen taking after-
dinner drinks with Antony showed her that the
captain was also absent.

She went in the direction of the terrace, peering into the moonlit garden. Standing in the shadows, she saw Captain Fitzgerald walk along the terrace and into the house. His face was expressionless, his jaw set hard. Keeping out of sight, she saw him stride into the house and heard him ask one of the servants as to the whereabouts of Mr Singleton. A few minutes later the two of them left.

Leaving the terrace, she came face-to-face with Shona. Her sister-in-law shot Carmelita a guilty look and went to join the other ladies without a word. The look in her eyes—what was it? Anger? Hurt? Disappointment? Carmelita was unable to tell, but whatever it was it told its own story.

She closed her eyes to hide the feral glitter in their depths, her thoughts upon how to bring the two of them together and ultimately get Shona off the island for good.

Chapter Three

Leaving the house and crossing the garden, Shona took a path that led into the forest. As she entered it she passed into a new, beautiful twilight world. Trees of enormous girth reared up two hundred feet in height, but their upper boughs could not be seen because they became lost in a smother of vegetation—a tangle of creepers which looped in all directions and cascaded down like green waterfalls, while others snaked upwards like green pythons. Mosses and ferns as large as small trees sprang out of the hollows, with stems as thick as a man's arm. Many trees were loaded with fruit: green avocadoes, golden mangoes, wild apricots and limes.

The path wound downwards and, after five minutes, she emerged into an open space floored with an outcrop of rock. Water cascaded over huge boulders into a deep pool in the centre of the outcrop. On one side of this clearing a tangle of great boulders sloped up to a twenty-foot-high cliff, overlapped with verdure where the forest began again. On the other sides of the clearing trees again towered skyward and between them the dense vegetation cut out any view of the open space.

Zack arrived at the house for his meeting with Antony just as Shona left. From the open French doors he watched her walk into the woods. Moving to his side, Carmelita saw the way he watched her sister-in-law.

'Shona is very beautiful. Do you not think so, Captain?'

'I do agree.'

'And—I suspect your visit is not just to see my husband?'

Zack's eyes narrowed slightly. Leaving her question unanswered, he said, 'I am here on your husband's invitation to see the island.'

'Then since Antony has been delayed at the mill and is not expected back for another half an hour, perhaps you would like to follow Shona. There is a creek where she likes to walk. It is very pretty. I am sure you would appreciate the view. Besides, for some reason she seems out of sorts today. Perhaps some company might cheer her.'

Zack was wary of her suggestion and felt that he was being manipulated in some way, but regretting his behaviour of the previous night and feeling he had to apologise to Shona for his harsh words and unable to quell the need to see her once more, he set off after her.

Her expression the quintessence of cunning, Carmelita watched him go. *So far so good,* she thought. By the time he reached the creek, Shona would have removed her gown and would be slipping into the deep waters. Having seen the lust burning in the depths of Captain Fitzgerald's eyes whenever they had fallen on Shona over dinner the night before, she was in no doubt that he would be unable to resist her.

But showing him the bait was the easy part. Now she had to get him on the hook.

Zack followed the path Shona had taken. The most troubling thing of all was the intensity of his physical reaction to her. The lust. The rock-hard lust that turned his body into a single, painful craving to smell her scent, to touch her skin, to see her eyes soaking him up, to feel her taking him into her, looking at her face in pleasure, insanely, obscenely hiding nothing she was holding back.

This was no ordinary reaction to a woman. This shook him to the core and interfered with his thoughts, his life, tormented him, overpowered him. He didn't understand why she had such a volatile effect on him, but he understood that he wanted her—he wanted her warm and willing in his arms.

In the dining room it had not gone unmissed that her sister-in-law's sharp eyes were fixed on her the entire evening, which led him to believe that all was not as it seemed at Melrose Hill. It hadn't been difficult for Zack to put the pieces together or to understand why Shona McKenzie had proposed to him afterwards. And he could sense her distress now as she sat at the side of the creek with her arms wrapped around her drawn-up knees, staring into the depths of the pool.

Zack distinctly felt his heart move and soften, then something speared him in the centre of his chest. She was a determined, wilful young woman, there was no doubt about that, but there was something vulnerable and sweet in her, something worth pursuing, something untapped, which she had allowed no one to see.

He had been overwhelmed when he had left her the night before by the stunning realisation that this woman, if he didn't take care, could mean something to him and he didn't want it. He ought to stay away, he warned himself as he descended the path, realising Shona McKenzie spelled trouble and more trouble.

In this secluded place she had removed her dress. Her hair was wet and slicked back from her face, her petticoat clinging to her body. Her flesh shimmered in the light filtering through the treetops, making her appear as tantalising and as elusive as a woodland sprite. She was the lovely, young yet feisty, naïve young woman he had seen on the quay and he'd been unable to think of anything but her since last night. The sight of her hypnotised him and he felt the peace thread through his veins and stitch itself to his heart. Whatever the danger she posed to his sensibilities, he knew he could not walk away.

But that was a far cry from wanting to marry her. He had no wish to sacrifice his life as a freedom-loving bachelor and he already had one obligation along that line—an obligation that made it impossible to marry Shona McKenzie.

He had a daughter, a child he was unable to openly acknowledge, a child he loved fiercely.

He had never expected to feel that way about another human being. When he last left England he would never have credited how profoundly he could be affected by a pair of innocent brown eyes and a dimpled smile from a small child. Nothing had ever claimed his heart like that before. Some day soon he would have to shackle himself to the mother in order to claim his daughter.

Occupied by her own thoughts, Shona didn't hear him approach until he was directly behind her. She started and turned. Her heart gave a traitorous leap at the sight of him. Glancing up at him in alarm, she scrambling to her feet.

'Captain Fitzgerald,' she gasped, extremely uncomfortable with the dark way he was regarding her, his gaze narrowed and assessing. Her hand crept to her throat. Her state of undress embarrassed her and she was mortified that he should see her thus.

Zack met her searching gaze with an amused smile, momentarily awed by her eyes as they caught a shaft of light from the sun. For the moment, they looked similar to emerald-green crystals, but then they seemed to change colour in the shifting light. He was awed by the exquisite creaminess of her complexion and the softness of her eyes. Slim and graceful, there was an air of lightness about her, as if at any minute she was about to break into a sprightly dance. With some difficulty he dragged his mind to full attention. He knew she was upset that he should see her in a state of undress and pondered how he might soothe her.

A smile tugged at his lips. 'I'll close my eyes if it makes you feel better,' he said softly, his voice imbued with warmth and humour.

'No,' she groaned. 'It's too late now. You've already seen me.'

'Believe me, Miss McKenzie, I am no lecher...'

'Neither are you blind!'

'Nay, I am not blind,' he admitted with a chuckle, 'and I cannot deny that I am pleasured by the sight of your perfection.'

'Under different circumstances, I would thank you for the compliment. But standing before you with half my clothes missing, I find it would be inappropriate.'

'So would you mind if I stayed?'

'I don't mind at all.'

He laughed. 'But you are very serious. You don't really want me to stay. You are still cross with me.'

'If I was, I would say so. What are you doing here?'

The corner of his mouth twisted wryly in a gesture that was not quite a smile. 'I saw you leave the house. I wanted to apologise for my behaviour last night. I should have known better than to speak so harshly and to say the things I did.'

'Really? You mean to say you followed me all the way here to do that? I am surprised. No one ever comes here.'

'Your sister-in-law told me where to find you.'

'Did she?' Shona's lips twisted with scorn. 'Now, why am I not surprised? As you see, I came here to bathe. I'm quite amazed that, knowing this, Carmelita would suggest you follow me.' Although, she thought, turning from him and sitting back down on the rock, Carmelita did want rid of her. Seeing Captain Fitzgerald as a possible suitor, she would do her utmost to throw them together.

Feeling the heat of the afternoon sun, shrugging himself out of his jacket, Zack hunkered down beside her. 'I get the impression that the two of you do not get on.'

Shifting her gaze over the water to the feathered palms on the edge of the creek, she said quietly, 'I have no great love for my sister-in-law, Captain Fitzgerald. We tolerate each other only because the situation demands it. In fact, we seem to exist only to antagonise each other.' She tilted her head. 'You look worried, Captain. You needn't. It wasn't particularly flattering for me to have to plead with you to consider marrying me and now I can only regret my foolishness in doing so. I'm not fool enough to repeat what I asked you last night.'

'I suppose that's a relief. Although being proposed to by a beautiful young lady was a unique occasion for me. You have a way of knocking a man between the eyes.'

'Sometimes it means grasping opportunities even though we might be making the greatest mistake of our lives.'

'What matters is that we learn from our mistakes and not to stand about licking our wounds. You don't want to be my wife, I assure you.'

She shrugged, tossing her hair over her shoulder. It was already drying in fine wisps and floating back to caress her bare shoulders. 'Perhaps you're right.' Turning her head, she looked at him directly. 'You don't want to marry me. I do understand.'

'You do?' He studied her face. She was no

fool—her eyes were bright with an unexpected intelligence he had recognised from the first. Involuntarily, he dropped his gaze to her mouth. It was a tantalising mouth, moist and carnation-pink and made to be kissed, generous, with a lush bottom lip that begged for a man's caress.

Shona nodded and caught her breath. She felt the impact of his gaze as she realised how intently he was studying her face. Around his neck there was a silver chain—what was suspended from it was hidden in the folds of his shirt. Did he perhaps wear a crucifix? She wanted to touch him very badly, to feel under the pious necessity of finding out what it was that was hidden. He was too close, she thought suddenly. Too close and too masculine. She could feel his warmth, could feel the vital power within him. His potent virility made her feel entirely too vulnerable and more than a little afraid. But for some reason she could not explain she did not want to move.

'I would appreciate it if you would refrain from mentioning to anyone what I proposed last night. Unless you already have...'

'No,' he answered quietly. 'It remains between ourselves. I won't marry you. I can't.'

'But—you told me you are not married.'

'True,' he said, looking beyond her and squinting his eyes in the sun, 'but back in England I have a duty I am obliged to fulfil.'

'I see. As I said, I understand. We are strangers, Captain. You do not have to explain anything to me.'

Zack gritted his teeth. She was a glorious creature, lovely and demure in her clinging wet petticoat. It moulded every line of her shapely body. She was cool and virginal and stunningly arousing, yet with a mysterious allure he found hard to ignore. He could feel himself responding, a fact that only inflamed his ardour. He searched the flushed contours of her face, the thick crescent of her lashes and the fine line of her eyebrows for a long moment, then reached up to gently touch her chin. He felt it tremble slightly beneath his finger.

'Shona,' he murmured, addressing her by her Christian name for the first time, liking the feel of saying it on his lips. 'If I were free, I really think I might be tempted.'

She forced a smile at his gallantry, but couldn't manage an answer. Instead she slipped away from him into the pool. The water had an iridescent green glow. It was warm and welcoming, the gentle swell sending her petticoats swirling around her thighs. Stretching out her slender legs behind her, she glanced up at him, finding him watching her intently with a smouldering silver glow in his eyes. She swam across the pond and back again, disappearing now and then beneath the surface. After a moment she hoisted herself out of the water on to the rock beside him, dripping water. Leaning over, she wrung out her long, heavy hair before tossing it back. She stretched out her long legs beneath the wet petticoats, her feet small and perfectly shaped.

Zack continued to watch her, devouring her with his eyes, having resisted the temptation to fling off his clothes and join her. The mere sight of her abandonment had left him throbbing for her like a youth hungering for his first woman. Yet there was little he could do to control either the lust licking at his veins or the disquietingly tender feelings that were prodding at his heart. Something in his chest tightened.

'You are competent in the water,' he remarked. 'Do you often come down here?'

'Every day. I come here to swim and to cool off.'

'And, I suspect, to escape your sister-in-law.'

She laughed. 'Something like that. I look on the creek as my own special place. It's private, so I have it all to myself—although today is an exception.'

'Do you mind? It wasn't my intention to intrude. When I arrived at the house, your sister-in-law informed me your brother had been delayed. You were just disappearing into the trees and she suggested I might like to walk with you. I wanted to see you anyway—as I said, to apologise.'

Shona scrambled to her feet. 'There really was no need.'

Zack stood up and stepped towards her and as she turned to retrieve her dress, he caught her arm and turned her back to face him. 'Yes, there was.' His other hand rose and he gently took hold of her chin. 'I couldn't leave things as they were.' Releasing her chin, he dropped his arm, his fingers, just like last night, unintentionally brushing her breast. He was instantly aware of the contact. And so was she.

It was an intense moment for Shona. Her breath caught sharply in her throat. Suddenly he seemed enormous and very near. His powerful body emanated heat, matching the heat that was rising in her cheeks. She attempted to ignore the effect of his unintentional caress. 'Would you please not touch me?'

It was a supremely proper response, just the kind Zack would expect from a woman of her innocence and reserved manner. But her reticence to let him touch her and the state he was in were like a red rag to a bull. 'Had I agreed to wed you, Shona, you would have to accept my attentions.' When she did not move away he lowered his head, his face close and threatening. 'Shall I show you what you could expect?'

'I'd rather you didn't,' she said breathlessly. His suggestive tone made her uncomfortably aware of the raw sensuality emanating from his long, muscular frame outlined in the closely fitted breeches and white shirt, open at the throat. A muscle throbbed in his neck. A shudder ran through her as his gaze moved over her face, lingering on her soft full lips, before dropping to leisurely study the thrusting curves of her breasts beneath the clinging fabric of her petticoat. She was unable to move away as his fingers gently brushed the droplets of water away from her cheek.

Running his hands gently up her arms, quietly, he said, 'Come now. A kiss is all I want. I would be as gentle with you as you wish me to be.'

Shona turned liquid inside at the meaning she read into his words.

'Am I bothering you, Shona?' he asked in a husky whisper.

'You know you are,' she murmured before she could stop herself. She heard his satisfied chuckle and turned her head away from him. 'You're doing it on purpose and it's making me nervous.'

'In that case, try to relax.'

Without giving her time to protest, he lowered his mouth and assaulted her lips with a controlled expertise that left her gasping. It was a warmly seductive, lingering kiss that bestirred some strange, unexplainable pleasure in the pit of her womanly being and sent her vow not to wed Captain Fitzgerald soaring into the wide blue yonder. It was a heady brew that sapped her strength from her limbs and made her head swim and her heart race wildly out of control. When he raised his head, he slipped his arm around her waist and drew her closer still. Again his lips descended to hers. She gave herself up to him, completely abandoned, clinging to him as ivy might cling to oak, and the strength in that hard, lean body gave promise of pleasure she had never imagined.

Their kiss seemed to go on for ever, became more passionate, arousing Shona's blood to madness. She was no longer aware of what Zack was doing. It was not until his lips left hers and he buried his head between her breasts that she remembered she was half-naked in his arms. But the sight of her own flesh, rosy in the heat of the sun, still rosier in contrast with the dark hair brushing her face, did not embarrass her in the least. It was as though, from all eternity, she had been created merely to give herself to this man, as though she had been made for him alone.

Passionately he sought her mouth again and pulled her supple body close to his, arching her slender waist. Shona moaned, a soft moan that was almost a call. She laid her hand against the reassuring strength of his chest and surrendered to delight as his hands caressed her bare shoulders and back, then slid lower, splaying against her spine to force her pliant body into intimate contact with every hard line of his legs and thighs. One hand lifted and curved around her nape, stroking it sensuously. The kiss advanced rapidly, startling her virginal senses as his tongue silkily plied her mouth and greedily consumed the sweetness within.

Even though she'd only known him for

forty-eight hours, Shona wanted this man, this stranger, to make love to her. She wanted it so badly she was shaken and amazed. The feel of him was just as masculine as she expected it to be, iron-hard flesh and sinews beneath his shirt. She had never imagined such a shocking thing could happen in a kiss and didn't know how to respond, but one thing she did know was that, considering his rejection of her proposal, she must not give him access.

Drawing back her head, she stared up at him, unable to believe he had dared to do this to her. 'What are you doing?'

Zack had the definite impression he had almost lost control of the situation, so soft and warm her lips had felt. 'Am I to gather you didn't particularly relish my kiss?'

'I could say it was most illuminating, but I've never been kissed exactly like that before.'

'Before I kissed you last night, have you *ever* been kissed before?' Zack asked, continuing to hold her within the circle of his arms, reluctant to release her.

'If I were to answer that, I'd be giving away secrets I'd rather not confess.'

'I'd like to be made privy to your most intimate secrets, Shona.'

'Intimate? Is that what you want, Captain, to be intimate with me?'

Zack wasn't at all sure he could answer that truthfully without destroying the moment. For her benefit he seemed to ponder her question. 'Would you like us to become intimate?'

Shona held his gaze. 'I think I'm beginning to understand you, Captain Fitzgerald. You want to be intimate with me, but you have no desire to have your freedom curtailed for the rest of your life. So if you are making overtures to me, perhaps you should consider that I will not accept them without a lasting commitment. I do not do things by halves.'

Zack sighed. 'I thought you might say that.'

'Disappointed, Captain?' she asked with feigned concern.

He looked down at her, his brows drawn together in bemusement. 'Naturally. You're too tempting by half,' he breathed, his voice quite husky now. Bending his head, he claimed her lips once more, drawing her down on to the rocks, where he pulled her hungrily towards him.

Subdued by the moment, she had neither the desire nor the strength to resist. Unconsciously she had waited all her life for this moment. She gave herself up to him, with complete abandon.

Their kiss seemed to go on for ever, became more passionate, arousing her blood to madness. She moaned as with great gentleness he caressed her body, his fingers seeming to hesitate before each new discovery. Then, in joy and wonderment, they closed on each new discovery.

Her loose hair was a glorious jasmine-perfumed silk tent that covered them both as they kissed. It fell on Zack's cheeks, his lips and twisted in and out of his fingers. It was the thread that wove them together, that would keep them from ever separating.

Absorbed in the enchantment of the moment, their ears were deaf to the approach of others into their own private world.

'Good Lord!' The exclamation exploded the silence of the creek. 'You blackguard! What the hell do you think you're doing? Get away from my sister, this *instant!*'

Recognising Antony's voice, supple as an eel, Shona somehow managed to slip out of his arms and scramble to her feet. Zack, uttering a quiet curse, did so at a more leisurely pace. Springing back guiltily from her compromising embrace, Shona turned to see her brother striding towards them. His fists were clenched by his sides, his face darkened to a raging purple. She had to bite her lips to stop herself crying out in horror. Behind him were Carmelita and two of his planter friends with their wives.

Crimson with shame, she drew back. She went cold and her throat tightened convulsively. Her disgrace was total. To have her virtue questioned before the elite ranks of Santamaria society was nearly as damning as if she had paraded naked through the town. To find herself half-naked before her neighbours, whose eyes fastened upon her greedily, their faces expectant… She reached for her dress and held it to her in an attempt to maintain her modesty. She heard the captain curse under his breath, but she was too numb to do likewise, even if she had known the proper words.

Antony stared at his sister's scantily clad form in icy stillness—silent accusation that promised there would be consequences later. 'Just look at you. Have you no shame? Return to the house at once, where I will decide how to deal with this.' He turned to his friends. 'I owe you an apology. I invited you down here to introduce you to Captain Fitzgerald. What we saw speaks for itself. However, I ask for your discretion and hope you will have the goodness to overlook the unfortunate incident. Please—will you excuse us and return to the house where you will be served refreshments. I will be up shortly.'

Both gentlemen bowed, politely enough, but stiff with reproach, and turned and walked side by side back along the path, the ladies with their heads close together quietly discussing what had transpired.

Antony turned his fury on Captain Fitzgerald. 'Damnation, sir, what do you mean by this? How dare you make a move like that on my sister! What do you think this house is? A brothel?'

'That is exactly what he must think,' Carmelita sneered with her harsh Spanish accent. 'Although I must congratulate you, Shona,' she said, looking at her sister-in-law, who chose to disobey her brother's order to return to the house. 'If you set out to seduce him, then what we have just witnessed confirms that you have succeeded admirably.'

In a few seconds the captain's face expressed first stupefaction, then fury as the full meaning of her words sank in, then a look of implacable contempt transformed his features. Although she was quaking inside, Shona remained where she was and faced him with outward calm. His eyes remained riveted on her. Those eyes of his, which only moments before had been soft with passion, were as hard as iron as they stared into hers. They raked Shona's stricken face and she watched in agony as they registered first disbelief, and then a terrible anger—anger so deep that all the muscles in his face tightened into a mask of cold rage. She stood there, irate, guilty and confused, as his fury exploded around her.

'You planned this!' he hissed, his eyes turning to shards of ice, and in that moment he was absolutely convinced that Shona McKenzie was the most consummate actress on earth.

'No,' she cried, stricken that he should think that. His expression was as murderous as his feelings.

Zack gave her in icy look, unable to disprove her contention that she had deliberately set out to deceive him.

Shona sensed his desire to disbelieve anything she said. She was daunted by his glacial manner in the midst of his rampaging emotions.

'You're a liar and an ambitious schemer, a woman who doesn't set too high a price on her charms. You lured me down here. You had me believing you were not upset by my rejection to your proposal, when all the time you were colluding with your sister-in-law to compromise me. You scheming, manipulative little… Well, whatever you cooked up between you, it won't work.'

He spat the words at her and Shona felt an agonising pain stab through her as sharp as a blow from a dagger. The blood left her face and rushed tumultuously to her heart, which seemed to have stopped beating. At this cruel attack she stepped back as if he had hit her. Her courage seemed to have abandoned her. The whole gentle interlude of a moment earlier had turned into a grotesque and humiliating farce. It was no use arguing, she realised, because he was blinded and deafened by fury. She now clearly saw the scene had been deliberately rigged by her sister-in-law, knowing Carmelita's devious mind had worked to manipulate the situation towards her own gain.

Desperately she sought something to cling to, some sort of help in her present plight. She felt Carmelita's sharp eyes watching her, no doubt reassured by the reaction of the people she had assembled for this scene, and Shona had to make superhuman efforts to hide her distress. There was a strange look in Carmelita's eyes. At first Shona could not read the expression—then, after a moment, she understood…and she was frightened.

It was a look of triumph.

Zack turned to Antony, hoping to appeal to his common sense. Instinct told him that he had gone too far and was near to making a deadly enemy of a man who had welcomed him to the island and shown him the hospitality of his house. 'I think you're in danger of letting this get out of proportion. All I did was kiss your sister—not an unusual occurrence, considering.'

Antony bristled. 'Explain what you mean by that.'

'Considering Miss McKenzie—as you see,' Zack said, indicating Shona's absence of apparel with an insolent sweep of his cold eyes, 'has removed her clothes. I am a hot-blooded male, Mr McKenzie, after all, and she certainly raised no objection to my attentions.'

'That is not good enough.'

'Then what do you want from me?'

'Allow *me* to tell you what we want,' Carmelita said, stepping forward, more assertive than her husband. Shona watched her and Captain Fitzgerald try to face each other down—the captain hard and cold and Carmelita aggressive, her eyes bright. Antony looked faintly alarmed and uncomfortable at the way things were going, but he was unable to stop his wife when she argued a matter of principle. 'We welcomed you to Santamaria and into our home, and in return you have ruined my sister-in-law's reputation.'

Zack sounded ready to explode. 'I did *what?*' he grated ominously.

'You followed a respectable young woman down here and tried to seduce her, leaving her open to ridicule and insult.'

'I think you will find she will survive,' Zack ground out.

'Heaven knows how far it would have gone had we not arrived when we did.'

'You seem to forget, Mrs McKenzie, that you were the one who suggested I follow your sister-in-law down here. I am a man of passion. I allowed my admiration for a pretty girl to carry me away and for that I am regretful.'

'We may be far removed from London, Captain, but the people who live on Santamaria have a moral code, just like everybody else, and you publicly breached that code. Mr Frobisher and Mr Carpenter are two of the most important men on the island. Now their wives have been made privy to what has happened, there will be no stopping the gossip.'

'And those two gentlemen and their wives just happened to come here by chance,' Zack ground out sarcastically. 'I am not stupid, Mrs McKenzie, and nor will I be manipulated by a woman who, it is clear to me, rigged the whole thing.'

Antony's face went white with fury. 'Captain Fitzgerald! It is my wife you are speaking to. I do not like your tone, sir. Carmelita is not to blame for your irresponsible behaviour.'

'Your wife cannot be absolved from blame. She knew *exactly* what you would find when she suggested I come here.' He eyed Carmelita scathingly. 'By God, you must be desperate to rid yourself of your sister-in-law to go to such lengths.'

'I am concerned, Captain Fitzgerald,' she said, glancing at her husband for his complicity. 'There is bound to be a huge scandal over this and Shona's marriage prospects reduced to nothing since no decent gentleman will marry her after what you have done.'

'What my wife says is correct, Captain,' Antony seconded. 'You must surely realise that no decent man is going to look at my sister now.'

'If the self-righteous citizens of the island can make a scandal out of something so paltry, they need their minds examined.'

'That is your opinion, Captain,' Carmelita uttered brusquely, 'but the fact remains that from this day forward, wherever she goes, scandal will follow her. For that you must pay, and dearly. Therefore, I am sure my husband will agree there is only one solution. You shall not leave this island until you agree to do the right thing by her.'

Zack could not have been more astonished if a thunderbolt had struck him. The Spanish woman's imperious tone appeared to be enough to daunt the most vigorous captain. Carmelita McKenzie was certainly no weak-minded woman who sheltered behind her husband, but Zack was not the man to be easily intimidated.

'And that is?'

'If you have any sense of honour, any sense of responsibility, to save her from disgrace you must wed her.'

With the look of pure bloody-minded rebellion on his face, a nerve jerking in his cheek, Zack was so consumed with fury over the thought of wedding that scheming, deceitful fair-haired witch that he could hardly utter a word. Everything in him rebelled. When he could finally trust himself to speak, his voice erupted like hissing steam. 'You ask the impossible. There is nothing I *must* do, Mrs McKenzie.' Shifting his gaze to Shona, Zack's eyes swept over her in the most insulting manner, contemptuous of what he was certain she had done. In cold, frigid silence, for an endless moment their gazes locked as they assessed one another.

He cursed himself for having touched her, but he had been unable to resist the mad desire which she awoke in him. The first time he had set eyes on her he'd made no attempt to disguise the fact that he was violently attracted to her. And now, he had not stopped to think, but simply because she was beautiful and he wanted her, he had taken her in his arms and would have made her his without the blessing of matrimony. But from that moment when spontaneous attraction had drawn them together, fate had stepped in and taken malicious pleasure in separating them— before forcing his hand into marriage.

Shona was half-clad, but felt entirely naked. Everything about Captain Fitzgerald exuded an unbending will and that in turn made Shona more wretched and helpless as she searched the forbidding countenance for some sign of the man she had seen earlier. But there was none. His face was frozen into a hardened mask of rage and his grey eyes, having turned to an icy, metallic silver, impaled her, accusing her of complicity and treachery. She could imagine how his mind must be recoiling from it, but all she saw were the hard lines of his face, the tautness of his jaw.

Trembling beneath the blast of his gaze, at the cost of a violent effort of will, she made herself step towards him on legs that were wooden. 'I—I know how this must look— I know what you imagine—'

Zack's laugh was even more insolent than his words. 'Imagine?'

'I know what you think—but I assure you, I did not plan this...'

'Don't bother trying to explain. Let us not pretend. Do not play the innocent,' he ground out, his voice quiet, with all the deadly calm of approaching peril. 'Let me congratulate you. You are as clever as I credited you as being. You are a consummate deceiver, Miss McKenzie, and a magnificent actress. I congratulate you. With your talent you should have been on the stage with the rest of the ambitious harlots who cavort and dance for the amusement of the crowd.'

In a state of acute misery, Shona swallowed convulsively. 'You are quite mistaken. I have done absolutely nothing wrong.'

In his current mood he was not inclined to deal kindly with her. Fed up with all the convoluted lies and his own disastrous blunder, he would not spare her. His tone was merciless and cutting. 'Spare me your lies. It's not difficult to see what sort of a woman you are. You planned this with all the deviousness of a born schemer.' His eyes were bright and as sharp as the teeth of a trap. 'When I leave the island, I never wish to set eyes on it again,' he said, his voice hard and smooth as polished steel. 'I never wish to think of you again, Miss McKenzie, unless it be with disgust.' His cold eyes swept over Antony and his wife. 'Excuse me. I have work to do. The sooner I leave this damned island the better.'

With a cold nod he turned on his heel and headed up the path, fury a hard lump in his throat, like a nut swallowed whole. He cursed ever setting eyes on Shona McKenzie. She had got under his skin the minute he'd stepped ashore and began to disrupt his life. In the heat of the creek passion had replaced all reason. Like the idiot he was, he'd watched transfixed as she'd shaken out her wealth of golden hair, slipped into the water and snaked her tantalising body back and forth, and all the time she'd been waiting for the moment when her brother and his wife would arrive to witness their actions.

McKenzie must be laughing himself into a

seizure that he'd fallen into the trap. After all his experience, his alleged sophistication, he thought as his wrath continued to mount, he'd fallen like a rock for the oldest female trick in the world. Leaving Melrose Hill, he tried to decide the most expedient way to extricate himself from this mess and get the woman off his hands for good. Reaching his ship, he immediately issued orders to stock up and be ready to leave within twenty-four hours. Any outstanding repairs would be completed in Martinique.

In the creek, Shona was left still hugging her dress to her chest. Her thoughts were unpleasant and for the first time ever she doubted her own worth. She felt as if she had been physically beaten. Her mind was too dazed to absorb the shock, too numb to feel the full enormity of pain she had brought on herself.

'Make yourself decent and come back to the house,' Carmelita ordered sharply, turning from her. Having gained her end, she forgot the means and, in high spirits, clutched her husband's arm and walked close to his side. 'Captain Fitzgerald's actions were without precedent. I see now it was unwise to welcome him so freely. I think we have set a lion loose in an arena filled with lambs. You must pay him a visit on his ship, Antony—let him see that the matter is by no means closed.'

With unsteady fingers Shona began to rearrange her garments. She followed them back to the house, relieved that the dreadful moment was over. There seemed to be an overwhelming emptiness about it all now, but her young body burned with a yearning she had never experienced before—but there was no solace in it now, for her arms were achingly empty.

But she would never forget the accusing look of treachery the captain had given her, a look that lay like a dead weight upon her mind. He had withered her with a look of crushing scorn and contempt. There were some things a man as hard and inflexible as Captain Fitzgerald would never forgive and in his mind she had set out to seduce and entrap him into marriage.

But what of her? The gossip created by their liaison would be endless and the humiliation she would suffer as a result of it would be immeasurable.

Zack drove himself relentlessly, getting the ship seaworthy, barking orders at his crew as if he could burn some of the anger out of his system. And that night he lay awake in his oversize bunk, restless and dissatisfied as he listened to the sound of revelry from the waterfront taverns and thought about Shona McKenzie.

Chapter Four

Shortly after lunch the day after the unpleasantness in the grove, feeling in need of strenuous exercise and to escape her brother's and Carmelita's reproving looks and to tire her mind and body, Shona ordered her horse to be saddled. She rode inland towards the cane fields, riding past the sugar mill and then beyond to the high cliffs. The day was pleasant, with a light breeze that billowed out the skirt of her light blue riding habit and loosened the tendrils of hair about her face.

Drawing near the cliff edge, her horse began to prance, tossing her fine head and lifting her legs smartly as she sidled along the edge, scattering loose rocks into the sea below. Suddenly another horse appeared beside her and a large brown hand shot out and took the bridle. Her horse halted with a bounce, bringing Shona's teeth together. Trotting away from the dangerous edge, she turned her head to see who had halted her ride. On seeing Captain Fitzgerald, Shona could have screamed her ire at him.

Anger sounded in his voice. 'If you must ride so close to the edge, you might do so with some care for your safety.'

The rebuke did not sit well with Shona and was even more irritating because she knew he spoke the truth. Her horse was spirited and eager to gallop and needed a firm, attentive hand on the reins. Today Shona was distracted and it was all down to this man. With a very feminine gesture she threw back her head, the gold treasure of her hair rippling down her spine. The captain did not so much as blink. His silver-grey eyes remained fixed on her face without the trace of a smile to soften their steely expression.

'Do you like Santamaria so much, Captain Fitzgerald, that you cannot bear to leave it? Go away. I should not be talking to you. It isn't proper.'

'Don't you think it's too late to worry about what's proper?'

Sorely piqued, Shona looked away. 'Yes, it is and it's all thanks to you.'

'You've every right to be angry. And so do I.'

So much for holding her feelings in check, she thought, then she closed her eyes and inhaled deeply, struggling against a wave of anger and uncertainty and despair. 'What are you doing here?'

'What does it look like? I am unable to leave for Martinique until the repairs to my ship are completed. Owing to recent events, the crew have been instructed to put their backs into it. The sooner I leave your island the better.'

'Santamaria is not my island, Captain. I just happen to live here—for the time being. I am every bit as eager as you are to leave.'

'Then you'll just have to wait for another ship with a captain gullible enough to fall into your trap,' he ground out sarcastically.

'Perhaps I shall,' Shona replied without preamble. 'A captain who is more amiable than you. But if you are so keen to be on your way, then shouldn't you be assisting your crew with patching up your ship?'

'The work is in the capable hands of my first mate, Miss McKenzie. Having heard of the beauty of this place, I hired a horse to see for myself.'

Careful to keep a distance between them,

Zack kept his horse on a tight rein. With a fire-
storm of humiliated fury erupting from his heart,
he had been watching her for some time. His
pulse had pounded out a primal drumbeat as he
watched her riding her fine white horse with expert grace, a ruthless, beautiful huntress in light
blue skirts, the bright gold of her hair blowing in
the breeze. Not only did he owe her for colluding with her sister-in-law to lure him to the creek
yesterday, but looked at in a certain way, her
brother's insistence that they wed, which would
result in his loss of freedom, was all down to
this maddening chit. If he had not been out of
his head over her, he would have stayed away
from Melrose Hill. Well, this was where it had
got him, he thought, and he was determined to
get himself out of it.

'Until you appeared, I was enjoying the ride,'
Shona said haughtily. 'Had I known you were
about, I would have sought a different route.'

'Why? Do you fear me, Miss McKenzie?' He
gave her a hard look, his mouth tightening as
he stared at her softly heaving bosom and the
tantalising mouth that he had so enjoyed kissing yesterday.

His gaze touched a quickness within Shona
and she quickly averted her eyes. No one before

this man had ever set her to trembling for any
reason, much less with a look or mere words.
What was there about this captain that aroused
her so? She could not think of those moments she
had spent in his arms. She could not allow herself to revisit the memory. It would not happen
again. Did she want it to? A part of her yearned
for him every moment—for his arms, his lips,
his warm flesh pressed to hers. Another part
of her cringed in horror. What was she? A har-
lot? What had her proper upbringing brought
her to—that she could propose marriage to a
stranger and then behave most shamelessly after
he rejected her? What would her father think of
her now?

She could understand her physical attraction
to him. What she could not understand, and what
frightened her, was this strange, magnetic pull
she felt towards him emotionally. There were
times when he spoke to her in that deep, compelling voice of his, or looked at her with those
silver-grey penetrating eyes, that she almost felt
as if he were quietly reaching out to her and in-
exorably drawing her closer and closer to him.

Greatly disturbed by the path of her mind, she
straightened her back indignantly and pushed
her hair back from her face, trying to control

her restive mount. Unlike yesterday when he had sought her out, today he made no effort to conceal the contempt he felt for her.

'I do not fear you, Captain. It is only that I prefer not to be mauled and ogled as you seemed to have a penchant for doing yesterday.'

'That's the last thing on my mind. That's what precipitated this mess, and I'm not fool enough to repeat it.'

'So, your run-in with my brother yesterday has cooled your lusts.'

The corner of his mouth twisted wryly in a gesture that was not quite a smile. 'Trust me, after yesterday the last thing you evoke in me is lust. Damn it, none of this would have happened if you'd kept your clothes on.'

'How could I know that?'

'Perhaps you make a habit of it. How would I know? How many more *gentlemen* have you entertained for your own pleasure in what you would have me believe is your own private little pool?'

Shona paled visibly as she listened to his flow of calculated insults with incredulity, delivered in a cordial, conversational tone. He was mocking her, showing her that the warmth of their passionate interlude, which had developed in the creek, had changed into a quiet contempt. 'How dare you say that? No one ever goes to the pool when I am there. Carmelita knows that and she was being malicious when she sent you there.'

'Was she? I would say your co-conspirator is an amazing actress to have pulled off the whole sham so well,' Zack said with a fresh surge of disgust for his own gullibility. Shona McKenzie was also a stellar actress, he decided wrathfully, remembering the softness in her eyes during the time they had spent together on the side of the pool. She'd looked straight at him with her heart in her eyes, unflinching. Except she had no heart. And no conscience either, obviously. It would appear that she was so eager to go to England that she would stop at nothing to achieve that. 'Your sister-in-law certainly had more to say than your brother, who doesn't seem to mind being undermined by his wife.'

'Antony is his own master, Captain. Carmelita is his only weakness.'

'He came to the ship earlier.' A muscle flexed in his jaw. 'Your brother doesn't intend to let my ship or crew leave the island unless I do the honourable thing and make you my wife. I do not underestimate your brother. He has told me the island is well fortified to stop undesirables landing. It would appear it is equally as impossible to leave with one's ship and one's life intact if he has a mind. He is still insisting that I marry you—soon.' His biting tone carried anger and frustration.

'He feels responsible for me.'

'He made that quite clear! I won't marry you. I have already told you that.' His voice was hoarse with anger, his tone adamant. He wouldn't let her or her brother or anyone else deny him the chance to still win his daughter. 'What happened between us yesterday doesn't change anything.'

Her eyes began to flash quietly. 'I didn't expect it to,' she returned with frozen civility. 'I don't wish to marry you either, Captain, so at least we are in accord about something.'

Zack stared down at her. He hadn't missed the flare of temper in her green eyes. 'Your brother has threatened to confiscate my ship if I don't go through with it.'

'Yes, I thought he might,' she said quietly. 'He is adamant. I'll speak to him if that will satisfy you.'

'And tell him what?'

'That we don't want to wed.'

'He won't accept that. His wife is determined that we will.'

'I'm sorry, but that is the best I can do. What happened yesterday is already being talked about.'

'I can't help that. You knew perfectly well what you were doing when you fell into my arms. You will have to weather the slurs and accusations as best you can. Any concerns I may have do not extend to actually marrying you. I am done with you. Your brother's timely arrival yesterday brought me back to my senses—and his ultimatum is a cutting reminder of the impossibility of any further association between us. It seems we have reached an impasse, which is a problem.' He clenched his fists, anger sweeping through him as he remembered her brother's ultimatum. Devil take it, he would not be forced into marriage, not even to a woman as lovely and bewitching as Shona McKenzie.

'For you, maybe, but not for me,' Shona said tightly, pulling on the reins to turn her horse about.

His hand shot out and he took her wrist and gripped it hard. 'I am not a stupid youth, Miss McKenzie. I am not a man you flirt with. I will not allow you and your family to enjoy yourselves at my expense.'

'Enjoy?' she scoffed, her eyes flashing irately. 'I am not enjoying this. Far from it.'

'So, what then?'

'Antony *does* mean for you to marry me.'

'Your brother be damned. I'm not some trained underling to do as he is told. I am not afraid of him.'

'Perhaps you should be. Antony is a powerful man, Captain. He will never forgive you for compromising me.'

'I don't think I shall miss his affections.'

'You should have a care. He's a man of much influence.'

'He's a man of much arrogance.'

'He means what he says.'

Zack's eyes narrowed dangerously. 'Are you threatening me?'

She nodded. 'I suppose I am. I suppose I must be.'

He thrust her arm away and his eyes glittered down at her from a face that was full of rage. 'You are nothing but an eager body and an empty heart,' he said viciously. 'Did you think I would be so desperate for your body I would be glad to marry you? Good God, lady, you do not know me! Good day, Miss McKenzie. I have nothing further to say to you.' He urged his mount away, as if he couldn't bear to be near her.

Shona watched him go. On reflection, as she realised how the situation must look to him, she gradually became more sympathetic and found herself coming up with excuses for him. After all, why should he trust her? She was a woman he did not know and yet she had asked him to marry her. Then, following his refusal, Carmelita had sent him to the creek where he had found her half-naked. She had made no attempt to run away or cover herself and had raised no objection when he'd kissed her. He knew of her desperation to leave the island and must have thought they had colluded to entrap him.

Riding away from Shona, Zack's thoughts turned to his daughter, the small child he loved fiercely. He had never expected to feel that way about anybody. He revered his parents and he held his brother and sisters in great affection, yet the bond between a father and his child was stronger—deeper...

He shook his head in frustration. He could not marry Shona McKenzie, not at the risk of losing his daughter, but he was determined not to let what had happened between them ruin his peace or spoil his last seafaring days. Riding his horse in the direction of the cove, he urged it into a gallop before bringing it to a halt and looking back.

'Damn it all!' he muttered, wondering how she had managed to make him feel like an utter cad for refusing her. Riding back to his ship, he felt every eye turn to him and the fact that they were all equated with what had transpired between him and Shona McKenzie made his blood boil, for he was a man of honour, but he knew there was little he could do to counter the thoughts of those around him. He'd heard the talk around the town, the rumours and speculation, and he'd learned long ago to let most of what was said in ignorance roll off his broad back.

Boarding his ship, Zack saw Singleton give him a questioning glance and knew his first mate was curious about what he would decide, for it was becoming increasingly evident that leaving Santamaria was becoming more difficult by the hour. He did not underestimate Antony McKenzie. He had told him the island was well protected against undesirables. Two ships patrolled the entrance to the cove and an increasing number of armed men were watching the ship. In fact, the whole island was bristling with weapons.

* * *

It wasn't long before Antony McKenzie paid him another visit. Zack received him cordially. Radiating command, he dominated the spacious cabin. If he could talk his way out of this mess he would, so if it meant having to be polite to McKenzie then so be it.

'You have presented me with a grave dilemma, Captain Fitzgerald,' Antony remarked, his hands behind his back as he slowly paced Zack's private cabin. He did not bother to hide his irritation. As he and Fitzgerald faced each other, anger was brittle in the air between them.

'I did not mean to,' Zack answered, his face holding a bland, cordial expression by ingrained politeness alone. 'Circumstances…' he omitted to say *and McKenzie's own wife* '…conspired to keep me alone with your sister.'

'And circumstances conspired to have her within your embrace?' Antony said dourly, his eyes hard and steady.

A mildly tolerant smile touched Zack's handsome visage, but the glint in the silver-grey eyes was hard as steel. 'Come now, it was but a kiss. I didn't attempt to touch her in any other way.'

Antony knew the captain to be a proud and

noble man, a man who had earned the confidence and respect of businessmen in England and Virginia. It was dangerous to question the honour of such a man. He decided to do so and said quietly, 'You know you will have to marry her. You style yourself a man of honour—do, then, the honourable thing.'

Zack stood before Antony with narrowed eyes, absorbing this and weighing his words carefully before he spoke. 'With all due respect, much as I would like to protect her from the scandal, I will not make her my wife.'

'And if I insist?'

Zack shrugged casually. 'Insist all you like, the answer is no. I'm afraid it is impossible.'

'Why? You are a single man and, if what I witnessed yesterday was anything to go by, you do not have an aversion to my sister.'

'The answer is still no. But I am not without eyes in my head and I realise your sister would be a most charming companion. But when— *if*—I do marry, the lady will be of *my* choosing, not because her brother holds an axe over my head. I shall be ready to leave Santamaria shortly. I trust I will be free to do so? If you do not choose to make mourners of your friends, I suggest you promptly call off your guards,' he warned in a mild reproof.

'If you take Shona with you—as your wife. However, there is a drawback.'

'Which is?'

'The ceremony cannot be performed just now. Reverend Trimble, the island clergyman, is visiting a neighbouring island and is not expected back for another month.'

Zack was incredulous. 'And you expect me to remain on Santamaria kicking my heels for this…this clergyman, to materialise?'

'Of course there is a solution.'

'There is?' Zack eyed him warily.

'I believe you have your own clergyman aboard the *Ocean Pearl*. I trust he is of the Protestant persuasion?'

Zack stared at him. Then, when understanding dawned, subdued amusement played on his face. 'Reverend Cornelius Clay.' Rubbing the side of his face, he laughed softly, a sharp, calculating gleam in his eyes. He could be just as shrewd and clever as McKenzie. This was one of those times which demanded all of his cunning. *Yes—why not?* he thought. Perhaps there was a solution to this dilemma after all. 'Yes,' he said quietly. 'Reverend Clay is of that persuasion.'

* * *

'Prepare for a wedding, Singleton, and pour us both some celebratory wine,' Zack said heartily when Antony had departed and his first mate came to enquire how the meeting had gone. 'I am to wed the delectable Shona McKenzie within the week.'

Singleton thought he could not be more surprised. The immediate aftermath of the previous day's grim events and Zack's determination not to be browbeaten into marriage, and now his request for a celebration, were both a little odd. 'I thought you'd made up your mind on that,' he remarked, doing as he was asked and pouring two glasses of wine.

'I have—and I haven't changed my mind,' Zack said, quirking an amused brow at his first mate and picking up his wine and lifting the glass in a mock toast. 'To our happiness,' he said drily.

In the moment it took Zack to drain the glass, Singleton recovered his composure, carefully disguising his confusion with the turn of events and picking up his glass of wine. But instead of drinking it, he turned it absently in his fingers while he eyed his captain with unhidden amusement.

'Are you wondering if I'm making a mistake?' Zack asked finally.

'You could say it's crossed my mind.'

'You'll understand when I tell you that our very own Reverend Cornelius Clay—a more pious man one couldn't hope to meet—is to perform the ceremony.'

For a moment Singleton stared at him as if convinced that he had taken leave of his senses. Then abruptly he slapped the flat of his hand upon the table and began to guffaw in rampant amusement. He left no doubt that he considered the captain's pronouncement absurd. Finally he calmed and peered at him askance with merriment still lighting his ruddy face. 'A more pious drunk, you mean—and a defrocked clergyman, or however they're referred to when the church has kicked them out.'

'Precisely! Convenient for me, eh?'

'And McKenzie? He doesn't know? He doesn't mistrust your intentions and integrity?'

'No. He made the suggestion.'

'He'll never forgive you for this.'

A low chuckle preceded Zack's reply. 'I don't think I'll miss his affection.'

'Be careful,' Singleton warned. 'McKenzie's a man of much influence.'

'He's a man of much arrogance and I couldn't resist deflating him a bit.

'For obvious reasons I shall not enlighten him about Reverend Clay's fall from grace within the church—unless, of course, it comes up. After the ceremony when the security is dropped, we shall slip quietly away from Santamaria and head for Martinique.'

'And Miss McKenzie?'

Zack's face hardened. 'My anger at being tricked by Shona McKenzie overpowers my desire for her—providing me with a motive to enter into a fake wedding. You will vow me mad, I know, but after what she contrived to do to me yesterday, it's with a devil's desire to have revenge upon the beautiful witch. She will have no objections to marrying me if she believes I'm to take her to England. After the sham ceremony I intend to tell her the truth before we leave—I'll tie her up if necessary to prevent her raising the alarm. I am sure this can work.'

There was tension in the McKenzie household. Carmelita was avoiding Shona and Shona was avoiding everybody. The evening meal, a splendid meal, was consumed in silence. At one point Shona met the guarded face of her brother, encountering the usual cold expression, and, glancing at her sister-in-law, a silent challenge flared between them. Shona's eyes, full on her, matched the icy disapproval of her tightly compressed lips. Afterwards Shona took her coffee out on to the terrace. It wasn't long before Antony sought her out. It was plain to her he had something on his mind. Taking his time to light a cheroot, he stood looking out over the garden into the darkness beyond.

Shona, in whom patience had been a lesson painfully learned and not always completely, sipped her coffee and waited for Antony to speak. There was a hard knot, she didn't really know what it was, in the centre of her chest, and try as she might she could not get rid of it. After her encounter with Captain Fitzgerald earlier, she was tense, her face strained.

'What is it, Antony?' she prompted. 'Is something troubling you? Is it to do with Captain Fitzgerald?'

'I spoke to him today,' Antony told her.

'And?'

'You must know what we discussed. It has been decided that the two of you are to be wed. When he leaves the island, you will go with him as his wife.'

Shona's cup rattled on the saucer and she almost spilled the hot liquid over her lap before she managed to reclaim her poise. She gulped and swallowed hard, unprepared for the hurt her brother's pronouncement caused her. She was being banished from home and it was obvious that she mattered less to Antony than his wife. She meant nothing to the one person who should have loved and cherished her. She was unwanted and unloved. But then, wasn't this what she had wanted all along—a long-awaited chance to leave the island?

'This cannot be happening,' she murmured. 'You can't turn against me like this, Antony.' She held her hand out to him in a plea for understanding and forgiveness, but her brother's face remained cold and aloof.

'It's no use complaining, Shona. It is decided. I know you are a woman who likes to feel she has a will of her own. Very well. I can understand that. I do not resent you falling for this fellow. He is a handsome enough man—and much as I hate saying so to my own sister, undoubtedly, considerably attractive physically. Such infatuations are common. They are expected— permitted even—as long as you do not become emotionally involved and you conduct yourself with absolute discretion. But you have done neither and in the process embarrassed everyone concerned. Which is why you have to marry him.'

Shona knew her brother well enough to know it was useless arguing with him. She wanted Captain Fitzgerald in the way a woman wants a certain man. She had watched unmoved, contemptuous even, the gyrations of other men, many willing to marry her to get their hands on some of her father's money, listened to their flattery, which came from their falsely smiling mouths, and been ready to yawn in their faces. Now, out of the blue had come this force, this transformation which had caused her heart to perform a whole new beat, to be moved by one man and no other.

A man who did not want her, a man who was prepared to marry her for no other reason than to get off the island. It was not to be borne—she could not...

'Of course you will want for nothing, you know that.' Antony suddenly became aware that his sister was looking at him as though he was speaking in a foreign language, her eyes wide and staring and stunned. He looked at her anxiously, for all his plans were made and if she should refuse... 'Shona, you *will* have him, won't you?' he demanded menacingly.

She wanted him. Yes, she admitted it to herself, recognising it at last. She wanted him more than she had ever wanted anything in her life before. She would repay him, she vowed. She would be a good wife to him, a good mother to his children. Perhaps, she thought wistfully, they would deal well together. They had much to learn about each other, yet many couples began life together with less in common than she and Captain Fitzgerald. In spite of everything that had happened between them, he was a man she could respect and admire. Even his rugged vitality she found attractive—and she had found it extremely pleasurable when he'd kissed her.

'Yes, Antony, I'll have him. I'll be his wife.' *Wife.* The word had a pleasant ring to it—a wonderful ring. A glow warmed her. 'I'm merely surprised he's agreed.'

'I remain somewhat puzzled by his sudden change of heart to comply with my demands.'

'How soon?'

'Before the week is out.'

'You mean to forgo the reading of the banns?'

'There will be enough witnesses to make the marriage valid.'

'And who will perform the ceremony? Reverend Trimble is still away just now.'

'There is a clergyman aboard the *Ocean Pearl*. He will do the honours—providing his credentials are in order.'

'Have you some doubt about it?'

'Let's just say I will make quite sure that Fitzgerald isn't trying to pull the wool over my eyes. I've ordered Deverell to make discreet enquiries concerning the Reverend Cornelius Clay.'

Deverell, trustworthy and dependable, but as sharp-faced and cunning as a ferret, was Antony's right-hand man. With Deverell to guarantee that Shona abided by her brother's demands, she had known no opportunity to be anything but compliant to his wishes. If deception was afoot, then Deverell would sniff it out.

The following day, when Antony went off about his business at the sugar mill and Carmelita was resting, Shona rode down to the harbour. Dismounting, she secured her horse to a hitching post close to the pier. Further along Captain Fitzgerald's ship was tethered by her bow fast and stern lines. A figurehead of a woman with flowing dark tresses graced the head of the ship, and the name *Ocean Pearl* was carved into the stern. Other ships were in dock, but none compared to the *Ocean Pearl*. Like a proud queen she stood tall and serene amid her consorts. Shona walked past kegs and barrels towards the gangplank of the vessel. A man in a blue coat came to where the gangplank touched the ship. When he espied her, he smiled.

'Can I help you, miss?'

'Is Captain Fitzgerald on board?'

'And what, may I ask, has drawn the fair Shona McKenzie from her roost?' a voice behind her asked.

Shona whirled round at that familiar deep voice. Her heart set up a wild thumping as she realised it was Captain Fitzgerald, grinning from ear to ear, silver-grey eyes as clear as crystal. He radiated the same strong, masculine appeal. The problem was, now he had agreed to make her his wife, she found it difficult staying away from him. It was as if everything was out of control. She didn't like being out of control, but where this man was concerned she couldn't seem to help herself. She watched him as he doffed his hat to her, experiencing again the depth to which her mind and body was stirred whenever she was in his presence.

He bowed, smiling at her. The even white

teeth flashed against his bronze skin and Shona could only mark the resemblance he bore to a swarthy pirate. Garbed in a loose white shirt that gaped open from neck to waist, the brown skin gleamed with the healthy sweat of one who enjoyed the freedom of his time at sea.

However, she found something resentful about the way his gaze slid boldly over her body, from the hat perched atop her shining curls to the swelling flesh exposed above her bodice and right down to the toes of her shoes. She was somewhat accustomed to the admiring glances of gentlemen, but there was nothing gentlemanly about Captain Fitzgerald's insolent, lazy perusal of her body.

'Are you quite finished?' she asked tersely.

His unhurried gaze lifted to her eyes and a wry smile quirked his stern lips. He heard the antagonism in her voice. 'Have I made another social blunder by approaching you?' he enquired in a low, amused voice.

'No. I—I wanted to see you.'

'Then may I entice you aboard?'

Her gaze flicked over the faces of the men who had come to the rail to appease their curiosity. She was unable to hear what was being said as they murmured and chuckled together, but she sensed that she and Captain Fitzgerald were the topic of their animated conversation.

'Are you sure I will be safe?'

An amused chuckle and a wicked twinkle in his eyes came with his reply. 'Miss McKenzie, if we were cast upon a lonely shore with the members of my crew, I'm sure the torment of your beauty would soon overwhelm them and you would depend upon me to provide protection for you.'

Finding no appropriate retort, she accepted the arm he offered and allowed him to escort her across the plank. She gazed up at the tallest mast, which rose to a dizzying height, and she looked down quickly, glad for the support of her escort's arm.

'You have a fine ship, Captain Fitzgerald. You must be proud of her.'

'At any other time I would be honoured to give you a tour, but I have a feeling you have other things on your mind. Come. We will go to my cabin.'

Some members of the crew stopped what they were doing and stared outright as she passed, while others cast surreptitious glances in her direction, but each in his fashion paused to admire her beauty. The cabin into which she was shown was spacious and well furnished with panelled walls, the smell of tobacco heavy on the air.

Zack poured her a light cordial and handed it to her, perching his hip on the edge of his desk, the surface strewn with charts and ledgers and quills. 'I didn't expect to see you down here,' he said, his expression unreadable. His head, a tumble of dark curls, cocked characteristically, but his eyes narrowed against the brilliant shaft of sunlight slanting through the expanse of window, wrinkled at their corners. 'I was under the impression that your brother didn't approve of you coming to the docks and mixing with the common folk.'

'He doesn't.' She sipped at the cordial, finding the taste delicious. 'He doesn't know I'm here. I wanted to see you.'

Mocking eyes gazed back at her. 'I see. I'm honoured, Miss McKenzie—although I suppose it's perfectly natural that a bride should want to meet with her intended before the wedding. I assume he's informed you that I have agreed to his demands.'

The remembrance of their last meeting, of the bitter things that had been said, touched Shona deeply, and his implication that Antony had *demanded* this marriage added to her humiliation.

'Yes—yes, he has. He is naturally angry at what has occurred.'

'That arrogant brother of yours—'

'No, he is not. He is my brother—my guardian. He's upset and disappointed. He doesn't understand what has happened between us. He feels as if he's losing control and he can't function unless he controls all he considers his. But I am surprised that you gave in—which is why I am here. After your firm refusal to agree to a marriage between us, I am puzzled as to your sudden change of heart.'

'The answer to that is simple. I need to leave this island, Miss McKenzie. I would negotiate with the Devil to achieve that.'

She stiffened, embarrassed, aware of her pounding head and thudding heart. 'I would like to explain about the other day—'

'Don't bother,' he interrupted. 'I know exactly how it was.'

'For what it's worth, Captain, I'm sorry—about the way things have turned out.'

A muscle in his jaw flexed and his eyes hardened. 'Why? You've got what you wanted all along. A proposal of marriage which will enable you to leave the island. Whatever you may be expecting after that, I cannot imagine. But don't for one minute imagine that marriage to me will be easy, Miss McKenzie, because you will be sorely disappointed.'

Shona took a shuddering breath, putting her glass on the desk. 'I don't know what I expect. I haven't thought that far ahead.'

'Then don't look at me like I've just read you a death sentence. I am sure you will find that marriage to me will be full of surprises.'

She glanced away, looking down at her hands, knowing then that she must never nurture any illusions that Zack Fitzgerald would ever come to love her. But what role she would play in his life she did not yet know, only that she would be the mother of his children. Whether he took her with him on his voyages in the future or left her conveniently behind was his decision and one in which she would have no say. But she was determined to face life head-on, taking whatever small pleasure her husband allowed her and being content.

'I—I imagine it will,' she said quietly.

Zack looked at her, trying to see her face, which was partially hidden by shadow. 'And don't look so wounded. I think I like you better when you're angry.'

Shona raised her head and met his gaze. 'I do

have a temper. I admit to that. So did my father. Do you have brothers and sisters, Captain?'

He nodded. 'My name is Zack. If you are to be my wife, you might bring yourself to address me by my given name. The answer to your question is yes, I do have siblings. One brother and two sisters.'

'Are you close?'

Zack shrugged. 'As close as we can be considering I've spent most of my adult life at sea.'

'I should like to have had sisters,' Shona said wistfully.

'And instead you have one brother and a controversial, acid-tongued sister-in-law.'

Shona sighed and gave him a tremulous smile. 'Something like that. You don't trust her?'

Zack gazed down at her with grudging admiration. If he didn't know better he would think this situation must be devastating for her. She believed she would be leaving everything to face a new way of life...

If it wasn't for his daughter, he thought with a twinge of regret, he might have been willing to go through with a marriage ceremony that wasn't a sham and give their marriage a chance. Having a wealthy sugar-planter's sister for a wife would be a benefit to him. And Shona McKenzie was undeniably lovely. He felt an overwhelming desire to take her in his arms. Her fragrance beckoned him, her soft, ripe curves made him ache with the want of her, stirring his mind with imaginings of what loveliness lay hidden from view. There was a need in him to feel the warmth of her beneath him, to sweep her up in his arms and ease the lust in his loins. But he was painfully aware of what he was about to do to her and suddenly he wanted to make his leave-taking as painless as possible.

'The woman is a true master of deception,' he said in answer to her question, 'so the answer is no, I don't.'

'I am hardly surprised. Not many people do.'

Zack raised a dark brow and considered her flushed cheeks and soft, trembling mouth. His gaze moved even lower and surveyed her heaving bosom, until Shona wondered wildly if he could see through her dress. Beneath his steady regard, her breasts burned, and she could not control her rapid breathing. Feebly she crossed her arms before her as if naked beneath that stare. Zack smiled evilly and gazed again into her eyes.

'Ever since we parted yesterday my mind has been tormented by your loveliness and I have been unable to forget even the smallest detail of you in my arms. That image was seared upon my memory as if you had branded me.'

He stared at her for a long time with a serious light in his eyes that made Shona doubt her sanity at ever having sought him out.

As the world seemed to dwindle to just the two of them, the ever-watchful Deverell's voice cut between them.

Shona was quick to note his arrival in the open doorway of the cabin and the smile playing about his normally taciturn lips as his gaze settled smugly on Captain Fitzgerald.

'Come, Miss Shona! Your brother has sent me to look for you. He'll be none too pleased to know you've been down to the quay unaccompanied—and even less when he learns Captain Fitzgerald has been entertaining you alone in his cabin.'

'Yes—yes, Deverell, I was just coming.' Zack pushed himself away from the desk, his body uncurling to its full, intimidating height.

She looked up at him, unsmiling. 'Please excuse me. I must go. Thank you for the cordial. Good day.'

'Good day.' He bowed slightly to her and watched her follow Deverell out of the cabin.

A moment later he went on deck and watched her walk towards her horse. She moved lightly, her radiant gold hair flowing loose behind her like spun sunshine, her white-sprigged dress pressed against her legs to reveal their perfect form of which he was so enamoured. Zack tensed imperceptibly, sensing the constriction of his heart. He would remember this image of her always, come what may.

In the silence that followed as she left him, the captain's words lived on in Shona's mind, filling her with the restlessness of many questions. She was moved by her admiration of him, by what he said, and disconcerted by the sudden violence of her feelings. He interested her, intrigued her more deeply than she ever cared to acknowledge. Staring back at the ship, she felt oddly disappointed that she had left him.

If we had met in other times, she thought as she rode beside Deverell back to the house, and not as the two people we are, perhaps then things between us would have been different.

Antony rose to his feet and asked Deverell, 'And how do you know Reverend Cornelius Clay is not an ordained minister of the church?'

'Oh, he was ordained all right, but his right to exercise the functions of the ordained ministry was removed when his criminal activities were uncovered.'

Antony sauntered to the window and stood looking down the hill, paying little attention to the lone man who was riding up to the house. 'And they were?'

'Smuggling. He was the minister of a small parish in Cornwall. He was also the leader of men who plied the trade. One of the smugglers, who believed Clay had cheated him, informed on him and he was apprehended and convicted of smuggling. He was tried and sentenced to hang, but he had clever friends in the fraternity, who organised his escape. He ended up in America, where he became quite a character and continued to be addressed as *the Reverend*. He is also a drunkard.'

'And how do you know all this?'

Deverell grinned thinly. 'For a price, there is always someone willing to talk.'

Antony nodded thoughtfully. 'And this is the man Fitzgerald has arranged to officiate at his marriage to my sister.'

'It looks like it.'

Antony's mouth twisted. 'Well, well.' Fitzgerald's intended deception tore at the very mettle of his pride. Now he knew exactly why he had suddenly been willing to agree to his demands. He had chosen Cornelius Clay. It made the most perfect sense. After the bogus ceremony, Fitzgerald intended to slip away when the coast was clear, leaving Shona to bear the shame and humiliation of it all.

'What will you do?' Deverell asked, eyeing his master carefully. 'Confront him?'

Antony was a cautious man, a man who weighed a situation. He was watching the rider approach. The man was close enough now for him to see his face beneath the circular brim of his hat. And then a slow smile stretched his lips and he shook his head. 'No, Deverell. Fitzgerald is to have no notion that I know he is trying to double-cross me. I will play him at his own game—and I will win.' He turned to Deverell. 'Not a word to my sister, you understand. The less she knows the better. In the meantime we have a visitor. Show Cousin Thomas in, will you? He couldn't have chosen a more opportune moment to arrive on Santamaria.'

Deverell frowned. 'Cousin Thomas?'

Antony nodded. 'You might say he is the answer to our prayers, but his relationship to me is not to be made known, Deverell. Secrecy is of the utmost importance.'

Chapter Five

Thomas Franklyn was tall and lanky and bone thin. His light brown curly hair was cut short. His coat had shiny cuffs and his linen was worn. Various expressions chased themselves across his face. He was a great one for practical jokes and there were times when what he said was serious or not serious, it was difficult to tell. He had visited Shona often when she had been in England and it had always been something of a novelty among her friends when he had turned up unexpectedly at her school. Life was never quiet or dull when he was present.

His home was in England. The youngest of three sons raised at Ferndene, the family's ancestral home in Sussex, his ambition had been to go on the stage, but his father had frowned on this ignoble profession, unable to countenance any son of his treading the boards, so Thomas had succumbed to the pressure placed on him by his family and made the church his living.

Eight years spent as a parish parson in the provinces had endowed him with an air of philosophic indifference. Having become disillusioned with his profession, critical and outspoken about the church's doctrines, with a spurt of rebellion to amuse himself he had written what he considered to be some light verse.

Some of the clergy had expressed outrage at the titillating content, the general consensus being that, instead of filling his head with poetry and writing heathen words, he should be reciting psalms or the gospels. They declared his position untenable, but with friends in high places and highly thought of by some who saw nothing wrong with his verse, by mutual consent he had been granted some time away to indulge his mind in philosophical thought. Seeing it as the perfect opportunity to travel and broaden his mind, Thomas had taken ship for America, deciding to visit his family on Santamaria on the return journey.

Shona looked down at the man who had just entered the house, dumping his baggage on the floor. Surprise widened her eyes. 'Thomas!'

Laughing delightedly, raising her skirts slightly, she hurried down the stairs, straight into his outstretched arms. 'This is wonderful—but why didn't you write and let us know you were coming? And look at you,' she said, taking in his well-worn clothes and his mop of unruly brown curls. 'Why, it's plain to see you have no one to take care of you. What you need is a wife, Thomas.'

'And why should I want that? I am perfectly happy and content the way I am, without the encumbrance of a wife. But look at you,' he said, frowning, holding her at arm's length and studying her features. 'You have lost weight since last we met—and you are pale. Dearest coz, are you all right? If not, that is easily remedied. The Ship Inn down in the town is close by. They serve the finest meat pies this side of the Caribbean.' His eyes twinkled mischievously. 'Or are you too proud to accept your disreputable cousin's invitation?'

Shona was so happy to see him that she forgot her meeting with Captain Fitzgerald earlier. 'Thomas, we are family. How can you think that? And much as I would like to accompany you to the Ship Inn, I'm afraid Antony would certainly not approve.'

'That is what I expected you to say,' Thomas said with a grin. 'How is Cousin Antony? Last I heard he had married a beautiful Spanish *señorita*. I look forward to meeting her—although I doubt her beauty can match yours, fair coz.'

Shona refrained from showing her distaste and telling him that in her opinion her brother had made a poor choice for a wife. 'I had no idea you were so taken with my looks, Thomas. I always thought you favoured my good friend Maria.'

'Given the opportunity I would disabuse you of that opinion.' He smiled. It was impossible not to respond to the charm of that smile. This was the light-hearted flirtation her friend Maria had so enjoyed when he had visited her at school. Maria kept her apace of what was happening in London and to other friends she had been at school with. She wrote of carriage rides in Hyde Park and new ballgowns. The gentleman she was to wed was busy training hunting dogs at his country estate in Cheshire and he had presented her with a small English poodle. They were to attend a wedding in London and she was to wear a pearl-blue dress with silver threads. How Shona envied her, but not for much longer. She would soon be taking her place in London society when she reached London as Zack's wife.

'And how was Aunt Augusta when you left England? She must visit us here, Thomas.'

Thomas's mother, who had left her humble origins behind on the rise to power of her brother, Shona's father, had married into the nobility.

'Since my father died, my mother is rarely at home in Surrey,' Thomas replied with a smile. 'She prefers St James's and the gaieties of the London Season. I know she would like to visit Santamaria, but as you know she is not a good sailor. Now,' he said, looking about at the grand surroundings, 'when am I going to see my cousin and meet his lovely wife?'

'My wife is very lovely, Thomas,' said Antony, striding out of his study to greet his cousin, 'and shortly to give birth to our first child. She is resting at present, but you will meet her later. It's good to see you.'

'My visit is brief, I'm afraid—a week or so, no more. I'm on my way back home after spending some time in Virginia. I could not come all this way without stopping off to see my cousins.'

'You are most welcome. Your arrival at this time is most fortuitous.'

'How so?'

'Shona is to be wed—before the week is out. But come. I will put you in the picture over refreshment.' He glanced at his sister. 'Order refreshment, Shona. We'll be on the terrace.' In a quiet voice he said to Thomas, 'There is something I would like you to do for me—or I should say for Shona.'

As Antony led their cousin off to the terrace to tell him all about Shona's fall from grace, Thomas looked back and winked at her.

When Antony told Thomas what had transpired, he looked incredulous.

'I'd welcome your help in this, Thomas. Fitzgerald is out to cheat me. I'd let him leave the island, but that's not the point. He's ruined Shona. Besides, she is impatient to return to England. Santamaria is not enough for her any more. She adored Father. Now he is no longer with us there is nothing to keep her here.'

'Then allow her to go to England. She doesn't have to wed to do that. My mother will be more than happy to take care of her.'

'No disrespect to Aunt Augusta, but I can't let her go alone.'

'And my mother would not exactly be a good influence. Oh, don't worry.' He laughed when

Antony would have contradicted him to spare his feelings. 'Always one to live her life as though it were one long party, my mother is hardly the perfect role model to take on the chaperonage of a young girl.'

'It's not just that, Thomas. Because of the way she looks and the large dowry Father settled on her before his death, he was certain Shona was vulnerable to fortune hunters. I promised him I would see her suitably married before she left the island. I will abide by that. But by God, Thomas, how long can I stand Carmelita and my sister being at each other's throats day in and day out? Something has to be done and soon.'

'And how does Shona view Captain Fitzgerald?'

'After what I witnessed when I came upon them in the creek, she is certainly not averse to him. Quite the opposite. They were all over each other. At present there is no cleric on the island. This man that Fitzgerald has arranged to marry them is a fake cleric. He intends to dupe me. I cannot allow it to pass. I will not tolerate being made a fool of. Co-operate with me, Thomas.'

'What you ask of me is against everything I represent. My life has always been conducted on the highest principles.'

'You mean nobody knows anything about you,' Antony pointed out drily. 'Come, Thomas. You may be a man of the church, but you are no saint.'

'Try not to offend me, Antony.' Thomas chuckled.

'Will you do it? Cornelius Clay is a drunk. It should not be too difficult rendering him incapable and putting yourself forward to perform the ceremony.'

Thomas hesitated, aware of the enormity of what Antony was asking of him and knowing that he was about to risk his credibility in the church. But the thought of Shona's suffering as Antony had detailed to him, made him feel he had no choice. His expression suddenly became serious and he fixed his cousin with a level gaze.

'I have developed a great fondness for Shona. She is a fine young woman and it grieves me to think of her in such unhappy circumstances. I had no idea things were so—difficult for her on the island. I'll have to think about it.'

'There is no time, Thomas. A decision has to be made.'

Antony felt quietly confident. If Thomas had not meant to accept his request, he would have rejected it firmly. His promise to think about it was almost as good as acceptance. He would consider it and do battle with his conscience, but he would do it.

Antony was right. Thomas had reached a decision. 'If marriage to this…this Captain Fitzgerald is what she wants, then I am more than happy to do this small service for her. I can only hope that he makes her happy.'

There was no mistaking the sincerity in his voice and Antony, exultant but somewhat shame-faced, turned away. 'It's settled, then?'

Thomas nodded. 'It's settled.' He grinned. 'I give you my word, coz, that I shall keep Mr Cornelius Clay sinfully occupied, thus rendering him incapable of conducting a wedding ceremony—bogus or otherwise.'

The only cloud hanging over Shona at this time was the island's gossip circle. The ladies were already clucking their tongues in disapproval of her behaviour, echoing one another's vicious words. After all that fine schooling, more than one said, didn't she know how to behave…? How could she? There were some kind souls who tried to defend her, but the gossipmongers were no longer listening.

In the eyes of the elite on the island she was a

shameless wanton, soiled and used, unfit company for unsullied young ladies and gullible young men. She had broken the rules governing moral conduct and not even with someone that she was acquainted with. She might as well start packing now, they said.

To avoid causing any more trouble for herself, Shona threw herself into preparing for her new role in life as the wife of a shipping magnate. There would be much to learn and, in truth, more responsibility involved than she had expected. But she was excited and impatient to be Zack's wife. Her marriage became more real by the hour.

To avoid coming into contact with her neighbours she limited the days' activities to reading in her room and short walks around the garden. She had looked forward to spending time with Thomas, but he had left the house shortly after his arrival, which she thought most odd. With brusque impatience, Carmelita told her he had returned to the ship which had brought him to Santamaria, that he had things to do and could by no means stay at the house until the end of the week. Both Antony and Carmelita had about them the air of grim irresolution that Shona recognised as the prelude to crisis. She noted Carmelita's tone as she told her, the haste. Hastily she memorised the signs on her face, to puzzle over and interpret later.

With the wedding just days away, disconcerted by Shona's silence and long seclusion in her room, feeling better disposed to her now she was to leave Santamaria, Carmelita sought her out in her chambers. The walls of her bedchamber were a soft magnolia complemented by the subtle hue of pastel-green and the vibrant turquoise of the chairs and sofa. A luxurious Aubusson carpet combined all the colours in the room and a green silk canopy hung from the large tester bed.

'You mustn't take things so hard, Shona,' she said, crossing to where the young woman was curled up in a wicker chair on the balcony, an unopened book in her lap. 'Despite that unfortunate incident in the creek, this marriage is really rather a good thing when you think about it. A lot of girls will envy you and not a few grand ladies, too. And Captain Fitzgerald is very handsome. You may even grow to love him. Whatever happens, you will be a titled lady and kept in the manner to which you are accustomed.'

'I am sure you are right, Carmelita,' Shona

replied drily. 'Although I don't imagine for one minute you are concerned one way or the other.'

Ignoring her sarcastic remark, Carmelita let her eyes stray towards the rows of Shona's shimmering gowns through the open door to her dressing room. 'You must instruct Morag to begin packing your things, Shona. Captain Fitzgerald has insisted that as soon as the ceremony is over he wishes to leave the island.'

'Do not concern yourself, Carmelita,' Shona said, opening her book and looking down. 'I'll be ready when the time comes.'

Three days later, on the day that Zack was to marry Shona, but with no sign of the reverend on board, cursing quietly, Zack went in search of him. He was directed to the Ship Inn. A chorus of rowdy voices greeted him when he pushed his way into the dim interior. A fiddler's bow scraping a jarring note on the strings battled to be heard above the din of voices. The place was crowded, the air thick with the fug of tobacco smoke, stale ale and unwashed bodies. Zack's nostrils flared in disgust. Men seated on upturned barrels argued over a turn of a card, or squatted in circles wagering upon a throw of the dice. His eyes narrowed and his lips set in a grim line as his eyes located the reverend propped in a corner—it soon became apparent that he had been there for some time. Zack strode towards him, taking hold of his shoulder.

'You mule-headed idiot,' he barked. 'You sure pick your time to get stinking drunk. Get up, you laggard. Have you forgotten where we're meant to be in an hour's time?'

His command penetrated the reverend's deep torpor and sluggishly he raised himself to a sitting position. Through half-open eyes he looked up at his captain. Something must have penetrated his inebriated brain for he managed to shove himself to his feet. Taking a few tentative steps, he slumped back down and his eyes rolled back.

With his shoulder propped against the frame of the open door, Thomas watched with unbridled amusement as the captain again tried to force the Reverend Clay to his feet. 'Look at that, will you?' He laughed. 'The man can't even walk without stumbling.'

Zack let go and stepped back. 'God damn it! The man's drunk!' The problem now was what to do next. He could hardly parade a drunken cleric in front of the McKenzies.

Thomas looked at him and cocked a brow. 'Can I be of help?'

'Not unless you're a damned good actor,' Zack growled.

'Oh, I can act all right,' Thomas said, cocksure of himself, 'for a price... Why, didn't I appear in *The Merchant of Venice* as Shylock once—and again as Romeo to a rather delectable Juliet!'

He had Zack's attention. He looked at him hard. 'How much?'

'That depends on the part.'

'What's your name?'

Thomas shrugged himself away from the door and made a flourish of a bow. 'Thomas Franklyn—at your service, Captain.'

'Come with me.'

'It will be my pleasure.'

'Wait until you hear what I'm about to ask of you before you consider it a pleasure.'

Quietly triumphant, with a smug smile and a spring to his step, Thomas followed jauntily in the captain's wake.

Quietly confident that he had everything under control and that things would go his way, accompanied by Singleton and Thomas Franklyn, Zack arrived at Melrose Hill as the light was fading.

From the window of her bedchamber, Shona watched him leap from his black horse with a strange tight feeling round her heart. As always he looked striking, in his buckled shoes, lace at his throat and olive-green coat. She was not surprised to see Thomas with him—Antony had told her that in the absence of the island's curate, he was to perform the ceremony. He had also told her that for reasons that he would make clear to her later, she must treat Thomas as if he were a stranger to her. Knowing Antony would have his reasons and wishing to avoid further argument, she had not questioned this, but she did consider it an odd request.

As soon as she had seen the two of them disappear into the house, Shona left the window and waited till she was summoned. It was hot, but she shivered in her embroidered ivory dress. Looking at the trunks ready to be taken to the ship the following day, she felt a sudden terror seize her now the moment had come for her to confront the man who would take her away from Santamaria. Her hands were icy and she shivered all over in a sudden panic.

Muffled but ominous noises through the house

reached her ears. Suddenly the door opened and Carmelita appeared. She pursed her lips when she caught sight of Shona standing there.

'What are you doing? They have sent for you. Come along and try to put a good face on things,' she advised, turning and walking ahead of Shona. Incapable of showing any reaction by now, Shona followed docilely.

Entering the drawing room, where the ceremony was to be performed, Shona was aware of people standing around, but her eyes became fixed on Zack Fitzgerald conversing quietly with Mr Singleton. With a prayer book in his hands, Thomas, standing alone, appeared a sombre figure in his black surplice. When she appeared, however, Zack and his first mate stopped talking and looked at her. She was acutely conscious of Zack's unrelenting gaze. He watched her with a slow, unhurried intensity that unnerved her.

There was a certain tension in Zack's body, his eyes transfixed by Shona's beauty, as he watched her slowly walk into the centre of the room. Shona's lowered eyes prevented her seeing the look of wondering admiration which spread across his face.

Taking her place by his side, Shona drew herself upright. Her slender figure seemed taller in the rose, dancing sunlight. Her resplendent golden hair enveloped her in a sort of radiance, which suddenly made Zack's heart ache. Her beauty was almost blinding and Zack, more drawn to her than he cared to admit, had a presentiment that she was one of the rare women for whom wars were fought, for whom men killed themselves—women who rarely bring happiness to the men who love them.

But as he stood by her side to recite the words that, unbeknown to him, would bind them together for all eternity, his expression was one of resolve. However much he wanted to, he couldn't let himself make love to her. He couldn't let his objectives slide. He swore Shona McKenzie and her brother would pay for intimidating him and trying to manipulate him, and by damned, they would! No one could blackmail him, then be as sublimely happy and content for doing so—as the woman by his side was at this moment. It was the devil in him that wouldn't let him be tested and pride was the devil's name.

Thomas made sure that the marriage ceremony was brief. He was uncomfortable with what he was about to do. His desire to please Antony, and at the same time grant Shona her heart's desire to return to England, had overcome his reservations. Now he was set on a path of deception that might have disastrous consequences.

Shona heard herself answer 'yes' to Thomas's questions as though in a dream. Her voice had sunk to a whisper and he had to lean forward to catch her responses. Zack, for his part, had spoken up in a calm, indifferent voice.

The warmth of his hand replaced the coldness that had threatened to engulf Shona only moments ago when she had sat waiting in her chamber. From time to time she stole a glance at this man who was shortly to be her husband. She thought back to the moment he had arrived on Santamaria, relived each breathless, daring second—the pressure of his lips, the taste, the wanton way her body had responded to his touch. So long ago now, it seemed. So many ages past, yet it was only days.

Is that what love should be like?

The thought that it should be struck her like a thunderbolt. Her heart was suddenly full, almost bursting with excitement beyond words. Surely she didn't…couldn't…be in love with him?

How handsome he looks, she thought. He had his eyes fixed straight ahead. Without warning, she knew a moment's panic. Somewhere in her mind a voice cried out that she was making a terrible mistake, committing herself to a man whom, deep in her heart, she knew held a deep resentment for her. From this point there would be no turning back. They were caught up in an implacable destiny, that whatever the future held, they would have to endure together all their lives. There was a curiously unreal, almost sinister air about the whole thing. Recalling the happy ceremonies she had attended when friends of her family had married, Shona told herself that this was easily the most depressing wedding she had ever been to.

The words that bound them together were spoken quietly. Shona's eyes misted over when Zack promised to love, honour and cherish her. With all her being she wanted the words to be true. The ring was placed on her finger and the ceremony was concluded when Thomas pronounced them man and wife.

He gave a nod to Zack. 'You may now kiss the bride.'

Shona flushed and would have turned away for fear of being rebuffed. A small gasp of surprise escaped her as Zack tightened his arm about her waist and pulled her round to face him. Slanting its way across his firm lips was a rather wicked, wayward grin and slowly he lowered his head to hers. All reason fled as his lips hovered close above her own.

'Bear with my kiss, Shona,' he murmured, his breath warm on her mouth. 'Everyone would be disappointed if I were remiss in not doing so.'

Suddenly his lips were moving over hers in a warmly seductive kiss that stirred some strange, unexplainable brew that sapped the strength from her limbs and made her head spin and her heart race wildly. Without her being aware of it, she placed her hand on his waist, causing a murmur of approval from those present. It acted on her like a douche of cold water. Coming to her senses, she stepped back and turned her face aside. Zack straightened and turned away.

A small banquet awaited the few wedding guests in the dining room. It was a quiet, strained affair in spite of Mr Singleton's efforts to lighten the atmosphere. Shona, seated beside Zack, scarcely touched the food which was placed before her. She ate a morsel or two of the superb fish course, cooked in herbs, but the food stuck in her throat when she swallowed.

The champagne had a cheering effect on the company. Antony had mellowed enough to try to draw Zack into the conversation, and even though he maintained a reserved composure and was well skilled at putting a fine cutting edge on his civility, the atmosphere became quite convivial. Shona felt isolated and alone like a spectator at a play as she sat back and watched them all laughing and talking. She couldn't wait to escape.

When the meal was over, Carmelita escorted Shona to her room, where she instructed Morag to prepare her mistress for bed. Fully aware of the deception that had preceded this marriage, positively preening with her success in getting her irritating sister-in-law married off at last, Carmelita couldn't help her lips forming a semblance of a smile.

'There, you see. Everything went well. That wasn't too difficult, was it?'

'Not for you, maybe, but I wouldn't say that.'

Carmelita dismissed her comment with a careless shrug of her shoulders and returned to the guests.

From where he sat Zack watched Shona leave, knowing he was expected to follow when he had given her enough time to get ready for him. He had thought he had solved the problem of his lovely wife by refusing to go near her, but his plight somehow only became more unbearable at the thought of leaving her.

When Morag helped her remove her clothes, Shona took a new and intense pleasure in the beauty of her own body, which was very soon to be presented to her husband. While Morag stood behind her, combing out her golden hair till it shone as brightly as the sun, Shona dabbed a few drops of jasmine on her neck and wrists. When she moved she felt herself enveloped in a cloud of fresh, delicious but subtle fragrance.

The polished mirror in its elaborate frame reflected back a charming picture, all rose-pink and pale gold. It was such a ravishing sight that Shona's eyes sparkled with excitement and anticipation, confident that the grooming of her body would prove to be an irresistible magnet, a delicious trap for her husband. She longed for him with all the ardour of her proud heart and all the passion and vigour of blooming youth.

When Morag had finished, with a happy tear in her eye, she, too, stood back a little distance to admire the enchanting vision of womanhood reflected in the mirror. 'There, you look lovely,

Shona. If there's nothing else, I'll leave you now. Your husband will be with you shortly.'

'Yes—yes, Morag,' Shona said, throwing her arms about her maid's neck and hugging her. 'Tomorrow we sail for Martinique and then England. I'm so excited and happy I'll have you with me. In fact, I'm so excited I have to keep pinching myself.'

Shona stood motionless when Morag had left, her nervousness returning as she waited for Zack to come. One minute she longed for his presence and the next she prayed he would not come. She both feared and desired him.

When Zack opened the door the first thing he saw was Shona standing in the middle of the room, her slender body outlined beneath the gossamer-thin nightdress, the golden nimbus of hair drawn back from her face so as to reveal her long, supple neck. She looked like some pagan goddess. His glance flickered over the shadow of her breasts through the soft folds of material, provocative and arresting. Yet the gown was so simply cut that her nakedness beneath seemed innocent, almost vulnerable. He stood looking at her, as if not wanting to spoil the lovely picture she made, not wanting to disturb the beguiling innocence that hid the burning fire within.

Closing the door, unable to take his eyes from her, he moved slowly to where she stood. 'Your sister-in-law told me it was time I retired.'

Shona looked up into his saturnine face, her lips forming a trembling smile. 'And there's no disobeying Carmelita. I feel like a wayward child who has just been sent to bed by a strict governess,' she said with an awkward laugh.

'The woman is an arrogant fool. You are no child, Shona—though more than a tad wayward,' he said, giving the first carefree laugh Shona had heard from him all day.

In the pale light his sensual features were darkly handsome and she knew the desire in his eyes was mirrored unashamedly in her own.

He turned from her.

'Please—look at me, Zack.'

She heard him groan softly. Slowly he turned back to her and saw the face of an enchanting temptress, with parted lips and eyes soft with promise. He touched her hair, wrapping a lock around his forefinger. 'Such a colour,' he murmured. 'Golden like the sun and yet with a hint of fire.'

Shona stood in silent fascination, watching

him as he removed his jacket and neckcloth and opened the front of his shirt. His body glowed with strength, energy and vigour. Her eyes took in the flexing iron-hard muscles of his wide shoulders, the broad chest, the lean belly and the length of his powerful legs. She could feel the warmth of his body close to hers as he stood looking down at her, and her whole being reached out to him, yearning for him to seize her, hold her and possess her.

As if he read her thoughts, taking her arms and pulling her close, Zack felt each curve of her young, supple body against him. The sudden, sharp coldness of the locket he wore around his neck made her gasp and draw back. Smiling an apology, he took it off and placed it on a small table beside the bed. Then slowly, gently, he slipped her nightgown down over one shoulder, so that first one breast, then the other appeared from beneath the concealing shadows of the garment and, little by little, the rest of her glowing flesh was revealed to him. The candlelight washed over her and there was the pungent smell of aromatic shrubs and trees outside.

His eyes caressed every curve of her body, every indentation of her skin, and his obvious delight in her sent the blood singing in his veins.

She was offering herself to him and she was maddeningly desirable. His gaze was drawn to her trembling lips. Slowly, he bent his head, covering her mouth with his. He heard her sigh and, when he felt her arms tentatively reach up to rest on his shoulders, he deepened his kiss, thrusting gently into her mouth. His arms went around her then, his hands tracing her curves without volition.

The fierceness of his wanting her startled him. He wanted to fill his mouth with the taste of her, to span that impossibly narrow waist with his hands and draw those inviting hips beneath him, to have those long, lithe legs wrapped around him, to bury himself in her silky sweetness.

Somehow he found himself leading her to the bed and lowering her down on to the mattress so that she was lying beneath him. He hovered over her. All he could see was the quiver of her tantalising mouth urging him to kiss her into dazed insensibility. He was aware that the days of being around her, of wanting her, of self-denial and frustration, were in danger of driving him beyond restraint. Her appearance was a striking contrast between angelic and wanton. One part of him wanted nothing to do with her. Another wanted to punish her for bringing him to such a pass. And yet another—by far the greatest part—wanted to take her in his arms and awaken all the exquisite, undiscovered passion in her lovely body.

The mere sight of her aroused carnal feelings in him that he had no business feeling since he meant to leave her, so whatever happened he must not take his fill of her. He could not afford to father another child out of wedlock. But a kiss, a caress—a memory to take with him from Santamaria to warm his empty bed on the long voyage back to England.

'I know this is insane,' he said hoarsely.

'No, it isn't,' she whispered, caressing his lips with her own. 'It's perfectly normal for a husband to want to make love to his wife.'

She drew a quick breath as his hands slid upwards to cup her breasts. His touch was incredibly sensual, and as he filled his hands with her breasts, a quiver built deep in her stomach. Closing her eyes, she let her head fall back.

He heard the soft sound and his eyes flared with silver lights. 'Wife,' he murmured. The word was a mere whisper and lost as he slowly leaned forward to press his lips against her neck, his arousing fingers caressing her nipples. If only it were possible for him to experience the full depth of pleasure between a man and a woman before the night was over.

'Aren't you going to remove your clothes?' she asked, reaching up and gently caressing his face, aching with unfulfilled need.

Zack was aware of her need. The quick rise and fall of her breasts, her shallow breathing, the fast beating of her heart—all told him. Her trembling innocence was incredibly erotic. Lowering his body so that he was kneeling between her thighs, he lowered his head to scatter hot, open-mouthed kisses over the taut skin of her belly.

Shocked to the core, Shona had no idea how to respond to his attentions. She lay there, open to him, taut and trembling, and when he kissed her lips again, she instinctively reached up to curl her fingers in his hair. He was stirring such sensations in her—desire and heat and staggering pleasure. Feeling the chafing of his shirt against her flesh, she opened her eyes and looked up at him.

'Please,' she whispered, 'take off your shirt.'

Her softly spoken words brought him to his senses. Recollecting himself, he gently pushed away her outstretched arms and stood up. 'Forgive me, Shona. I must leave you a moment.'

Shona experienced a moment's panic. 'You will come back?'

Knowing her world was about to be ripped apart, that he was powerless to prevent the disgrace and disaster soon to descend on her, and consumed with guilt, Zack suddenly looked away.

'Of course you will. I trust you.' She sighed, drawing the coverlet up to her chin.

Feeling profoundly wretched he closed his eyes tight for a moment, having to fight the temptation to go back to her. He couldn't believe he was letting the chance to make love to this beautiful woman slip through his fingers. Leaving the rosy figure stretched out upon the bed, shrugging on his coat, he strode to the door. He placed something on her dressing table before he went out and vanished into the darkness of the house.

Chapter Six

Shona heard Zack's footsteps grow fainter. Snuggling into her pillows, she waited, fully expecting him to return.

But he didn't return. Feeling bereft, she sat up and swung her legs to the floor and looked around the room. A gentle breeze blowing in through the open balcony windows stirred the curtains. On a sigh she stood up and went to her dressing table. That was the moment when her eyes lighted on the letter propped up against the mirror.

Tentatively she reached out and picked it up, looking at it curiously, suddenly reluctant to open it, for she feared the contents. She was right to, for in his bold hand, Zack had written down what he'd not had the courage to say to her face. In stunned silence she read how their marriage was a sham, the curate an actor playing a part. The words puzzled her. None of it made sense to her just then. The only thing that penetrated her mind was that Zack had left her and he was not coming back.

Seeing the locket, she picked it up, the silver chain sliding through her fingers. She looked at it for what seemed an age before she had the courage to snap it open. Inside was a single lock of dark brown hair. A lump of unexplained emotion suddenly appeared in her throat. Whoever it had belonged to the woman must mean a great deal to Zack for him to carry a lock of her hair. Who was she?

Thrusting the note and the locket away from her, still Shona waited, thinking—hoping—desperately he might return when he realised he had left the locket behind. In front of her the sight of her rumpled sheets reminded her of him. All her emotions surged and eddied in her mind. The union she had dreamed of had never happened. The delight she had envisioned during the magic of preparing for bed had been but a mirage. In vain she fought to control the tears that threatened to brim and flow down her cheeks.

She had thought they had overcome the bitter recriminations that had beset their relationship in the beginning. All her hopes and dreams of weaving lovely threads into their marriage, the love and the trust that would come with knowledge of each other, the delight and laughter, the companionship, the stability, reliability, comfort and trust which would be theirs to last a lifetime, were shattered in a moment. It was unprecedented, unmatched and hopeless. Zack's desertion had exploded the very roots of the life she had hoped they would build together. She felt she might wither away and die, like a flower that is left unprotected in the hot sun. She held herself tightly, arms locked about her breast, for if she did not keep a firm grip on herself she would scream. She quite simply could not stand the pain.

Control shattered with full realisation. He wasn't coming back. Zachariah Fitzgerald had gone, fleeing the wreck that he had brought about. Now she, Shona, must think what to do about the disaster he had left behind. A blurred vision of her face in the mirror across the room struck her, tore at the very fabric of her soul, the treacherous catalyst being her lips still swollen from his kisses. The girl in the mirror stiffened and stared at herself as the tears ran down her face. The precious spark of life left the parted lips and the hurt and questioning set in.

Through the vision her own rage took form and grew. She fought for control and won. The woman in front of her changed, stared back at her with tight, angry eyes. *What had Zack Fitzgerald done to her? What had she allowed him to do to her? She was Shona McKenzie, the most sought-after young woman in the Caribbean.* She squared her shoulders, trying to convince the woman in the mirror. *Who does he think he is?* The woman in the mirror stared coldly back at her. *Zack Fitzgerald was a domineering, stubborn, ill-bred blackguard.*

It took a moment to convince herself that she was not trapped in some bad dream, but as her power of thought returned she tried to sort out her situation, but this only left her feeling bitter. She had been living in a sort of trance all these past few days, ever since the moment, in fact, when Zack had first stepped on to the island. And now the return to reality left an ashen taste in her mouth. When she thought of Zack Fitzgerald, a flush of shame and anger left her crimson and she was even more angry with herself.

Brushing back the long gold tresses from her face, she dressed and left the house.

* * *

The hour was late when she entered the town and, slowing her horse's pace, passed through the streets like a wraith. The tropic night was warm and still. The moon was high in a cloudless sky. Its brilliant light eclipsed the stars. Flooding the scene, it splashed the ground ahead of her with patches of silver between the stark black shadows of lounging sailors on the quay and threw their features into stark relief. Apart from raucous laughter coming from the taverns around the harbour, it was quiet. She looked towards the pier. As she expected the *Ocean Pearl* had left her moorings. Shifting her gaze to the mouth of the cove, in the moon's silver glow she watched the ship head for the open sea.

A quiet, cold anger stirred in her breast. *This is not over, Zack Fitzgerald,* she vowed. *This changes nothing. I am still your wife. I shall give you no respite. One day you will come to repent what you have done.* A fierce desire for revenge had suddenly taken hold of her. In truth, her feelings towards Zachariah Fitzgerald were complex. She desired him and hated him at the same time, this man who had so coldly and unhesitatingly entered into what he'd believed was a bogus marriage, gone wild with passion in her arms and then left her.

His tortured face when he had left her awoke a streak of malicious glee in Shona. By the time she had finished, he would realise that pride did not solve everything or protect him from everything.

As soon as Zack stepped aboard, amid soft commands the sails were unfurled, the anchor raised. Soon a freshening breeze was licking at Zack's face and the *Ocean Pearl* was ploughing onwards. He bent his neck around and watched as the lights of Santamaria began to fade from view. At last he had escaped the island. He tried to follow his standard policy of never looking back where females were concerned, but Shona McKenzie was not so easily forgotten. In spite of himself he brooded on how she had looked when he had left her, how her lovely face had been flushed with passion. Though he had gone through the sham ceremony without expression, he could not escape the guilty sense that he was abandoning her to a life of loneliness on Santamaria, much like a pirate abandoning one of his crew on a deserted island for some nefarious misdeed.

Don't think about her, he told himself. She was tough. Life was tough. Shona McKenzie would survive. When they'd been together she'd told him she trusted him. Inwardly he scoffed at the words. *Trust!* By now she would have read his note and would share his opinion that he was an all-round bastard.

His mind went back to their meeting in the creek which had precipitated this mess. He was unable to shake off the image of the tempestuous beauty as she had strenuously attempted to defend herself, to deny that she had deliberately set out to deceive him. The picture branded itself on his mind along with a voice that shook with emotion. She had actually looked and sounded as if she meant every single thing she'd said to him.

His fingers shook as they brushed his hair from his brow. Dear God, she was a superb actress, but she had failed to pull this particular act off. Or she'd been innocent of deviousness all along and it was her sister-in-law who had masterminded the plot all alone to get rid of her.

Zack hesitated uneasily and then coldly rejected the possibility. Had Shona been innocent of deviousness she would have tried harder to defend herself instead of going along with her brother and forcing the marriage. She was just a woman and women were all alike. She could be forced from his mind. He had never known one who couldn't be.

Closing his mind and hardening his heart, thinking of his daughter, he fixed his eyes on the unforgiving sea.

When Shona emerged from her room the following morning, she felt as though she had been born anew as a result of some painful and unaccustomed new process of gestation. Very little remained of the innocent young Shona McKenzie who had plunged headlong with such blind stupidity into the arms of Zachariah Fitzgerald. Now her only feeling was anger, an anger that nothing but vengeance could assuage.

In the midst of the ruins she was alone. Of her world, the world of her childhood, nothing remained. Her home and all her most cherished illusions had been destroyed the moment Zachariah Fitzgerald had moored his ship in the harbour of Santamaria.

After she calmly read the note he had left her once more, her instinct told her that somehow Antony wasn't innocent in all this and that he, too, had deceived her in some way. But Zack had been a participant in the deception and entered into what he believed was a sham marriage, leaving her without realising Thomas was a minister of the church and she was truly his wife, and for that he would pay.

Calmly she slipped out of her flimsy nightdress for which she no longer had any use. Dressing and tying her hair into a knot at the nape of her neck, she went in search of her brother. She glided soundlessly along the landing and down the stairs, struck by the heavy, almost brooding silence of the house, an ominous, waiting silence like the calm before a storm. She found Antony drinking coffee on the terrace with Thomas.

Thomas, looking ashen and rather shamefaced, rose on seeing his young cousin. 'Shona! What can I say…?'

'Nothing, Thomas,' she said coldly. 'Zack left me a note explaining that our marriage was a sham—before leaving me and sailing off like a thief in the night.'

'For what it's worth, I am sorry…'

'I'm glad to hear it. Although why on earth Zack had reason to think you were an actor is beyond me for the moment.' Her gaze shifted to her brother. 'And you, Antony? Are you sorry? I suspect your hand in this. I await your explanation, for I sense there is a good deal more that I should know about and I insist you tell me everything.'

Lifting his gaze to hers, Antony shrugged casually. 'Very well, I will, but one thing you can be sure of is that you are Fitzgerald's true wife.' He went on to reveal even more of Fitzgerald's treachery, about the drunken reverend who was to perform the ceremony even though he was aware that he had been excommunicated, of how Antony had found out and cunningly replaced Zack's reverend with Thomas. 'The only thing I'm sorry about is that I lifted the guard on Fitzgerald's ship, which enabled him to slip away.'

The scheming and treachery that had taken place without her knowledge shocked Shona to the very core of her being. 'Is that all you have to say after your outrageous conduct? You might at least show some shame or remorse. But, no, you are as carelessly at ease as ever. And you dare to mock me! You're not sorry about hurting me?'

'You brought it on yourself—with your wanton behaviour.'

A wave of sick disgust swept over her. 'And what of your behaviour, Antony? You played with my life like you would indulge in a game of cards. From what you have told me, there

was some misunderstanding about a minister
to perform the ceremony. Without a curate on
the island, Zack offered to put forward one of his
own—a man excommunicated by the church—
and you found out. Anyone else would have been
outraged, but not you. Instead of confronting
him, you decided to play him at his own game.
By making me the object of your game of cat
and mouse, you offered me, your own sister, a
gross insult.'

With a sigh of irritation, Antony hoisted himself forward in the chair. 'A damnable game it
turned out to be. The man had the devil in him.
He would have rolled me up if Thomas hadn't
arrived in time.'

'Providing you with the perfect opportunity
to get your own back. How much alcohol did it
take to render Mr Clay unconscious?' She fixed
her hard gaze on Thomas. 'I have heard of your
acting skills, Thomas, but to succeed in fooling
Zack tells me your talent would be more appropriate on the stage rather than in the church. I
trust Zack rewarded you for your services.'

'Indeed. Had I refused to accept recompense
he might have become suspicious. I assure you
that the proceeds will go to a worthy cause.

There is an orphanage in my parish that will benefit.'

'How noble of you, Thomas,' she said, her lips twisting with sarcasm. 'I'm pleased to hear something worthwhile has come out of this treachery.'

'I'm sorry, Shona,' Thomas said, profoundly ashamed of the part he had played. 'What is to be done?'

'You might well ask. Zack and I are properly married. My place is with him now, so naturally I shall follow him to England.'

A dark flush of anger swept over Antony's face. 'You will not. I forbid it.'

Shona gave him a haughty look. 'It won't make any difference whether I go after him or not. Thanks to your meddling, my life is a disaster whichever way you look at it.'

'A disaster of your own making. Go into to the house, Shona. We shall decide on a course of action when Carmelita comes down.'

'I will not go back to the house until this is resolved,' Shona said, filled with sudden bravado. 'You did me a great wrong, Antony. You married me off in the most disgraceful manner— you, my brother—and you, Thomas, a man of the church. Shame on you—both of you! Am I alone in feeling that the church should not be used and abused like this?' Indeed, it caused a feeling of profound revulsion in her.

'It's unfortunate, I grant you,' Antony said. 'The marriage will be annulled, of course.'

Colour flooded Shona's face. She knew what her brother was implying. 'No,' she said. 'You can't do that. It's not possible. I— We...'

Antony stared at her hard. 'Are you telling me that...that...renegade had you?'

Shona raised her head haughtily. When she spoke, her tone was one of complete defiance. 'Yes,' she lied. 'I am his wife in every way. I am not beholden to you any longer, Antony. I am the *legal* wife of Captain Zachariah Fitzgerald. It is to him that I belong now—even though he does not know it and is as deserving of my contempt as you are. When Thomas sails for England I shall go with him. How soon does your ship sail, Thomas?'

'About a week. But the captain—'

'Arrange for me to be on it,' she interrupted sharply, determined she would leave with the ship even if she had to stow away. 'It's the least you can do. Carmelita must be disappointed with the way things have turned out. She will have no objections to my leaving the island.'

* * *

Shona was right. Carmelita was beside herself with fury that Captain Fitzgerald had outwitted them. But she was not to be deterred. She had every intention of seeing Shona off the island for good.

When Shona was ready to board the ship, Antony's unwavering gaze bore into her. 'You are determined to stand by your decision to go after him?'

'Yes, Antony, I am.'

He stood unflinching. Every trace of emotion drained from his face. When he spoke his voice was as cold and devoid of feeling as a wind blowing through an empty house. 'Very well, then. Follow him if you must.'

Shona forced herself to stand straight, having to force down the hard lump that had appeared in her throat. 'Antony, I didn't want it this way. Won't you please—'

'The decision is your own, Shona. Freely made. There is nothing more to be said.'

And there wasn't. Shona's mind was made up.

London

Shona renewed her passion for London the moment she left the ship. They had arrived at the height of the Season. As the hired carriage drove away from the docks and headed towards Mayfair and Aunt Augusta's town house, the atmosphere of gaiety was entrancing. On reaching the Strand the streets were so overcrowded that their carriage was forced to slow almost to a halt. Shona stared out of the window. Shopkeepers shouted the excellence of their goods. Pedlars and street vendors praised their wares, vying with each other to attract customers. Not only the noise, but smells invaded the carriage—mouth-watering aromas of freshly baked bread, pies and cakes.

'Do you intend to stay in London, Thomas?'

'Only for a short time. I must return to my parish in Berkshire. But don't worry. My mother will be happy for you to stay with her for the time being—until things are sorted out between you and Captain Fitzgerald. As you are aware, Shona, both my parents led rather unconventional lifestyles. My brothers and I accepted the fact that they were living their lives as they wanted, even though they were frowned on by society in general. You will soon grow accustomed to Mother's ways.'

Shona was silent for a moment as she considered this statement. Antony had not been so generous and had condemned their aunt for her wayward behaviour after the death of her husband, which was why, considering her unfit company for a respectably reared young woman, he had been unwilling for his sister to come to England and for Aunt Augusta to act as her chaperon.

They entered the fine house in Upper Brook Street to find Thomas's mother reclining on a *chaise longue*. Her abundant deep red hair streaked with grey was confined loosely by a red satin ribbon that matched her velvet robe richly embroidered in gold thread. It was open to the waist to reveal a frilled and ruffled gown. There were the inevitable lines of age on her face and her cheeks owed some of their glow to the rouge pot, but there was no denying that Augusta Franklyn was still a handsome woman.

On seeing her son, she rose to her feet in one sinuous movement to glide across the carpet with her arms outstretched and her garments flowing around her in a diaphanous cloud.

'My darling boy! Here you are at last— And Shona! What a lovely surprise.'

Before Shona could react, after Augusta embraced her son she clasped Shona in a fond embrace and a cloud of expensive perfume heavy with musk.

'Aunt Augusta,' she murmured, at a loss for anything better to say. She liked her aunt and always felt comfortable with her. She could understand how her garish clothes and forceful personality might be forgiven when she gave so generously of the warmth of her personality.

Augusta held her at arm's length, gazing at her fondly. 'Why, look at you! How you've grown. You're no longer the skinny schoolgirl who used to come and visit me during your holidays. I can see you are going to turn heads here in London. It was mean of your brother not to let you come to me before, foolishly accusing me of being a bad influence on one so young. It would seem he's had a change of heart and we are going to have such fun.'

'Don't be too hasty, Mother,' Thomas remarked, making himself comfortable in a large armchair. 'Our darling Shona is now a married woman. For reasons which are…complicated— we will explain later—she is here to become reunited with her husband.'

Augusta expressed both her surprise and delight, insisting on knowing the identity of the gentleman. On being told she shook her head.

The name was not unknown to her, but she was not acquainted with the family. 'But don't worry,' she enthused, drawing Shona down beside her on to the *chaise longue,* 'I shall find out. And you, Thomas? I do hope you're not going to go tearing off to Berkshire without spending time with me. I was so upset when you sailed off to Virginia like that. I missed you so much.'

'Really, Mother, I don't recall you being too upset at the time.'

'Darling, don't be horrid. Of course I was upset. A mother's heart is a delicate thing and easily bruised, if not broken, when her children leave home. With your older brother and his wife in the country at Ferndene and Alex and his family in Northumberland, as the youngest I hated the thought of you being so far away. I suffered in silence.'

'My dearest mama, you never do anything in silence,' Thomas said with a mischievous twinkle in his eyes. 'I have no doubt you buried your sorrows in a continuous round of fashionable soirées with your innumerable friends. You are much in demand wherever you go.'

Augusta laughed happily and gave her son a coquettish smile, reminiscent of a schoolgirl, Shona thought. 'I confess they did help—as always. But you are a naughty boy for teasing your mama. Your brothers were always such serious boys, but you, like your dear father, have a wonderful capacity for fun and always make me laugh. It's such a pity you were denied your ambition to go on the stage, but your father refused to countenance such an ignoble profession for any of his sons. You've had plenty of time to consider what we discussed before you left for Virginia. What have you decided? Will you leave the church?'

Having no inclination that Thomas was even considering taking such a huge step, Shona stared at him in amazement. 'Thomas, you can't,' she gasped. 'Please don't. I can't bear to think you will go to such extremes.'

'I have to,' Thomas said calmly. 'My heart isn't in it. I've been thinking about leaving for some time, which was one of the reasons why I went to Virginia. I discussed my intentions with Mother before I left England. She is in agreement.'

Shona looked at her aunt, who nodded and smiled. 'Thomas is right. If that is what he wants, then he has my full support. He never wanted to enter the church in the first place, but as the youngest son and with his head on more frivolous pursuits at the time, his father believed it would be good for him. I was not in agreement, but even though I voiced my objections most forcefully, they went unheeded.'

'But—Thomas! What will you do?' Shona asked.

'When I've settled everything here, I intend to return to Virginia. I loved it there and I have friends—and employment with a shipping company if I want it.'

'You will have to consider it carefully, Thomas. Now ring for Standish and order him to bring some champagne. We must celebrate our reunion in style.'

'Anything you say, Mother, although I think Shona might prefer tea,' Thomas said, getting up to reach for the bell pull and winking at Shona.

'And you, my dear,' August said, gently tapping Shona's arm, 'must tell me all about this husband of yours. I insist. Is he handsome?'

'Yes, he is.' Shona laughed. 'Very.'

'Well, that's a start, I suppose.'

Augusta was intrigued to hear the facts of Shona's marriage to Zachariah Fitzgerald and was determined to play an important part in bringing them together. 'There is a grand charity event at the Earl and Countess of Whitchester's town house in Piccadilly in two weeks. It will be accompanied by a masquerade ball with an elaborate fireworks display to honour the occasion. It promises to be a jolly affair, where ladies will bid to spend some time in the company of unattached gentlemen. Everyone who is anyone will be there. If your husband is in London, my dear, I think you can guarantee he will be among the guests.

'But you must have a care. Everyone will be watching you to see what you are made of. I'm sure some of them will be happy for a new charming young lady to arrive on the scene, but you must remember that there are some who will be only too happy to see you fail in society. Your age, your wealth, the fact that you are practically a foreigner will make you conspicuous, not to mention your rank—you must remember you are Lady Harcourt, a title passed on to your husband from his mother's side. Just take care you get yourself noticed for the right reasons.'

Shona grimaced at the thought, but she understood her aunt's point.

'But that doesn't mean you can't have fun.' Augusta chuckled and Shona listened in rapt amazement as she related some of her madcap antics at masque balls in the early years of her marriage.

* * *

The night of the masquerade ball found Zack travelling alone in his long, jet-black town coach drawn by four fierce black horses, tossing their heads and snorting at the speed as they plunged through narrow streets. Lamp posts cast glowing orbs of light over the gilt trim of the coach.

Inside the coach Zack took a long drag of his cheroot and slowly blew the smoke out of the open window. Since his arrival back in London, it felt like a different world, his own place in it unclear since his meeting with Caroline. He was in a sombre mood. Subtle doubts tugged at him tonight.

Things weren't working out as planned. In his absence Caroline's husband, Lord Donnington, had died without issue. Having condemned his wife for her indiscretion and the shame of bearing a bastard daughter, he had left his entire estate to a distant much younger cousin, Lord Robert Byrne. Zack wanted Caroline to know that he was willing to take responsibility for his daughter and for her. But it would appear that Caroline—who Zack had discovered was more mercenary than he'd realised when it came to ambition—and Lord Byrne had begun an affair. In the hope of resuming her position as mistress of her late husband's country mansion, Caroline was hankering after a proposal of marriage. In the event that no such proposal was forthcoming, she had not ruled out Zack as a prospective husband.

Zack could still feel the anger and every second of his helpless fury when she had told him on his return that when her husband had refused to look at the result of his wife's indiscretion in his house, she'd had no choice but to place their daughter in the care of a foster mother. There the child remained, for it would seem that Robert Byrne was of the same opinion as her husband had been.

Zack was outraged at being placed in an impossible situation—that because of his commitment to their daughter, Caroline was assured of his dependability.

Profoundly disappointed and incensed by her attitude and the fact that Caroline was treating the situation in a casual manner, he was not looking forward to the evening ahead. Caroline had been invited to the ball—fortunately without her lover—and if he hoped to win his daughter, he would have to resort to the humiliating position of dancing attendance on a woman who was playing him for a fool.

He brushed off his dark musing as his coach slowed, reaching its destination. Stepping down, he flicked away his spent cheroot and smoothed his coat and strode up the steps into the brilliance of the mansion's interior.

Shona was excited as she prepared for the masquerade ball. Aunt Augusta had made discreet enquires and it was confirmed that Zack had been invited and had accepted the invitation. She stood in a dazzling pool of candlelight, surrounded by maids, a constant buzz of talk around her. She was being dressed for the ball and they were lacing up her stays. Her hair had been elegantly *coiffured* for the occasion, a white gardenia caught up with ribbons of silver tulle among the crown of glossy gold ringlets piled high on her head. A gown of ivory silk was laid out, its skirt frosted with intricate silver lace. Shona raised her hands so the maids could slip on her petticoats. By the time she was ready for the gown itself, she was beginning to weary of the preparations.

Her hands were clad in long white gloves. The silk gown rustled softly as she made a slow turn in front of the cheval mirror. She lingered a moment before the glass, enjoying her own radi-

ant reflection enhanced by the soft candlelight.
Her green eyes were sparkling and there was a
moist sheen on her lips. The silver lace sparkled.
Morag was looking out for any imperfections—a
loose thread, an unfastened hook. Shona smiled
at herself in the glass. Never, she thought, as
a maid draped an ermine-lined cloak over her
shoulders, had she looked so fine.

A little before ten when Shona and her aunt
arrived at Whitchester House the party had already begun. The house was lit up from the base-
ment to the handsome roof. The courtyard and
the street had been filled for some time with
the rattle of carriages and the jingle of harness,
accompanied by the shouts of coachmen and
lackeys, almost drowning the strains of violins
coming from the house.

Stepping down from the carriage, Shona
turned and looked at her aunt and caught her
breath in a gasp of pure admiration. Her lissom
figure struck a dramatic pose against the fine
house. With her elaborately arranged hair and
vast array of sparkling jewels, she positively dazzled, which, combined with her flamboyance, all
added to her striking personality and suggested

that she was a woman with many aspects to her character.

She smiled. 'You look wonderful, Aunt Augusta. You certainly know how to make an entrance.'

Accepting the compliment with a short laugh and taking her niece's arm, she led her up the wide flight of stone steps. 'We both do, my dear. Come. I'm so looking forward to tonight.'

They had arrived late, hoping to avoid the early influx of guests, but there was still a crush of an elegantly dressed assembly on the stairs. The smell was that unique mixture of powder, perfume and sweat that always heralded a society event. Music and flowers filled the rooms. Around Shona the din of voices melted into laughter. Stony-faced footmen made their way through the throng, balancing platters of food that vanished as fast as it was placed on tables. On one of the sideboards rose an elaborate creation made entirely of pastries and fruit. Shona picked out a pitted plum and slipped it into her mouth, casually taking a glass of wine from the tray of a passing waiter. In the cut-crystal goblet, French wine shimmered ruby-red as she drank to her forthcoming success.

Glancing through the open French doors on

to the wide terrace where the bidding was to take place later, a flock of peacocks passed by, stately and indifferent, their folded tails trailing on the damp grass. She smiled thinly. Their arrogance reminded her of her husband. Beside her aunt, who acknowledged guests she knew as they passed through the rooms connected through carved and gilded portals, floating in her luscious gown, her raised heels sliding on the polished floors, Shona took note of the velvet midnight-blue curtains drawn over the windows, the opulence of the soft carpets and gilded chairs. On a marble mantel an ornate gold clock chimed ten.

With her head held high, only her lips, chin and eyes visible behind the black mask that covered her face, filled with confidence Shona carried on walking down a long gallery, portraits of the earl's and countess's ancestors gazing down on her. Suddenly, the splendid gallery, the fashionable throng, even the music seemed to melt away and Shona was as cold as if she had been miraculously transported to a cold climate. Of their own volition her eyes were drawn to a sombre figure in a plain but perfectly cut black coat. He was alone and walking towards her, full of vigour and briskness. Like everyone else, a mask covered his features. Shona felt an iron band tighten suddenly around her forehead and there was a taste of ashes in her mouth. Her fingers tightened on her fan.

The man was Zachariah Fitzgerald, otherwise known as Lord Harcourt. Her husband. He was there, his presence a certainty beyond the proof of sight.

Shona's first instinct was to turn on her heels and run but, in a moment and remembering all he was guilty of where she was concerned, she carried on walking, her eyes never leaving his tall figure for a second as he came closer. He appeared to be preoccupied. On impulse, when he was almost directly in front of her, she let the fan slip from her hands. She stopped and looked down. So did he.

'Allow me,' he said, his deeply resonant voice, so well remembered by Shona, vibrating along her nerves. He retrieved her fan, a vague smile hovering on his lips. His silver-grey eyes behind his mask gleamed with sudden interest as they met hers. He handed her the fan.

Taking it from him, she forced a somewhat absent-minded smile and answered automatically. 'Thank you,' she murmured, lowering her eyes so she did not see the puzzlement enter his eyes as she went on her way. Shona felt his eyes burning holes into her back, her heart pounding in her chest. Much as she wanted to turn her head and look back at him, she straightened her spine, lifted her head and carried on walking. She wondered what she hated him more for— the turns her life had taken from that day she had first laid eyes on him, or the need, the obsession, she had allowed to creep into her heart.

The noise and faces about her became a blur as she recalled those last moments with Zack in her room at Melrose Hill. She discovered to her astonishment that, even after all this time, she could still taste the sweet violence of it, strange and overpowering in spite of the anger which had filled her at the time. It was not easily forgotten.

Feeling she was under inspection, she went through the motions of allowing her aunt to introduce her to her friends. A crowd of young gallants formed about her and she collected her thoughts sufficiently to respond politely to the compliments and to look as if she was enjoying the ball, allowing one or two of them to lead her on to the dance floor.

'Well?' Augusta said when she caught up with her niece. 'Is Lord Harcourt here?'

Shona nodded and turned to meet her gaze.

'Yes. We came close. He didn't recognise me.'
She smiled assuredly, her eyes cold. 'But he
will—before this night is done.'

Chapter Seven

Shona's eyes followed Zack as he walked towards the woman standing on the edge of the dance floor. She had dark brown hair. Of course! The same lustrous dark brown hair inside the locket Zack had left in her bedchamber. Shona was unprepared for the fierce stab of jealousy. The woman wasn't voluptuous, precisely, but her breasts were full and her features strikingly beautiful.

Shona took a step back, into the shadows. From behind her mask she watched Zack bow in front of the woman and lead her to the dance floor. Zack's turns and steps showed the mastery of practice and a delight in his own dexterity. Each time he bent his head and murmured to his partner, a warm smile softened the fine lines of his handsome face. There was not a sign of his arrogance, she decided. Just the worldly ease of someone who feels at home everywhere.

Shona would have been surprised to learn that Zack was not oblivious to the golden-haired woman with a commanding presence. He was intrigued. She seemed to prefer to observe the dance from a distance, because whenever she drew near, people paused to look at her, especially the gentlemen. It was understandable since she cut a striking figure. Perfectly proportioned, she was not a woman whom it was easy to ignore.

Later, Shona saw Zack and the woman she now knew to be called Lady Caroline Donnington standing by the refreshment table. Zack was smiling at something she had just said before lowering his head and whispering something into her shapely little ear.

Around midnight the rooms began to empty, shifting the party's centre of gravity, like iron filings unable to resist a magnetic field, on to the terrace, the guests clustering around the source of the attraction. There was general excitement among the younger members of the party as the bidding for the charity event was about to begin, while some of the older generation muttered that this kind of thing was a vulgar practice, but they stayed to watch and pass comment as each lady placed her bid to tumultuous laughter and applause. When there were no more bids the laughing gentlemen took their bows and went off with the ladies who had won their favour.

Submerged in a sea of silks and laces, Shona was pleased that she had found a spot where she could observe the proceedings without being overlooked herself. Zack was standing a little apart by the balustrade, illuminated by a soft pearly light. His shoulder was propped negligently against the door frame, his arms folded across his chest, watching the proceedings through narrowed eyes.

Until then Shona had thought she remembered exactly what he looked like, but she hadn't. His jacket clung to wide shoulders that were broader than she'd remembered. Beneath the mask that covered his eyes, there was still the masterful face—one of leashed sensuality and arrogant handsomeness with its sculpted mouth and striking eyes—but now she noticed the cynicism in those silver-grey eyes and the ruthless set of his jaw, things she'd been too naïve to see before. Everything about him exuded brute strength, and that in turn knocked her confidence as she searched his features for some sign that this aloof, forbidding man had actually held her and kissed her with seductive tenderness.

She gazed at him wonderingly, his strength and vitality incredibly appealing to her heightened senses, forgetting in an instant all he had made her suffer, but she quickly recollected herself. She must strengthen her resolve and not allow herself to lust after her husband when she knew that, for her own sake, she would have to hold him at arm's length, for he would *never* commit himself to their marriage.

With this thought in mind she watched and waited and bided her time. Eventually Zack climbed on to the stand. She was aware that his blatant masculinity appealed to the other females present. More than one favoured him with indiscreet glances, fluttering lashes and blushing prettily while wafting fans. He returned their interest with a roguish grin. Indeed, Shona realised he accorded the elderly matrons the same treatment as the young ladies—he treated both simply as women.

Yet she couldn't help experiencing an ungovernable jealousy at all the attention he was attracting, especially when she observed the brown-haired Lady Donnington securing her place for the bidding. A hush fell over the crowd as the bidding began. It started slow and with much hilarity, with one or two ladies offering a few guineas. Lady Donnington, her face flushed with laughter and expectancy, offered a hundred guineas, and, when there were no more bids, before the auctioneer's hammer could hit the block, in a loud, clear, confident voice, Shona said, 'Five hundred guineas.'

There was a silence, which was soon followed by a communal gasp. As people turned, craning their necks to see who had made the bid, there was a bobbing of all manner of elaborate and colourful hair adornments.

'Five hundred! Five hundred guineas for Lord Harcourt. Come, ladies, before it's too late. I beg you to consider the prize. Do I hear six hundred? Are there any more bids for Lord Harcourt?' the auctioneer called. Five hundred guineas was a sum that could not readily be challenged by the young, unattached ladies. 'Five hundred guineas it is, then!' the auctioneer declared cheerily. 'Five hundred! I say it once. Your last chance, ladies. Five hundred twice!' He glanced about, but found no takers. 'Five hundred guineas it is, then! To the lady at the back.' He grinned broadly in Shona's direction. 'You've purchased a rare prize for yourself, madam.'

Everyone was curious as to the identity of the unknown beautiful woman—especially Zack, who, as the throng parted to let her through, was intrigued. Not even when she moved towards him, pausing a moment to speak quietly to the auctioneer, did he know who she was. He recognised her as the woman whose fan he had retrieved, and again as she had kept to the shadows to watch the dancing.

Supremely confident, Shona smiled and turned to Caroline Donnington, who was bemused and clearly disappointed that she had come second in the bidding.

'Have you been keeping my husband company while I've been away?' Shona said calmly before fixing her gaze and a sublime smile on an astounded Zack, who recognised her at last and could not believe his eyes.

A world of feelings flashed for an instant across his face. The knowledge of her presence stunned him. He heard not a word that was being said around him for all sound was blocked out by a sudden roaring noise in his head.

Shona! She was here, incontrovertibly here, and his eyes were drawn to her automatically, his muscles taut by some unconscious force. For the first time in his life he was totally surprised.

She was heartbreakingly beautiful. More beautiful than he remembered. A radiant sunburst in a city choked with darkness.

He should have been prepared for this. He had been so sure that he had seen the last of Shona McKenzie. It had never occurred to him that she would follow him to England. He was neither prepared for the sight of her nor what it did to him. He stood quite still and looked at her, his face drawn, his eyes wide, fixed and unbelieving. In the silence, a hundred questions and emotions swept through his head. Then he was moving forward, very coolly, to stand before her.

All eyes were on Zack. It was as if everyone was waiting for him to laugh. But laughter was the last thing on his mind. He chose his next words carefully.

'Shona! I had hoped to have the pleasure of seeing you again, but I did not think to find you here.'

'No, of course you didn't. For myself, *your* presence did not take me entirely by surprise.' She laid the faintest of stresses on the 'your' and coolly handed him a card. 'This is where I am staying,' she told him haughtily. 'Don't be long in calling on me, will you, Zack? You've just cost me five hundred guineas.'

For a moment her glittering eyes swept the sea of faces that surrounded her, all with the same expectant and bemused expression, then, with her head held proudly erect, she left the terrace as the first rocket sent a gigantic spray of rose-and-white-coloured sparks rushing across the dark sky to fall back softly towards the gardens and the terrace, where the women's jewels rivalled the splendour. Her head on fire, her hands like ice, she walked stiffly on, the long train of her dress sweeping in her wake, ignoring the storm which broke out behind her. She would leave and wait for what was bound to follow—Zack's wrath. But for the moment, nothing mattered to her.

Zack's voice called after her. 'Shona! Wait!'

She went on down the grand staircase as if nothing had happened. Not until he caught up with her at the bottom did she finally stop and turn with an expression of complete indifference to face her husband, who, having torn off his mask, was clearly furious.

Taking her arm none too gently, he led her to an empty room and slammed the door shut. The room seemed to shrink around him. He was so tall that Shona thought he must surely have grown since she had last seen him.

'Take that damned thing off your face. I like to see who I am talking to.'

Calmly she did as he asked.

Zack stared at her. She had been lovely before. But then it had been a beauty without art. London had changed her. And, because she was one of those women so basically perfect that even fine clothes and diamonds heightened her, she had become something more than lovely. Now, Zack thought, she was glorious.

'So it is you. Good God, Shona! What the hell do you think you're playing at?'

For a moment Shona studied this man who had made such a big impact on her life. On their wedding day she had sworn happily to love, honour and obey him. It was the first time that she had been alone with him since that dreadful wedding night. Then she had been coldly sacrificed, a helpless victim in the hands of two heartless and unscrupulous men—her own brother and Zack.

'I am not *playing* at anything, Zack. You did not know me.'

'Not immediately. When I picked up your fan and watched you walk away, I had a vague feeling of familiarity which I was unable to place, a resemblance I failed to grasp. When you stepped forward to confront me and Lady Donnington, then I knew who you really were.'

Smiling thinly, she stepped away from him, casually running her fingers along the back of a chair. 'I see I failed to make an impression on you. Have you forgotten the charming circumstances attending our marriage? Do I have to remind you that while you swore to God to love and cherish me and forsake all others you were already planning to leave me? You had the audacity to destroy my life as if it were merely another of those delightful escapades you men discuss over your brandy. How stupid you must have thought me and how foolish of me to have believed you.'

'The ceremony was a sham, Shona, you know that. It was never made to last. How else was I to leave the island?'

'It does not alter the fact that what you did to me was despicable.'

'You are right. You see, when your brother impounded my ship, I think I somehow lost my reason. I had only one idea—to get her back and take her off the island. I felt as if I were trapped in a terrible swamp. The only way out as I saw it was to pretend to marry you.'

'Was there no limit to what you would do?'

'At the time, no. No limit whatsoever. I acted on an impulse stronger than myself and a similar impulse would probably have taken me back to look for you.'

'Ha!' she scoffed, throwing her head back haughtily. 'And I am expected to believe that.'

He shrugged. 'Believe what you like. I have regretted ever setting foot on that wretched island.' Turning his back on her, he went to the window and stood looking out. 'Why have you come here? I thought you would still be on Santamaria.'

'Hoped, more like, I'm sure,' she snapped. 'No doubt you would rather have me working on a treadmill for some fat slave owner.'

'Don't be ridiculous. Why are you here?'

The tone was harsh, clearly calculated to overwhelm her, but having learned her lesson in the creek on Santamaria, Shona now possessed the faculty of rising quickly to defend herself. He had been prepared to find her agitated and nervous. The confident woman who looked at him so calmly could not fail to rouse him to annoyance—and more than a little admiration, if she did but know.

Ignoring the ominous set of his shoulders, Shona risked a smile. 'To see you. We have some unfinished business to take care of. I am happy to see you are well, Zack, and none the worse for your time spent on Santamaria.'

There was no response. He continued to stare out of the window in silence, his hands clasped behind his back for what seemed to Shona an eternity. Realising that he was deliberately seeking to weaken her resolve, she gathered her courage for what she had to say, knowing that it was bound to be unpleasant.

'I came all this way because I am your wife. It is a situation that cannot be ignored.'

'Wife? I don't think so. Did you not read my note?'

'Yes. Every word.'

Abruptly, without turning, Zack spoke. 'I await your explanation, if you have one to offer, of your astounding conduct here tonight. Your explanation and your apologies—although it is to Lady Donnington you should apologise. It would appear that you were suddenly bereft of your senses, and of the most elementary notions of respect and the correct behaviour.'

'Apologies?' she said derisively. 'It so happens that I have done nothing, *nothing,* for which I require your forgiveness or for which I owe you explanations, for that matter. However,' she amended tightly, 'I will be happy to give any explanations you wish once you've made *yours* to me.'

He did turn round at this, his eyes alight with anger. 'What did you say?'

'That if anyone here has been insulted, it is me! What I did was within my rights and for my own dignity.'

'Within your rights? What rights?'

'As your *wife*. Not only did I come all this way to see you, I could no longer stay on the island— nor did I wish to. My position had become untenable. The capacity for warmth and gaiety and happiness that was present on Santamaria before you sailed into its harbour was cut off like the flowers in winter and the island society found me unfit company. On Santamaria reputation is everything. Once lost, it is impossible to regain.'

Something in the faint, despairing note in her voice hurt Zack with a savage pain that was as entirely physical as the touch of a hot coal. 'So you ran away.'

'Not exactly. It was necessary for me to leave. Whatever you think, I did not conspire with Carmelita to entrap you. Nothing was further from my mind. When I foolishly propositioned you that night on the terrace and you refused,

I accepted that. As far as I was concerned that was the end of it. What happened after that was purely coincidental. It was not until you left me and I read your note that I was able to comprehend the full magnitude of what you and Antony had done to me. I couldn't be blamed if I took it into my mind to hate you for what you've done.'

He stared at her. On the instant, he saw the blackness of Shona's loneliness that had driven her to leave Santamaria. Suddenly she looked vulnerable, somehow helpless. In a moment of weakness his heart went out to her. He wanted to hold her to him as he would a child. It was a totally new feeling for him. 'I don't intend to give you the opportunity,' he replied in an implacable voice that brooked no argument.

A faint smile touched Shona's lips. 'That's a start at least. You have cost me five hundred guineas.'

'You didn't have to go that far. I can spare you some of my time without you having to pay for it.'

'I was told it was for a worthy cause.' Her eyes softened. 'I won't let you forget that you owe me. Perhaps you would like to call at the house. I will introduce you to Aunt Augusta. I think you will like her. She is here tonight—somewhere—

she has such a wide circle of friends it's difficult keeping track of her. You might also like to
become reacquainted with my cousin, Thomas
Franklyn.'

His look was sharp, suspicious. 'Franklyn?
Cousin? You mean…?'

She nodded, watching him closely. 'The same
Thomas Franklyn who conducted our marriage
ceremony.'

His eyes narrowed on her, something unpleasant shifting in their depths. 'I get the distinct
feeling that this does not bode well for me.'

'That depends how you look at it. You see,
Thomas is also an ordained minister of the
church.'

Zack stared at her, trying to comprehend the
full meaning of what she was saying. As he absorbed this he began to see the truth at last. 'I
see,' he said in a terrible voice. 'So *you* are my
wife!'

The crucified look on Zack's face as he uttered these words in a voice thick with contempt
roused Shona to a primitive and savage rage by
an act of wanton cruelty and injustice.

'The situation is as abhorrent to me as it is
to you,' she snapped. 'You have only yourself
to blame.'

'And you knew about this?' he demanded.

'No. I swear that I had no idea what Antony had planned. It was a clever ruse—but it was risky. It could have gone quite badly, but it didn't. You really had no idea, did you?'

'Unfortunately your brother didn't take me into his confidence. He turned the tables on me. When he told me there was no curate on the island, I assumed I had the advantage. But your brother was alert. I see it all now. It would appear he made his own enquiries about Reverend Clay and set an ingeniously baited trap when your cousin turned up, making me look careless so that I entered into things with insufficient preparation. I should have conducted my own enquiries into Thomas Franklyn and not taken him at face value.'

'So now Antony will be looked on as your arch-enemy. It is fortunate you are on opposite sides of the Atlantic Ocean.'

'Shona,' he said in a cutting voice, 'your brother made a fool of me and caused me to make a fool of myself. Not many people manage to do that. Although he may have an equal in his wife.'

'Carmelita is a match for anyone. When I realised what you and Antony had done, the situation was devastating for me. You left Santamaria not realising we were properly married. The ceremony was not, as you planned, a sham. I asked myself what I should do. One thing became clear to me. I would not remain married to a man who didn't want me.'

'I see. And what did you decide?' he asked with infuriating calmness.

Shona drew a deep breath and slowly expelled it, knowing she was about to tread on dangerous ground. 'I want an annulment—a divorce—anything that can be done to end this farce of a marriage.'

The harsh words rebounded through the room, reverberating in the deafening silence, but not a flicker of emotion registered on Zack's impassive features. 'An annulment,' he finally repeated. Zack couldn't help the way his lips curled. 'Forgive me if I appear surprised. It's not often a man is told he has a wife he didn't know about and the next instant is being informed the lady wants a divorce,' he said carefully, trying to control his scorn.

His mind was still registering disbelief, even while something inside him slowly cracked and began to crumble. After all those months of treasuring the memory of the way Shona had surrendered in his arms on his last night on Santamaria, it had been a lie. He could still see her innocent smiling eyes warmly welcoming when he had entered her bedchamber—leading him to believe she was happy to see him. That tender scene had been an act. She had played it to the hilt in her desperation to get off the island and away from the suffocating authority of her brother and his wife. In that moment he was convinced that Shona McKenzie was the most consummate liar on earth.

Giving no hint of the cold, black rage that swept over him, he said, 'I think I'm beginning to get the picture. Even though I left you, as my wife your brother no longer had any authority over you and you were free to leave the island and follow me to England. I remember that night on the terrace at Melrose Hill when you spoke with such impassioned determination about your father and your longing to return to England— that you felt like a bird in a cage unable to fly free. I was the key to your cage and now I have served my purpose you want to be free of the marriage.' Mocking silver-grey eyes held hers. 'You have an instinct for survival, I'll give you that. And how do you intend to go about seeking an end to our sham of a marriage?'

Shona's ire at his condescending superiority was almost more than she could contain. 'I shall take advice from my aunt's solicitor.'

Zack nodded slowly, his eyes hardening. 'Our marriage has not been consummated, so it should not be a problem to have it declared invalid.'

His bold reminder of the night she had lain naked and willing in his arms was almost more than Shona's nerves could withstand, but she was determined to stand her ground. 'That is exactly what I thought,' she snapped.

'Although obtaining a divorce is a complicated and difficult process—and expensive. Just how do you intend to pay for it?'

'Before I left Santamaria, Antony settled a large sum of money on me—and you are a wealthy man, Zack. You must be as keen to put an end to this marriage as I am.' Hearing loud laughter from outside the door and fully expecting they were about to be interrupted, she crossed towards it. 'I will leave you to give the matter some thought. I must go.'

'I'll arrange for your carriage,' Zack said, impatient for her to leave so he could give the idea that she was his wife some thought. He needed time to come to terms with the situation and needed to determine what he was going to do about his daughter. She was his absolute responsibility, he couldn't change that, but when he looked at Shona his conscience was torn one way, his feelings the other. It left him with limited alternatives—and unlimited frustration.

Shona was surprised by the expression in his eyes. It had a yearning quality, nostalgic almost, as if he was crushed by some scarcely discernible problem, but she was too preoccupied with what Zack would decide to do about the situation to be moved by it.

'Is your aunt to accompany you home?'

'No. She's with friends. I'm perfectly capable of travelling alone. You must return to your companion—Lady Donnington. She must be feeling distressed by my sudden appearance.'

'Caroline will understand,' he replied coldly, thankful that Shona wasn't playing the betrayed wife.

'Will she have any reason to be upset about our marriage?'

'Upset? I doubt it. Surprised, yes.'

'Is she your mistress?'

It was said in a low, calm voice that made the directness of her conjecture all the more startling. Zack ran a finger along the edge of his cravat, for the cloth suddenly felt too tight. His relationship with Caroline had never been as permanent as that. How did he excuse his brief but consequential relationship with a woman who at the time had been a married woman? How did he tell Shona about his daughter?

'The sea has always been my mistress,' he uttered, providing what he thought was a diplomatic answer.

'She seems very nice,' Shona said, not allowing him to escape the issue so easily.

'Yes, she is,' he agreed testily, wishing he could have avoided exposing either Shona or Caroline to such an embarrassment. 'I've known Caroline for a long time—'

'Yes, I'm sure. Whatever the nature of your relationship, it is a matter of supreme indifference to me.'

At Shona's dry-voiced interruption, Zack shot her a hard look, suddenly angry at having to defend himself, even if he had just been hoping for the opportunity to do just that.

'But if you are in a relationship with her, Zack, then all the more reason for you to have our marriage annulled.'

This time his dark brows snapped together. 'I am no saint, Shona. I've always enjoyed the pleasures of life and the company of women happens to be one of the pleasures.'

Shona raised her chin as she returned his glare. 'Do you have to be so crude?'

'*I* crude? Lady, you do not know the meaning of the word.'

In tight-lipped silence, taking her arm, Zack escorted Shona through the hall and out to the carriage and assisted her inside. Closing the door, he placed his hand on the open window, holding her gaze.

'You, my dear wife, are beautiful, conniving and deceitful—a consummate actress. On two occasions you almost gave yourself to me. You pressed your body to mine and kissed me as if your whole heart were in it, because you saw me as a means to escape the island. I wanted to believe it was me you wanted. When I left you, feeling wretched and ashamed of what I had done to you, I even tried to convince myself of that. But now I know better.' His eyes were merciless as he spoke in the implacable, authoritative tone of one issuing an edict. 'This is all rather sudden. You will understand that your arrival and revelation has taken me wholly by surprise. I need to consider the matter carefully before I decide how it is to be dealt with. I will give the matter careful thought and call on you when I have decided what to do about it. In the meantime I want one thing understood.'

Shona looked down at him, succeeding in hiding the hurt his words caused her. 'And that is?'

'Until I decide on the course of our future,' Zack continued dispassionately, immune to the wrathful expression on her beautiful face, 'you will make no public appearances with any man but me. Is that clear?'

Indignation exploded in Shona's brain, but considering it sensible not to cause either of them further embarrassment by flaunting herself any more than she already had tonight, until the matter was settled she decided not to make an issue of it. Looking straight ahead, she swallowed down her ire and disappointment.

'Very well. But do not be long. I am impatient to have done with this unpleasant situation.'

Zack stood and watched Shona's carriage disappear down the street before making his way back inside. Her arrival in London and the knowledge that she was his legal wife gave him much to think about. He was surprised to discover he wasn't displeased by her appearance, but the thought that she might have used her body to secure her position was actually distasteful to him.

However, her protestations were having an impact on him and his instincts told him he was wrong. Whatever he had accused her of lying about in the creek that day, her reaction to his kisses had been real. He knew when a woman was feigning passion and when she was not. And Shona had definitely not. Her contemptuous scorn when he had accused her of conspiring with her family to trap him into marriage—that look had been real. No one could have fabricated that look of stunned horror or shocked outrage. Another kind of woman might have been so calculating, but while Shona might be hostile towards him, he didn't think she was cold-blooded. Yet he could not dismiss the thought entirely.

He became thoughtful as he tried to remind himself of his daughter, of how much depended on a successful annulment, but things weren't going well with Caroline and Shona had looked so damned lovely he knew he was in danger of losing the battle.

Caroline was waiting for him on a quiet part of the terrace. She would have to be told about this new development. She observed him calmly as he strode towards her, an expression of curiosity and bewilderment on her face. Zack also saw a hint of accusation or blame. To his intense disgust, he realised that he could not bring himself to make the romantic overtures to Caroline he knew she would welcome, even though she would spurn them in favour of her lover.

Seated in the carriage, Shona was too numb and angry to feel the full pain of her confrontation with Zack, but, as the shock of the angry words they had flung at each other melted away, then her real suffering began in all its agonising sharpness and cruelty. How cold and unemotional he had been, how hard and implacable his eyes as he had calmly told her what he expected of her. Her blood boiled afresh. *Oh, damn him,* she thought fiercely. Did he think he could dictate terms on how she was to behave while he enjoyed the pleasures of his mistress?

Without more ado, she ordered the driver to turn the coach around and go back.

Shona immediately sought out her aunt, took her aside and told her about her encounter with Zack.

'I heard about the bidding—I was in the card room at the time, but it's all everyone talks about.

And Lord Harcourt?' Augusta probed, her eyes sparkling with excited expectancy. 'How did he react when he saw you? What did he say?'

'He was…surprised.'

'I suspect that's an understatement. I expect he was surprised when you turned up at the ball without letting him know you were in London.'

It was an enquiry, Shona knew—phrased tactfully, but still a request for an explanation. 'Yes, he was,' she replied, meeting her aunt's eyes directly. And when the older woman remained silent, patiently waiting for her to reveal all, she told her the rest of the story, about his shock when she told him they were legally wed and that she wanted to have the marriage annulled.

'And is that what you want? To end the marriage?'

Shona lowered her eyes in confusion. 'Well, yes— No— I mean— Oh, I don't know, Aunt Augusta. I don't think I know what I want any more.'

Augusta relaxed visibly, sipping her wine appreciatively. 'There you are, then. That's all right. I wouldn't worry about how your marriage began.' Into Augusta's worldly eyes came a look of spontaneous sympathy and softness, followed by an understanding, rueful smile. 'My, my! It is all quite shocking, but you did right to return to the ball.'

'Yes, even though Zack will be furious.'

'What? More than he is already? You must continue to enjoy yourself,' Augusta said, her voice full of determination. 'You will be at your most charming and alluring. You will smile and laugh—but not too much. Make him a little jealous. Follow your instincts and you can't go wrong. You'll find he will be consumed with anger, but he will be unable to resist you. You'll see.'

Shona was not convinced. Her aunt had enormous influence and shamelessly loved forcing society to bend to her will, but Zack—with all the iron forces of his nature gathered together against her aunt's assault—would be quite another matter.

'Aunt Augusta, are you suggesting that I seduce my husband?' she asked with an amused tilt to her lips.

'And why not? After a short rest and a restorative glass of wine, you will feel at your best to cope with anything.' She smiled. 'It will be vastly amusing to see what his reaction will be when he sees you have defied him and returned to the ball to enjoy yourself.'

* * *

On the point of leaving the ball, Zack was waylaid by Sir Humphrey Seton, who was a friend of long standing. With people milling around them, for several minutes they engaged in social chit-chat, casually discussing the politics of the day and friends and acquaintances known to them both.

Suddenly distracted, Humphrey exclaimed, 'My God! Who is that simply gorgeous creature dancing with Lord Barrington? She can't be real.'

Zack raised his eyes and glanced at the dancers whirling by. Absently his eyes sought out Barrington—a notorious society rake—and the lady in his arms. Recognition hit him like a thunderbolt. He became frozen, staring in stunned silence, all his earlier tender thoughts vanishing like a morning mist. It was as if all the breath had been knocked out of him. Anger, uncurling from his stomach, surged through him. On discovering that as soon as his back was turned, Shona had flagrantly disobeyed him, for the first time in his life Zack experienced an acute feeling of jealousy, which caught him completely off guard. It was a feeling he found decidedly unpleasant.

Before he'd had time to think of the consequences, his next words sealed his public fate. 'That gorgeous creature, as you so aptly put it, Humphrey, is my wife,' he said through gritted teeth, his eyes burning across at her with fire that scorched her raw as she caught his gaze. 'And I can confirm that she is perfectly real. What the hell is she playing at?'

Zack's eyes remained fixed on Shona, whose whole presence seemed to blaze across the distance at him, eliminating all else. The dancers between them became like a multicoloured blur of moving bodies, but they could have been alone, facing each other across a dangerous, unbridgeable chasm. The loveliness of her smiling face was flushed with dancing and the champagne she had drunk between dances, and when she moved her slender, though softly rounded, form floated with a fluidity and grace over the floor in a swirl of elegance. He kept his eyes fixed on her, unable to believe she had returned to the ball without either his knowledge or his permission. How dared she defy him? How dared she force his hand in this manner?

When the music ceased and she left the floor on the arm of her partner, with her face partly screened by her fan and the mask, she seemed to be absorbed in what was taking place around her as she purposely avoided looking his way. He watched, growing angrier by the minute, as Barrington escorted her to a lady he presumed was Lady Franklyn. One by one gentlemen approached them with no other purpose than to be introduced to Shona, bending over her hand for far too long, he thought.

What the devil did she think she was up to, a flirtatious smile on her lips and a twinkle in her astonishing green eyes for anyone who looked at her, laughing and sighing with a demure playfulness, and inviting lingering, lascivious looks and indecent thoughts? He could see that none of the raffish young men were immune to her sparkling personality, for her beauty, coupled with the mischief in her eyes, was irresistible. He was struck afresh by jealousy—an emotion he did not handle at all well, but the frequent glances his young wife was receiving from the dozen or so other gentlemen gave him the urge to put his fists to good use.

'Excuse me, Humphrey,' Zack said, clenching his hands. 'It would appear that I am the only man here tonight who hasn't danced with my wife.'

Chapter Eight

Augusta, who was enjoying the enthusiastic attention she and Shona received, was in good spirits and full of smiles as she observed a hard-faced man she assumed must be Shona's husband bearing down on them. Ushering the gentleman who was bent over Shona's hand unceremoniously away, she cast her niece a sharp look.

'Chin up, my dear...' she smiled, waving her fan languidly '...and smile. Remember what I told you. Flirt just a little and be charm and graciousness personified. Mark my words—you'll have your husband eating out of your hand before the night is over. If the reception so far is anything to go by, you have already caused something of a stir.'

Shona took a deep breath. Now the moment had come when, for the second time that night, she must come face-to-face with her husband, she was afraid. Accompanied by another gentleman, he stepped in front of her and she was acutely conscious that his eyes were glued to her face as he introduced himself to her aunt, his manner cool yet polite.

'Why, I am honoured to meet you at last,' Augusta said, greeting him with a cheerful heartiness. 'Shona thought you might be here tonight. She was reluctant to come, but it seemed such a pity to leave her all alone when she could be here enjoying herself.'

'How considerate of you, Lady Franklyn— and how nice of Shona to honour us with her company,' Zack said, his voice and his eyes like ice as he looked at his wife.

The hard expression on his handsome face caused Shona an involuntary shiver, which was not one of pleasure, but, remembering the part she was playing, she smiled sweetly. Zack introduced Sir Humphrey Seton.

'I am pleased to make your acquaintance, sir,' she murmured, and, stirred by some feminine impulse of coquetry—and an urge to annoy her husband—she favoured Sir Humphrey with her most brilliant smile.

'It's a pleasure, Lady Harcourt. I had no idea

Zack had a wife, let alone such a beautiful one.' He stepped back and looked at Zack. 'You should bring your wife to London more often, Zack. Her presence would enhance any event.'

'Yes,' he said stiffly. 'Maybe you're right, Humphrey.' As the orchestra began playing a waltz, he held his hand out to his wife. 'Come, Shona. Let us dance.'

Leading her on to the floor he captured her waist and whirled her into the waltz. Only then did he look down at her.

'What the hell are you doing here?' he demanded, keeping his voice low so as not to be overheard by others in close proximity.

Beneath his icy calm, such was the force of his fury that Shona flinched, but, catching her aunt's sharp eyes, she took a deep breath and gave her husband a wide-eyed look of innocence.

'Why, the same as everyone else, I suppose. When I left you I suddenly realised I wasn't in the least tired, so I returned to enjoy what is left of the ball.'

'Are you out to incur my anger? Is that it?'

'What? More than I have already, you mean?'

'Don't be flippant,' he ground out, his face so close to Shona's that she could see the ice-cold satanic glitter in his silver-grey eyes. 'I told you that your behaviour must be beyond reproach. Yet within no time at all here you are. Not content with attending the ball alone and making yourself conspicuous, you have to make me appear ludicrous by flirting with every man present?' His eyes held hers, full of accusation. 'Well? What have you to say for yourself?'

With an effort Shona retained her composure as they moved over the dance floor, aswirl with couples moving gracefully to music, lovely and melodic.

'Nothing. When you're in this mood, whatever I say in my defence will be futile. For a start I wasn't flirting. I was merely being polite. Besides, I could hardly wait for my husband to escort me to a ball since we are estranged. What would you have me do? Go slinking around as if I've disgraced myself? We may be seeking an annulment, but that doesn't mean I have to make an outcast of myself. I am sorry if you're not pleased to see me, Zack, but it's too late to do anything about it now.' She spoke firmly, quietly, her eyes unwavering as she met his gaze. She refused to be drawn and, holding her head up, smiled engagingly. How she would like to give his handsome, angry face a resounding slap and cut his conceit, his arrogance down to size, but instead she forced her face to remain calm. 'I am your wife and will be your equal—not your chattel to be told what I will and will not do.'

'Will you not? We shall see about that.'

'If you insist on being disagreeable for what is left of the ball, I suggest you return to your friends. Perhaps they will tolerate your dour mood better than I,' she said, trying hard not to make eye contact with the brown-haired woman who was watching their every move from the edge of the dance floor. Lady Donnington had positioned herself so that she was in the direct line of vision. Shona caught something indefinable in her eyes. For a moment she couldn't think what it meant, and then she recognised it. It was the assessment of one woman for another.

'By introducing me as your wife to your friend, I can only assume you do not wish our marriage to remain a secret. You do realise that people will expect to see us together—will expect us to live together. How will you explain it?'

Struck afresh by her loveliness, it was easy for Zack to forget he hadn't wanted to marry her. What was difficult was controlling his physical reaction to her nearness. *An exercise in fortitude,* he thought grimly. His body was achingly aware of her. 'I don't have to explain anything to anyone,' he replied, studying her beneath half-lowered lids with tranquil amusement, torn between torment and tenderness. 'May I ask what your admirers talked to you about?'

'You may, but I will not tell you.'

'Do I have reason to call any of them out?'

Shona found herself smiling, her eyes glowing with repressed laughter. 'Several. But with so many, you would be hard-pressed to beat them all.'

'Don't count on it,' Zack replied, spinning her round with unnecessary force.

She laughed. 'Zack, please slow down. You swirl me round so fast I'm beginning to feel quite dizzy.'

'Perhaps you've drunk too many glasses of champagne.'

She was indignant. 'No, I have not.'

'Yes, you have—three—or was it four?'

His smile was amused and slightly mocking, which annoyed her. 'You were watching me?'

He nodded. 'I had nothing better to do.'

Gazing down at her sublimely flushed upturned face, he wondered how he could have imagined for one moment that he could live without her—that he could purge her from his heart and mind. Every time he looked at her the breath caught in his throat. He cursed himself for letting her affect him this way. She played havoc with his insides, a sensation not normal for him, a man who had always enjoyed a woman casually, on a whim, made love to her for his pleasure. Now this girl from Santamaria needed to be taught a lesson and he could hardly keep his hands off her. He couldn't believe that his passionate encounters with Shona had left him throbbing for her like a green youth. Yet now, holding her in his arms, there was little he could do to control either the lust throbbing through his veins or the disquietingly tender feelings that were prodding at his heart.

Where was his logic, his easy self-control? Had it all flown away when he had entered into what he believed was a bogus marriage, when he had sworn not to treat her as his wife, firmly subduing his carnal desire? Suddenly she had become the one thing he must have. But he had desired her all along, even when he thought he would never see her again. What in hell's name was the matter with him? The fact was undeniable. He wanted to make love to her. He wanted to take her immediately. He did not want to keep himself in restraint another moment. How long could he endure having her near without throwing her down and satisfying himself with her?

Now the anger and surprise of her reappearance in his life and her pronouncement had diminished somewhat and he could think more rationally, he reconsidered her request for an annulment. Despite everything that had transpired between them and unable to lie to himself, he realised he didn't want an annulment and he would be damned if he would give her one. It mattered to him what happened to this beautiful, intelligent, foolish young wife of his. For the first time in his life he had found a woman who was rare and unspoiled, a woman who had succeeded in touching his heart, which was something all the other women had failed to do. He had no intention of letting her go and this had nothing to do with his battle to gain custody of his daughter.

'What are you thinking?' Shona asked, amazed at how relaxed she felt in his arms.

'About your request for an annulment to our marriage.'

'And what have you decided?'

'There will be no annulment, Shona.'

Shona's eyes widened in amazement. 'But—I don't understand. What are you saying?'

He smiled down at her, his gaze dropping to

the tantalising creamy swell of her breasts exposed above the bodice of her gown, a sight in which he took a lustful delight.

'You heard me. I don't want a divorce—an annulment, call it what you like. I have no intention of letting you out of my sight ever again.'

Shona stared at him, reeling from his incredible words. 'And if I don't want to be your wife?' she said fiercely.

'But you *are* my wife, Shona.'

'I am also a free spirit with an independent will and I wish to leave you.'

'No, you don't. *You* asked *me* to marry you. Have you considered the consequences of a divorce?'

'The consequences for whom?'

'You. It will certainly be unpleasant.'

'I would imagine divorce is always unpleasant.'

'It is. You will become notorious in a way you do not deserve. What would you hope to gain?'

'My freedom.'

His eyes probed hers. 'And do you want to be free, Shona? Of me?'

Shona searched his face, feeling her heart turn over exactly the way it always did when he looked at her like he was looking at her now.

She saw the glow in his half-shuttered eyes kindle slowly into flame. Deep within her, she felt the answering stirrings of longing, a longing to feel the tormenting sweetness of his caress, the stormy passion of his kiss.

But she could not forget the terrible things he had accused her of—of the kind of person he still believed she was. How could a happy relationship be built on such rocky foundations?

The question remained unanswered when the dance ended. Zack led her off the dance floor. His anger was roused once more when other men flocked around her and did not abate as the night wore on. It was no easy matter for Shona to ignore his penetrating, enquiring gaze fixed on her, but she continued to smile more vividly, and to tease and laugh with the gentlemen who came to be introduced with what Zack considered to be infuriating persistence.

Shona smiled sweetly at him when she saw his dark scowl after yet another young rake went on his way on being confronted by Zack's black look of thunder.

'Must you look so put out, Zack?' she reproached. 'It should flatter your vanity having your friends envy you your wife.'

'It gives me no satisfaction to see other men coveting my wife.'

They danced together once more. Shona knew Zack was finding it difficult coming to terms with the fact that she was truly his wife. She also knew when he left her side and he and Lady Donnington each left the room via separate doors out on to the terrace. She had seen the subtle look the woman passed to him across the ballroom and the imperceptible nod he gave her in reply.

Suddenly the noise, the colour, the movement and cheerful laughter swirled all about her and she had the feeling she was in the centre of a swiftly moving kaleidoscope. It was all too much. She wanted to get away as soon as possible, to be quiet, secluded, in a space somewhere with no one in it, in which to recover her composure.

Unaware that Shona had observed anything untoward between her husband and Lady Donnington, taking note of her niece's pallor, Augusta moved to her side. 'Are you all right, Shona?'

She flashed her a brilliant smile from behind her fan, lifting her head to a queenly angle. 'Of course. Why ever should I not be? But I am rather tired and I have the beginnings of a head-ache, so if you don't mind I think I'll go home. Zack has gone off with one of his...his friends. If he should come looking for me, please don't tell him I've left just yet. I need some time on my own and the last thing I want is an irate hus-band arriving on the doorstep at this late hour.'

Augusta looked at her with genuine concern. 'Very well, but I'll come with you.'

'No, I won't hear of it. Please stay. See—Lady Smythe is beckoning to you. I'll be perfectly all right.'

'Well—if you're sure.'

'Absolutely.'

Without glancing at the terrace doors, through which Zack emerged at that moment alone, Shona hurried away.

Augusta stood for a moment and watched Zack glance around the ballroom in search of his wife. She had watched the changing expres-sions move across his fiercely handsome face all evening—from fury to the violent jealousy a man felt when the woman he loved was being coveted by others. From the moment Shona had returned to the ball he had clung to her side and watched her with all the substance of his being, his concentration glued to the slim and elegant figure by his side.

Augusta was certain that no matter what had prompted Shona to slip away from the ball while her husband was otherwise occupied, she was in for an exciting time over the following days. Suddenly, feeling very old, she sighed, envying Shona more than she would ever know her youth, her beauty and, she thought with irritation when she looked at an elderly gentleman looking at her expectantly—a rather gross, unappealing man and already showing signs of running to seed— her husband.

The house was quiet when Shona arrived with only a footman on duty to open the door. Thomas was on his way to bed when she entered the hall. Contemplating her downcast face, he tried not to show his concern.

'Ah, Shona. You're early. I didn't expect to see you back until the early hours. Mother not with you?'

She shook her head dejectedly. 'No. I—I'm rather tired and...'

'Did you meet Lord Harcourt?'

'Yes.'

'And you told him?'

'That we are properly married—yes.'

'How did he react?'

She shrugged. 'As I expected. He was shocked—angry. He believes I colluded with Antony to deceive him. I asked him for an annulment, Thomas. A marriage cannot be built on such rocky foundations.'

'What did he say?'

'He refused to give me one.'

'I see. Why did he not escort you home?'

'Because I didn't tell him I was leaving. When I saw him go out on to the terrace with Lady Donnington, I thought it was time to go.' She sighed, giving him an affectionate peck on the cheek before turning to the stairs. 'I'm sorry, Thomas. Forgive me, but I must go to bed.'

Thomas watched her climb the stairs. He was burdened with guilt. Had he not listened to Antony and believed the marriage was what Shona wanted, she would not be in this unhappy state.

Returning to the ballroom and finding Shona had left without a word, Zack was at a loss to know what to do about the unholy mess in which he found himself. He had just made arrangements with Caroline to take Victoria on an outing in a few days' time and now, with his pride

and his passions waging a terrible internal war,
Zack spent what was left of the night in an ex-
clusive gambling club in St James's, drinking brandy, playing cards and losing. Feeling
plagued by one woman in particular, he emphat-
ically declined the feminine company so will-
ingly offered to him.

At dawn, when he finally returned to his
brother's town house where he was presently
residing, he threw himself into bed and for a
short time was able to forget Shona McKenzie-
Fitzgerald.

His wife.

'Who is Lady Caroline Donnington, Aunt Augusta?' Shona asked as she swept into her aunt's
bedchamber the morning after the ball, showing
no trace of the troubled night she had spent worrying over Zack's relationship with Lady Donnington.

Having her breakfast in bed, as she was in
the habit of doing after a late night, Augusta
glanced up at her niece and smiled. 'My, my,
Shona! You look disgustingly bright this morning. I trust your headache is better.'

Shona smiled. 'Much better. Were you late home?'

'Not really. I went to the card room to watch a rather interesting game of piquet. Dear me…' she sighed, buttering a thin piece of bread '…Lord Griffith lost a monumental sum of money to Sir Mark Sedgefield, which he can ill afford.'

'I'm sorry to hear that,' Shona said, sitting on the edge of a chair beside the bed. 'But you haven't answered my question.'

'Didn't I? What was that, dear?' Augusta murmured rather absently as she spooned a generous helping of strawberry jam on to her bread.

'Lady Caroline Donnington? Are you acquainted with her?'

'Not personally, but I know *of* her. She was married to Lord Donnington. He was an old man when she married him. I believe she was reluctant to enter into it, but he was terribly wealthy and it was what her disgustingly ambitious parents wanted so they pushed her into it. She was such a shy little thing then. She had a child, I believe—although it's doubtful Donnington was the father. There was talk that she took a lover while her husband was on his deathbed. As a consequence, he didn't leave her as well off as she expected to be when he died.'

'And how long has she been a widow?'

'About two years—and she's certainly come out of her shell since. Her closeness to Lord Byrne—her husband's heir—has been duly noted. I didn't have the pleasure of conversing properly with Lord Harcourt last night by the way. I'm impatient for him to call. When he enquired after you and I told him you had left the ball, I could swear he looked fit to commit murder.'

It wasn't difficult for Thomas to locate where Lord Harcourt was staying. Arriving at the house, he was shown into a spacious, panelled library where Lord Harcourt was standing. The two men stood facing each other, Zack looking far more ominous than amiable. Thomas seemed unconcerned with the tangible danger emanating from Lord Harcourt. In fact, he appeared relieved that the confrontation was happening at last.

Zack acknowledged Thomas with a sardonic, questioning look. 'So we meet again, *Reverend* Franklyn. I think you have some explaining to do. Shall we indulge in polite trivialities for the next couple of minutes, or shall we come directly to the point?'

'I am sure Shona explained the situation precisely when you met last night. Before we go any further, you should know that she has no idea that I have come here. She would have been against it. I have to try to right the wrong my cousin inflicted on you. Yet the fact cannot be overlooked that both you and my cousin Antony resorted to dishonest practices in order to find a resourceful solution to a difficult situation.'

Zack's eyes were brittle, his tone ironic. 'And your own involvement was without reproach?'

'No, it was not. As far as you and Shona are concerned, I can confirm that you are indeed man and wife. The papers you signed are genuine. If you do not wish to remain married to each other, then you must seek a divorce. I am not proud of what I did. Indeed, I've had time to regret my actions.'

'A man in your position should be beyond corruption.'

'I agree. It was a mistake—a huge mistake. I deeply regret allowing Antony to play me for a fool. What I did, I did for Shona. I knew how unhappy she was on the island and that her presence at Melrose Hill with Carmelita had become unbearable. According to Antony she was not averse to you. Determined to abide by his father's wishes, he would not allow her to leave Santamaria without the protection of a husband. I only agreed to go through with the ceremony because I thought it was what Shona wanted. I had no idea Antony was deceiving Shona as well as me.'

'And you expect me to believe this?'

'Your own actions could be held up for question. You are not entirely blameless. When you decided to play Antony at his own game, you entered into an arrangement devoid of honour and didn't care about the hurt it would cause Shona.'

'Because I believed she was part of the deception.'

'She wasn't. She really had no idea of the scheming going on behind her back. When she was made aware of the facts she was devastated. Believe me when I say that she was innocent of any wrongdoing.'

A pair of silver-grey eyes held his captive, measuring his response, judging it for truth.

Zack drew a long breath and nodded slightly, his expression no longer coldly forbidding. 'I know that now.'

'You do?'

'Absolutely. It wrenches my gut to think that I took part in something so despicable.' Regret surged upwards within him and was so intense he was nearly taken aback by surprise. 'Because I thought she'd tricked me so artfully, damaging both my ego and my pride, I insulted her by treating her as if she had. When I hatched my plan to deceive her, I never dreamed I would come to care so deeply for her. I treated her abominably. She deserved better from me.'

'You feel no worse than I do,' Thomas said. 'I think I should tell you that I've decided to leave the church.'

'Over this?'

Thomas shook his head. 'There are many reasons too numerous to go into just now. Suffice to say that I've been battling with my conscience for some time. You might say that circumstances on Santamaria forced my hand. But what now? I believe Shona has asked for an annulment.'

'There will be no annulment. I have made Shona aware of this. However, things are still rather complicated, I admit.'

'I'm happy to hear it. You must speak with her. At this present time she's at a pretty low point. Her pride has taken a battering, too. Go to her.'

Knowing that as each moment passed, Shona's hurt and anger would be hardening into hatred, naked pain flashed across Zack's handsome features. 'I'm on my way.'

It was one o'clock when Zack arrived to see Shona. She had just come in from the garden and gone to her room to refresh herself when Morag informed her that her husband had just arrived. Crossing to the window, she looked out and, sure enough, an ornate, shining black coach and four was outside her aunt's villa, the fine black horses tossing their heads, as if they had borne the devil to his destination.

With her heart in her throat Shona eventually entered her aunt's stately drawing room. On seeing Zack, she quivered, half with a spurt of apprehension about how he would react and half with relief that he had cared enough to come. As always, he was every bit as imposing in his dark, brooding way, a man any woman would be proud to call her husband—or lover. With clenched hands, she fought the memory that thought aroused. She didn't like to remember the night she had thought he was her husband and welcomed him into her bed as a bride. Sometimes she forgot the terribly wanton things they'd done, the pleasures they'd shared without the final act. And then a mere glimpse of him, the sound of his voice, would send them rushing back again.

With one of his long legs crossed over the other, he was in conversation with her aunt, apparently friends already. Shona could see that her aunt, arranged in elegant perfection on a graceful Egyptian-style couch with *The Morning Post* on her lap, was savouring every moment, positively eating up Zack's attention. The deep, velvet rumble of his cultured baritone made her stomach flutter.

She hadn't expected him to just turn up at the house like this—but then she hadn't known what to expect from him. Zack was a law unto himself. He was no foppish, romantic young gallant. With his jaw set with implacable determination, even in pensive pose he seemed to emanate the restrained power and unyielding authority she had always sensed in him.

Zack stood up the moment Shona entered. Their gazes locked—a tremor ran the entire length of Shona's body. As he approached her, she was filled with a disturbing surge of lust for him, despite her anger and hurt and her general desire to throttle the man.

'Here she is!' Augusta said sweetly.

Shona held her breath, her eyes wary the closer he came. He was looking every inch the handsome, elegant lord today, with his blue coat and darker blue trousers, his striped blue-and-silver waistcoat and his immaculate white linen, and it was clear by the admiring face of her aunt and the way she patted her hair and straightened her gown that she was quite overwhelmed.

He is no doubt accustomed to this sort of feminine reaction everywhere he goes, Shona thought wryly. Well, he might have fooled her aunt with that smooth charm of his, but she saw through this shrewd puppet master who was determined to control her now he'd decided not to set her free.

'Hello, Shona,' he greeted her, his silver-grey eyes aglow, a slight smile on his lips, with no sign of his fury of the night before.

He looked so pleased with himself, she thought. She smiled at him with an aloof lift of her chin as he bent and kissed her cheek, reproach shooting from her eyes. She refused to shrink from his touch and the intensity of his gaze, but the scent of his flesh lingered.

Augusta beamed from her chair. 'There now,' she enthused, 'this is so agreeable. Ring the bell

for tea, Shona.' But before her niece could move
to do her bidding, Zack protested.

'No, please, do not trouble yourself on my account,' he said. 'I will not trespass on your time
too long. I wanted to see Shona, but I also wished
to pay my respects to you, Lady Franklyn—and
your son Thomas.'

'I am delighted to receive you. Unfortunately,
Thomas is not at home at present, Lord Harcourt,
but I know he will regret having missed you.'
So taken was she with her visitor that she was
unaware of the powerful currents of tension that
passed between Shona and her husband at the
mention of her son's name. 'I have to say what
a perfectly beautiful couple you make!'

'It's kind of you to say so, Lady Franklyn,'
Zack said, not looking away from Shona.

'Isn't it just?' Shona retorted for his ears alone,
her look telling him that nothing had changed.

Zack took one look at her and saw he had
some making up to do. His young wife was not
the expert that he was at hiding her feelings—
what he read in her face told him that she was
still furious because he refused to grant her her
freedom. So he would have to pacify her and
help her see the wisdom of their marriage. Being
rather skilled at compartmentalising different

areas of his life, he was able to put the difficulties this would pose with Caroline and his daughter aside for the moment. Now he'd had time to get used to the idea of being married to Shona—of wanting her to be his wife—in his mind he had already begun to think of her as his. Strangely, any objection on her part merely strengthened his resolve.

When he had last seen her, she had been a radiant star in a shimmering gown of silver lace, almost untouchable in her pristine elegance, but today she was as warm as the sun. In a state of unpretentious loveliness she was demure in her floral-printed day dress, with three-quarter sleeves edged with lace and a white fichu tucked into the neckline. The sunlight, streaming in through the window behind her, illuminated her thick mane of golden hair, which hung free about her shoulders and was held back from her face with a simple pink ribbon.

Keeping a firm check on his desire, Zack smiled at her and took a step back.

'I did not expect you to call so soon,' Shona remarked. 'You find me unprepared for visitors.'

'I am no ordinary visitor, Shona.' He gave her a confident smile. 'I recall you telling me not to take too long in calling on you.'

'Did I?' she replied briskly, wishing he would leave, knowing he was not here to make idle chit-chat. 'I don't remember.'

'And I am no ordinary visitor.'

Her cheeks flushed suddenly. 'No, you're not.'

'My dear Shona.' He took both her hands between his own and gazed soberly into her eyes. 'It's a pleasant afternoon and I have my carriage outside. I want you to come for a ride with me.'

He didn't ask, he stated, Shona noted angrily. 'I don't think—'

'Oh, but you must, Shona,' Augusta said. 'A ride in the park is just what you need. It's too fine a day for you to remain cooped up indoors. Now run along and get your bonnet. I will entertain Lord Harcourt while you are gone.'

Zack sent her a small frown askance and the impatient look in his eyes brooked no argument. Raising her chin a notch, she turned from him. 'Very well. Who am I to argue?'

Upon leaving the house, with his hand placed possessively on Shona's elbow, Zack escorted her out into the street. Handing her up into the carriage, he then went around to the driver's seat as his groom climbed to his post in back. Gathering the reins, he snapped them smartly over the backs of his high-stepping horses. Their hoof-beats rebounded off the elegant houses as his carriage rolled down the cobbled street, urging them to a canter when they entered the main thoroughfare and drove the short distance to Hyde Park. The speed at which they travelled brought a reluctant smile to Shona's lips, her hair flying behind her and whipping around the sides of her bonnet.

Zack cast her an admiring sideways glance. 'Glad you came?'

Shona was surprised by his unexpected gentleness and, worse, completely at a loss as to how to answer. She wanted to appear haughty, coldly remote—anything but friendly, for that was tantamount to giving in. On the other hand, she could scarcely say *no, she wished she hadn't come.* 'It's a pleasant diversion, I suppose. I had nothing better to do.'

He smiled as the fetching creature pretended not to be over-enthused. 'Careful, Shona,' he said with underlying sarcasm. 'Your enthusiasm might show. At least we can be accorded some privacy out here.'

Shona was about to retort that the last thing she wanted was privacy with him, but, with her emotions all over the place, she decided to hold her tongue.

When they arrived in the park, being the height of the Season and a Sunday, they found the Ring crowded with mounted riders and open carriages occupied by persons of rank and fashion. The pace was fast and the park roadways muddy following an earlier rainfall.

Zack quickly noted the stares they drew from society ladies and how young men gawked at Shona. Word had quickly spread that the delectable creature who had graced the Whitchester Ball last night was his wife, generating a great deal of attention. Turning off the Ring, he drove away from the crowds towards Kensington Gardens, where he slowed the trotting horses to a halt.

'I thought we might stretch our legs and walk for a while.' Climbing out, he went round to assist her down while the groom alighted to take care of the horses. 'The fresh air agrees with you,' he said, noting the blooming colour in her cheeks.

Leaving the carriage, they strolled along a gravelled path beneath the trees.

Shona glanced at the lazily relaxed man beside her. She knew he was trying to break the

ice and carry on reasonably normal conversation with her. Sullenness was foreign to her nature and she felt horribly churlish for remaining
cross. Unaware that Thomas had paid him a visit
earlier, finally she said, 'Do you intend going
back to sea?' She was suddenly curious about
what he intended now he was back in England.

'I might, but not yet. I shall conduct my business from London—or my home in Surrey—for
the time being and let others bring back sugar,
indigo, rum and other goods from Virginia and
the Indies.'

Shona shot him a curious look. 'I didn't know
you had a house in Surrey.'

'There's a lot about me that you don't know,
Shona. Yes, I have a house in Surrey—Harcourt
Hall. It was where my mother was raised. It's
very beautiful.'

'I suspect you will miss your life at sea. What
will you do with your time?'

'I will have much to occupy me. It will give
me time to meet with investors, to watch the
stock prices—and,' he said, looking at her, 'to
put down roots. My father is the Earl of Halland
and the ancestral home is in Kent.'

'Is your mother still alive?'

'Very much so.' He grinned. 'She's the stalwart of the family. I doubt my father could function without her. My older brother, Harry—who is married to Miranda with two young sons—will inherit Halland Park one day. I also have two sisters. They are both married and live north and west of London. That leaves me.'

His face softened and his eyes warmed at the mention of his home. Against her better judgement Shona kept him talking about a subject that obviously meant something special to him. 'What's Halland Park like?'

'It's a beautiful place,' he said with a soft smile. 'It's been in the family for six centuries. The original earl built a castle on it. I believe different aggressors coveted it and laid siege to it, but no one could take it. The castle was demolished by another ancestor, who built a mansion. Then the next earls enhanced and enlarged it until it became the place it is. It's the responsibility of my brother to preserve it.'

'Do you regret not being the elder brother?'

He shook his head. 'No, I never did. My heart was set on sailing ships and building up a fleet of my own.'

'And sailing to foreign shores.'

'Something like that. I succeeded and now it's time for me to settle down at Harcourt.'

He fell silent, as if unwilling to show how much he would miss the adventure of life at sea, and when he lapsed into silence, she realised he must be reflecting on how drastically different his new life would be.

'I hope the transition will be as smooth and painless as possible for you.'

'Thank you. Tell me about the time you spent in England as a schoolgirl.'

'There's very little to tell, really. I was at school in Hertfordshire and during the holidays I went to stay with my friend's family in Northamptonshire or in London with Aunt Augusta—when she was in town. She wanted to bring me out, to make my début, but my father had died and Antony insisted I went home to Santamaria.'

'And would you have liked to be a débutante?'

'Yes, I think it would have been fun. My friends wrote telling me of their experiences— the balls they attended and the assemblies—and I confess I was envious at the time, being so far away. But it couldn't be helped.'

'And now you're a married lady who has been denied the frivolous fun that would have been yours as a débutante.' He clasped his hands behind him and, looking every inch the proper lord, his expression became serious. 'Please believe that I have nothing but regret for what has happened. What I did was thoughtless and cruel, and I realise you must have been deeply hurt.'

'You don't need to soothe my pride. It isn't necessary. My heart was not broken, although my pride was bruised and I am still hurting,' she confessed. 'You and my brother treated me very badly.'

'I won't do it again, I swear to you.'

'You say that, but you made me believe a lie before, so how can I know that you aren't deceiving me now?'

'You don't. But when you get to know me better, you will learn to trust me.'

Zack turned and studied her profile. He had developed a deep attraction for her on the island, strong enough that one could safely describe it as a sort of madness with him. He wanted her so badly. She had become in his eyes a woman as alluring and desirable as any he had ever known. Even now, when the consequences of what he had done were so grave, he wanted her. Even now, when all the things he valued most—his home, the honour of his name, his daughter and the legitimacy of a possible heir—were in jeopardy, even now, he wanted her.

Yes, Shona had become a passion to him, a beautiful and vibrant woman. A woman he had hurt very badly. These were not the most romantic circumstances under which to begin their life together. And having the subject of Caroline come out had not helped.

'I can only wonder at your refusal to end our marriage,' she remarked. 'Would you not value your freedom?'

For a lengthy moment, Zack's translucent grey eyes probed the dark depths of hers. That had been the question haunting him since the moment she had told him she was indeed his wife, but knowing the bliss of holding her in his arms and the taste of her lips, he found it impossible to dismiss his enthralment with this beautiful woman.

'When I returned to England I was determined that my life would change, Shona, and now, since I found that also entails being married to you, that is how it will be.'

'You needn't go to such extremes,' she stated, wounded by his callous commitment to the existing contract. 'How are we supposed to have any kind of life together if you don't tell me what is going on between you and Lady Donnington?'

His look became sharp. 'Nothing is going on, Shona. You have got to *trust* me.'

'How can I? I don't even know you. Will you let her go?'

'There are reasons why I cannot end the connection, but I have every intention of respecting our marriage vows.'

'No. I'm sorry, Zack. You can't have it both ways. I will not accept this. You're my husband and yet at this moment I have no idea who you really are. I'm trying, but you have to decide. You can either explain your situation with Lady Donnington,' she told him slowly, meaningfully, 'or you can divorce me. The choice is yours.'

'You are ruthless,' he said quietly, shaking his head as he stared at her. 'You have learned well, Shona.'

'I was taught by the best,' she answered. 'My brother was noted for it. You're intentionally dismissing the importance of what I'm trying to tell you. Don't you understand that I am giving you leave to dispense with this whole thing?'

Zack lifted his chin thoughtfully. Losing Shona was the last thing he wanted, of that he was confident. Capturing her gaze, he plumbed the dark depths as he stated with conviction, 'This is all rather sudden, but I mean to abide by my part of the marriage. I sincerely hope you intend to do the same.'

Shona bristled. 'I confess that was not my purpose when I came here. I offered to withdraw whatever claims I have on you because of the nature of our marriage and not because I thought you would wish to be free of the agreement.'

'Now you know better.'

'I have difficulty discerning your thoughts. Your actions seem to suggest the converse.'

'And your actions, my dear Shona, suggest to me that you are the most contrary young lady I have ever met,' he countered. 'I should hope in all truth that is not the case.'

Zack swept a warm gaze over her. Shona McKenzie—or Fitzgerald as she now was—was so different from any of the women in his past, he thought, watching the sun's glow glint on her hair like a silver halo. Observing her quiet, cool beauty, he could hardly remember what he had seen in any other woman. Her loveliness held such powerful allure that his body began to throb as it had always done when he was near her.

The thought of drawing her into his arms now and removing her clothes—here, beneath the canopy of leaves—of drawing her down on to the grass and burying himself in her enchanting body, beckoned him like a strong elixir. And the visual image of her naked, of her long limbs clasping his hips, her eyes liquid with heat, brought him to a pulsing arousal. Clenching his hands, he cursed himself for inviting such fantasies. Perhaps she didn't realise her deepening effect on him and was actually trying to do the honourable thing by releasing him from his commitment, but as much as his pride might have rallied at his freedom to claim his daughter, the idea of losing his firm grasp upon Shona went sorely against the grain.

She was the one. He knew it. And as his gaze consumed her, a single, searing thought filled his mind, body and soul. She belonged to him. She was his. He would not be parted from her.

Chapter Nine

They returned to the carriage and drove out of the park.

'This isn't the way we came,' Shona remarked when they failed to turn into Upper Brook Street. 'Where are you taking me?'

'Not far. There's something I want you to see.'

Proceeding to drive along spacious Grosvenor Street, the carriage finally drew up before a striking house. It was the perfect location for the home of a wealthy man of distinction.

'What is this?' Shona asked, looking up at the elegant façade.

'This, Shona, is to be my town house. It has undergone some changes since I purchased it and will very soon be habitable. The whole house has been redecorated and most of the rooms are already furnished. I've installed a butler and a couple of footmen to oversee the final stages. At present I'm residing at my brother's house not far from here. He's down at Halland Park just now with the family so I have the house to myself. Come,' he said, jumping down from the carriage and holding his hand out to her. 'I'll show you around.'

Jessen, the butler, opened the door and bowed to them, and they stepped into a magnificent marble entryway with an ornately plastered ceiling three storeys above. He then retired to the domestic quarters when Zack informed him he wanted to show Lady Harcourt the house.

Shona couldn't help but be impressed as Zack conducted her through spacious rooms that were graced with high ceilings, gleaming woodwork, elegant furnishings and floors covered with plush carpets.

Once they had covered the whole house Shona was surprised how reluctant she felt to leave.

'It really is a fine house and beautifully decorated. The furnishings are exquisite. Thank you for showing it to me. The grounds are lovely.'

'There is still a lot to be done,' Zack said with a sigh as he gazed out of the window overlooking the terrace. 'I do appreciate your opinion and welcome any suggestions you care to make.'

'Why? What I think is of no account. I have not changed my mind, Zack.' She took a deep breath, willing herself to be calm. Being his temporary wife certainly had its drawbacks, but only because their marriage was destined to end. She knew that by delaying the task, her heart would be entangled that much more when it came time for her to sign the papers. 'I think we should have our marriage annulled.' Quietly she murmured, 'Perhaps the sooner the better.'

Zack flinched, but showed no signs of backing down. 'Is that what you want, Shona? Truly? Tell me.'

Feeling herself weakening beneath his penetrating gaze, she averted her eyes, lest he saw the truth mirrored in their depths. 'I—I don't know…'

'Then let me help you. I don't want to be divorced from you,' he said quietly. 'I have no intention of letting you go, Shona. I don't want to be parted from you any more than you want to be parted from me.'

Zack's eyes burned into Shona's and she could feel the resistance melting within her. The thought began to run through her mind that he was, after all, her husband and it was quite proper to yield to anything he had in mind.

'Come,' he said, taking her hand and steering her along the landing. 'I think it's time to settle the matter and put an end to any more talk of an annulment.'

Flinging open a pair of polished double doors with ornate brass handles, they entered a large stately room which was clearly to be his bedroom—already a large bed had been erected on a dais in the middle.

Zack had no idea until now just how deep his hunger for Shona was. For the time they had been together, of wanting her, of frustrating selfdenial, his need for her had built up to such a pitch that he was almost beyond restraint. All he could think of was shattering her demureness and reserve and laying bare the woman of passion—a woman he had every right to make love to. Whatever it took he knew he would do anything to bring her into his life. He was shaken by the intensity of his desire—his very soul flamed with a whole new motivation to complete what had been, until now, a complete misunderstanding.

'I treated you very badly, Shona. I regret that

profoundly. I know you were innocent of any wrongdoing.'

'How do you know? What has changed—unless, of course, you have spoken to Thomas?'

'He called to see me earlier and told me everything. On Santamaria I treated you with a brutal viciousness of which I'd never thought myself capable, for which I am profoundly sorry and beg your forgiveness. Now I aim to do right by you.'

'And you really have no intention of letting me go,' she whispered, hope and gladness flooding her heart.

'Not a chance. I know my wants.'

'That's a start, I suppose. An attitude like that does bode well for our future together.'

Zack raised a dark brow and considered her flushed cheeks and trembling mouth. His heated gaze moved even lower and surveyed her heaving bosom. 'It does. Despite what happened on Santamaria, when I left my mind was tortured by your beauty and I could not forget even the smallest detail of you in my arms. That image was seared into my memory as if you had branded me. Now you've found me I will not let you go.'

Shona swallowed, her voice suddenly deserting her as she gazed into his mesmerising eyes. She felt herself being drawn into his gaze, into the vital, rugged aura that was so much a part of him. Being this close to him was having a strange effect on her senses. She was too much aware of his masculinity, of his power, his strength.

'Are you not going to take me back?'

In answer Zack tipped his head back and closed his eyes, looking like a man in the throes of some deep internal battle. 'Why?' he said.

'Because you've shown me the house and it's time to leave.'

'I did not bring you here just to show you the house, Shona.'

Shona's sense of security began to disintegrate. 'You didn't? Then—then why are we here? Do you have an ulterior motive?' she asked.

'You might say that. It appears to have slipped your mind that you bid five hundred guineas to spend time alone with me. It's time for you to collect, Shona. Besides, I wanted to be alone with you.'

'You did?'

He turned his head towards her, and his relentless gaze locked with hers. 'Come here and I'll show you why.'

Shona's entire body began to vibrate with a

mixture of shock, desire and fear, but somehow her mind remained in control. It was one thing to want to be kissed by him when there were others close by, but here, in his house, with absolute privacy and nothing to prevent him from taking all sorts of liberties, it was another matter entirely. Far more dangerous. And based on her behaviour on Santamaria, she couldn't even blame him for thinking she'd be willing now. Struggling desperately to ignore the sensual pull he was exerting on her, she drew a long, shaky breath.

Zack sighed. 'Considering what has transpired between us, don't you think it's a little ridiculous to behave like this?'

Shona tried to keep her voice steady. 'Since you left me on the island, I've begun to see things more clearly. The truth is that my actions that first day we met, when we were on the terrace and I asked you to marry me, were foolish—no, shameless. And again in the creek that day when we were alone together, I behaved like a shameless wanton. I should have known better than to flirt with a man of your years and experience. I can't completely blame you for thinking that's exactly what I was.'

'And you *know* that is what I thought, Shona?'

His deep voice made her senses jolt almost as

much as the way he was looking at her. 'What else could you have thought?'

'I thought you were very lovely and it was despicable of me to accuse you of being all those things I accused you of. Fear had something to do with it. You see, there were reasons why I couldn't marry you, Shona.' He watched her, waiting for her to comment and question his words. When she didn't, he said, 'It would mean a great deal to me, and to our future together, if you could forget the things I said.'

'Only if you can believe that they weren't true. If we try to hide from it, to pretend it didn't happen, it will always be there, lurking. It will come back to haunt both of us at odd times, for odd reasons, and when it does, it will come between us. Something one of us says or does will open the wound and create mistrust. I swear to you that I did not set out to compromise you into marriage. It's important to me that you know that and believe it.'

'I have already told you that I believe you are innocent of any wrongdoing. How did you come to be so wise?' he asked with a soft smile.

'If I were wise,' she said drily, 'I would not have allowed this situation to arise in the first place. Why, when we spoke our vows, did you come to my chamber when you believed I was not your wife?'

'For the same reason that you wanted me to.'

'It was wrong,' she protested. 'It was both dangerous and foolish.'

'Foolish or not,' he said grimly, 'I wanted you. That was something I had no control over. I want you now.'

Shona made the mistake of looking at him and his silver-grey eyes captured hers against her will, holding them imprisoned. His husky blandishments quickened her own hunger for what she had once tasted.

'I've remembered you all this time,' he went on, 'and I know damn well you've remembered me.'

Shona wanted to deny it, but she sensed that if she did, he'd be so disgusted he'd despise her for her deceit. Besides, she was too deeply affected by the things he'd just said to her to lie to him. 'Yes, I admit it,' she said weakly. 'No matter how hard I tried, I have never forgotten you or what happened between us the night you left me. How could I?' she added defensively.

Zack's eyes softened and his voice deepened to the timbre of rough velvet. 'I'm glad to hear you admit it. Come here,' he said, holding out his hand.

'Why?' she whispered shakily.

'So that I can finish what we began on San-tamaria. Let's see if it's as good as we remember. And then, when I've had my way with you, there will be no more talk of a divorce.'

Shona stared at him as his voice aroused the memory she had been unable to forget. Tentatively she took a step towards him, desperately wanting to seek the haven of his arms and solace from the turmoil of her emotions. Zack represented safety, warmth, security.

The look of desperation on her face and her trembling lips were Zack's undoing. Suddenly he crossed the short distance that separated them and caught her in his arms with such stunning force that the breath was knocked out of her. His embrace tightened about her until her toes almost cleared the floor and she was gasping for breath. His mouth swooped down upon hers, twisting, rousing, his lips searing hers, possessing her. As she was trying to rustle up some logic in her mind, pleasure began to seep through the barrier of her own will. The brutal crush of his lips on hers, his strong arms holding her clasped to his muscled frame became somehow bearable and she was answering, not fighting any more, returning his kiss with a fervour that betrayed her own longing.

Zack realised with a surge of lust that her demureness and reserve hid a woman of passion, of courage. He wanted her. Wanted to fill his mouth with the taste of her. The fierceness of his wanting startling him.

'I'll help you take off your clothes,' he forced himself to say in a voice suddenly grown deep and husky.

Panic seized Shona and her eyes flew to the door. 'But—someone might come…'

Taking her face between his strong hands, he gently kissed her lips. 'No one will come, my love. Jessen has instructions not to allow anyone to disturb us,' he told her softly, his warm breath fanning her mouth. 'Shona…' the word was a rasp '…I can't take much more of this. Any minute now I'm going to forget I'm supposed to be a gentleman…'

'Please—help me.'

'It will be my pleasure,' he said hoarsely, holding her away from him and helping to divest her of her gown, silently cursing what seemed to be hundreds of hooks and hoops and minute buttons.

Shona let the gown fall to the floor with an idle shrug. Thrusting off his jacket, Zack watched her with an avid, wolf-like stare as she stood in front of him and unfastened his cravat, tossing it on to the floor before setting about the buttons on his shirt. She saw the flash of startled delight in his eyes and he laughed softly, skimming his smiling lips along her neck even as she removed the shirt from his back.

Scooping her up in his arms, he carried her to the bed. He stood her to her feet beside it and immediately they were seized by a frenzied haste to finish undressing one another. Soon they faced each other in all their naked glory. Shona's gaze riveted on the bronzed skin that covered his broad chest and her treacherous heart began to beat a little faster. His body was a sculpture and she was enslaved. Zack's right hand lifted, and his knuckles stroked softly up her bare arm in a patient caress while his gaze held hers. The message in those compelling silver-grey eyes of what was about to happen was as clear as if he were whispering it.

Shona gazed at the sensual mouth only inches from hers. His hands moved down the length of her body, stroking her soft breasts, and, lowering his head, he covered her with greedy kisses.

In the next moment they were wrapped in each other's arms and tumbling to the mattress.

Zack's lips hovered over hers. He had endured a long abstinence and he wanted nothing to hinder his union with his exquisite wife. She was soft and willing, and he was hard and ready.

A tremor went through Shona as his hand claimed the softness of her, touching her where only he had once dared. The eyes above her own glowed intently as his caresses grew purposefully bolder. She held her breath as the strange sensations leapt through her, setting her whole being on fire, and she writhed, unable to stop her dizzying world. She curled against him and she felt his lips against her hair, heard her name hoarsely whispered.

Lowering his head, he traced with tantalising slowness over her breasts, venturing across the swelling mound to the pale pink crest, causing Shona to shiver as a delicious excitement rippled through her.

'You like that?' he queried, lifting his mouth to tease hers.

'You know I do.' She sighed as he continued to ply her mouth with kisses, his knowledgeable hands questing and caressing her womanly softness, setting her on fire for him. She writhed beneath his touch, wondering how long she could bear such rapture without being completely swept away.

Zack held himself back, clamping down on his own frenzied need, letting the heat build in her until her soft whimpers and arching body told him she was throbbing for him.

Following the urging pressure of her husband's hands, Shona relaxed back upon the pillows and welcomed him with opened limbs. His naked body covered hers and seemed to burn her with more than the fervour he exhibited. And then, down in the depths of her, as his narrow hips caressed hers in long, leisurely strokes that soothed the shock of his penetration, she could feel sparks beginning to flare in a core overflowing with womanly ardour.

The intensifying hunger within her became almost insatiable, driving her to a kind of wildness that made her dig her nails into his back. She was greedy, wanting to savour it all. Then she caught her breath in surprise as she felt the first pulsing waves of bliss begin to wash over her, a feverish warmth filling her, and she welcomed it into the cavern of her being.

Zack's rock-hard body, glistening with sweat, relaxed against her and she held him close, aware of the thudding of his heart and his harsh, laboured breath fanning her face.

When he could think again, Zack shifted himself to the side of her and propped himself up on his elbow, supporting his head with his hand. He remembered her request to end their marriage and smiled down at her. Shona lay there, rumpled and pink-cheeked and thoroughly kissed, her glorious green eyes sleepy with fulfilled desire.

'I imagine this means there won't be an annulment after all.'

With a mischievous little smile playing on her lips and her eyes gleaming with twinkling humour, she lifted her hand and caressed his face. 'I agree that an annulment is completely out of the question—and if you prove to be a good husband and continue to please me, I suppose that could also apply to a divorce.'

'Never fear, my love.' His smile was almost a leer. 'I have a thing or two more to teach you in the way of pleasing *me*.'

'I believe you,' she said, her gaze wandering leisurely over the broad expanse of his chest. With her mind intent on making love, she had not looked at the finer details of his body, but now, to see him naked was rather startling. He was a most impressive specimen and, since she was his wife, she would have to get used to seeing him without the adornment of clothes. She smiled, deciding such a task would not be so difficult.

Zack sighed with contentment. Shona looked so very sultry and seductive, lying there in his arms, breathtakingly alluring, her lips curved in a sublime smile. Her soft perfume mingled with the warm smell of their bodies, sending his senses reeling. Taking her hand, he gently placed his lips on her moist palm before looking at her, his eyes smouldering.

'Have you any idea how much I missed you when I left Santamaria?'

'Did you? I'm glad to hear it,' she said breathily, her dark-lashed eyes lustrous and warm. 'I belong to you now.'

Shona's skin had blushed to the colour of a soft pink rose—a flower well worth cultivating. The years ahead had suddenly taken on a rosier hue.

'Absolutely. I knew it the first time I held you in my arms. You have belonged to me since I first set eyes on you on Santamaria. You belonged to me then—my body knew it even if my eyes didn't see it. I want you and need you.

I don't want to lose you, Shona. I cannot, will not, let you go. I want what every man wants from his wife—for her to give him comfort and ease throughout the days, and nights, of their life together.'

'Me, too,' Shona murmured. Snuggling close to his side, she pressed a kiss to his chest, wanting to kiss all of him. 'What's this?' she exclaimed all of a sudden, pausing and staring at the pale narrow scar on his side while his hand caressed her back.

'Nothing,' he said. 'Just a wound some pirate inflicted on me when he tried to kill me.'

She looked at him in alarm. 'Was he very fierce?'

'Very.'

'Why did he want to kill you?'

'For profit. He tried to steal my ship.' He grinned. 'Don't worry, my love. It was all a long time ago and I escaped with my ship and my life intact.'

'And the pirate?'

'He wasn't so lucky,' he murmured, bending his head and nibbling her earlobe.

When his fingers traced the curve of her waist, she sighed, awed that a hand which dealt death so skilfully with a sword could be so infinitely tender. Her wandering fingers suddenly stopped. 'Zack,' she said, slightly perturbed.

'Yes, my sweet?' he answered, his deep voice gone slightly hoarse with renewed desire. It seemed her questing fingers were having a curious effect on him.

'There's another scar on the other side—much larger than the other.'

'There is?' The scent of her was quite amazing.

'Was this inflicted by the same pirate?'

'No. That was another reprobate.'

'Do people make a habit of trying to kill you?'

'Only when I annoy them.'

She pressed herself against him and gave a sensuous sigh, enjoying the way he nibbled her ear. 'Do you have any more scars I don't know about?'

'Keep looking,' he murmured in her ear.

Looping her arms about his neck, she pulled his head down to hers. 'You really are wicked, Captain Fitzgerald,' she whispered.

'Not beyond redemption, I hope.'

'I do hope not,' she murmured, breathing heavily.

'I'm happy to know your opinion of me is improving,' Zack said, laughing low in his throat.

'Aye, milord, but is it not time for us to go?'

'Not yet.' He reached for her once more, revelling in the satiny smoothness of her flesh and burying his face against her throat. 'I would savour once more the delights that you have brought within my grasp. I have waited too long for this. I will not let it end so quickly.'

Caught up in her intoxicating taste, again they made love. When he would have gathered her against him once more, Shona rolled to the edge of the bed and bounced to her feet, with light, lilting laughter floating from her lips. 'You, my lord, are insatiable.'

Zack sighed regretfully and relaxed back on the pillows. 'If you don't wish to experience another display of my ardour, you'd best put on your clothes.' He nodded towards a door across the room, his eyes gleaming with humour. 'I'm sure you would like to make use of my bathing chamber. I think you'll find everything you need in there. When you are dressed I'll return you to your Aunt Augusta—but I promise you, Shona, that I shall have you installed in my home within days.'

Turning her back on him and tripping across the carpet to sample the delights of his bathing chamber, Shona didn't doubt that for a moment—she no longer had any objections.

Zack looked up from fastening his shirt when Shona emerged from his bathing chamber. Her slender body was completely engulfed in his thick plum-coloured robe. Her bare white toes peeped from beneath the hem and the shoulder seams fell to her elbow. Earlier, Zack had thought she couldn't possibly look more desirable than she had when she had been naked, but he'd been wrong. Wrapped in an oversize robe, with her face flushed and her thick gold hair falling about her shoulders, she had the dewy freshness of a flower at dawn.

'How do you feel?' Zack enquired as she padded across the carpet to plant a kiss on his mouth.

'The same way I look,' she murmured, the oversize robe slipping off her right shoulder, leaving it bare. 'I'd better get dressed—although you're going to have to help me.'

'It will be my pleasure,' he said.

The warmth in his deep voice and the bold admiration in his eyes did astonishing things to Shona's heartbeat, a reaction that was so strong that her cheeks grew hot. She pulled away from him and gave him a playful smile. 'Perhaps it isn't such a good idea after all.'

Laughing softly, he pulled her into his arms and planted a kiss on her bare shoulder. 'I promise I shall behave. You will have no reason for complaint.'

Shona did not move out of Aunt Augusta's house as their time of courtship and getting to know each other began. Because Zack wanted her to enjoy the position of prestige in society she was entitled to—and because he enjoyed showing her off in the setting where she sparkled like the jewels he lavished on her—during the days that followed they attended a variety of social events.

These were blissful days. They passed as a lovely dream of laughter and loving, and hours of unbridled passion in the master bedchamber in what was to be their new town house. Shona quickly discovered that the day Zack had introduced her to the joys to be had in his bed had been but a small preview of the wild beauty and primitive splendour.

There were times when he could not hold her close enough or long enough. And then there were moments when he would turn to her in hunger and need, when she would listen to his husky voice grow thick with desire while he touched and caressed her in particular ways and without embarrassment she would return the favour, and when she did, his powerful muscles jumped beneath her touch. There were also times when he would change her into a creature she did not know, when he drew from her a stormy passion she had never known she was capable of, then shared it with her. And then there were times when he bathed her senses in pleasure, lingering over her endlessly, lavishing her senses with every exquisite sensation, prolonging their release, until Shona was pleading with him to end the torment. She gave herself to him completely—body, heart and soul.

Life became a rainbow of delights. She was aglow with happiness and loved the attention and care her husband lavished on her. Not since the death of her father had she known the joy of being adored and cherished for what she really was and the quiet, inner peace she felt was sheer bliss.

One afternoon when they left Zack's room following a particularly passionate interlude, Shona felt his hand tighten on hers and sensed instinctively that he was looking at her with that strange expression of tenderness on his handsome face. Raising his hand, she brought it up to her cheek and, turning her head, lightly kissed his fingers.

Zack bent his head and kissed her lips, wanting to tell her again what he felt, to explain that he'd never known there were feelings like this, but the emotions were still too raw and he was still in a daze.

They were halfway down the stairs when the doorbell rang and Jessen admitted a man and a woman into the hall.

'Good Lord!' Zack said softly, coming to a halt.

'Who is it?' Shona asked, still weak from the passion they'd shared.

'My brother, Harry, and his wife, Miranda.' He glanced at Shona, who looked completely alarmed, and whispered, 'Don't worry. They will like you once they recover from their surprise that you are my wife.' He knew there was nothing for it but to put a brave face on. 'Harry! What's this?' he said, proceeding down the stairs to greet his brother. 'Visitors already. I haven't even moved in.'

'I know. We've just arrived in town and thought we'd take a look at my brother's palatial residence.'

'Hardly palatial,' Zack contradicted.

'But very grand,' the petite brunette said, marching forward to press a kiss on her brother-in-law's cheek. 'In fact, it is much too grand for a man to live here all…' her bright blue eyes riveted on Shona and her voice trailed off lamely '…alone.' She regarded Shona with veiled puzzlement. 'But—where are your manners? Are you not going to introduce us, Zack?'

Cursing a perverse turn of fate for making a wonderful situation into a difficult one, for he suspected what they were thinking—that they had walked in on him entertaining an unchaperoned female in his home, which meant that her reputation was in serious question, or that she was some courtesan with whom he had been dallying and it would be an unforgivable breach of decency to introduce her to his sister-in-law. Shona's presence might also imply that her willingness to come to the house alone with him might misleadingly suggest a degree of sexual freedom that could obviously lead to trouble and must be quashed immediately.

Rather than descend to that, he put his hand beneath Shona's elbow, partly for support and partly to urge her forward. Giving her a reassuring smile, he took a moment to answer, clearing his throat first before saying, 'May I present Shona McKenzie-Fitzgerald—my wife. Shona, I would like to introduce my brother, Harry, and his wife, Miranda—Viscount and Viscountess Fitzgerald.'

There was a stunned silence while Zack's brother was regarding him with fascinated disbelief and his sister-in-law had gone perfectly still.

'Wife?' Harry echoed. 'Good Lord, Zack! When did this happen?'

'Shona and I were married on Santamaria—in the Caribbean.'

Harry Fitzgerald, a handsome, dark-haired man in his mid-thirties who bore a striking resemblance to Zack in his facial features and height, stepped forward and pressed a gallant kiss to the back of Shona's hand and told her that he was 'enchanted' to meet her.

Shona felt her cheeks flushing with embarrassment. She glanced at his wife and to her amazement, a warm and heartfelt smile dawned on Miranda's face before she turned to scold her brother-in-law. 'Zack, how could you? What do you intend doing about Caroline and Victoria?'

Zack's amusement faded abruptly. It was the moment he'd been dreading. Not that he had intentionally deceived Shona about his relationship with Caroline. Indeed, he'd already told her they had a connection, but the moment had not been appropriate to tell her about his daughter. Initially he'd been too angry at being duped into marriage to think she deserved an explanation. And he was enough of a gentleman to know the subject needed delicate handling. He could imagine the hurt look in Shona's eyes when he told her the real reason for not wanting to marry her when she had proposed to him on Santamaria— that he intended to wed another woman in order to claim his daughter.

From the moment he'd decided not to have their marriage annulled he had watched her with fascinated interest as, with the gracious ease with which she conducted herself, she effortlessly charmed everyone she came into contact with. His lovely young wife was fresh and unspoiled and there was a natural sophistication about her that came from an active mind, a lively wit and a genuine interest in others. She was a woman full of surprises, full of promise, vivid beauty moulded into every flawlessly sculpted feature of her face. But her allure was more than that—it was in her laughter and her graceful movements. There was something deep within her that made her sparkle and glow like a flawless jewel. He wanted to lay the world at her feet, but all Shona seemed to want was him and that knowledge filled him with profound tenderness.

He would have to tell her about Victoria, he knew that, but now he had started to feel that emotional bond, he was afraid the revelation that he had a daughter could put their newfound happiness at risk, which was why he had withheld telling her.

His eyes sought his wife's. Her expression was quizzical, puzzled and expectant. How did he tell her about Victoria? And how did he do it in a way that would shield Caroline's reputation *and* Victoria's? Surprisingly, she raised an eyebrow and gave him a smile. Zack realised she was giving him a reprieve, that she was avoiding the issue of Caroline for the present.

Shona wanted desperately to know about Caroline Donnington—and who was Victoria?—for Zack to reassure her that there was nothing to substantiate her jealous imaginings, but for the time being she would hold back. She hesitated for a split second before she smiled. The appearance of these two had taken her by surprise. If she had been forewarned, if she'd had time to think about her reaction to Miranda's thoughtless

remark, she might have prepared and rehearsed a
gracious set down. But she could not bring herself to be clumsily rude to this overwhelmingly
lovely woman.

'I'm very happy to make your acquaintance...'
Shona paused, not knowing how to address her.

Miranda's body seemed to relax and her expression to soften. 'Please call me Miranda—
and welcome to the family. I'm already looking
forward to getting to know you. You are my sister-in-law and I do hope it will make us friends.'
She cocked her head to one side. 'You really are
very pretty, Shona.'

'Miranda!' her husband admonished.

'Well, she is quite lovely, Harry. And I don't
see why it isn't good manners to say so.'

'Thank you for the compliment,' Shona said,
her throat unexpectedly tightening with emotion. She had never expected to be welcomed
so warmly. 'And even if it isn't proper to say
so on such short acquaintance, I think you are
very pretty, too.'

'Have the children accompanied you to
London?' Zack enquired.

Miranda shook her head. 'Harry and I had already arranged to come to town when your sisters arrived with their offspring. Our brood were

quite put out at the mere thought of leaving their cousins and the fun to be had so we left them in the care of nannies and nurses.'

'Was Santamaria your home?' Harry enquired of Shona, curious about this young woman who had suddenly become a member of his family.

'Yes,' Shona answered, telling him a little of her island home, a neutral subject she was happy to discuss.

'And have you been in England long?' Miranda asked.

'Over two weeks,' she said, thinking how different this kind and vivacious woman was to acid-tongued Carmelita, 'although my father sent me to England for my education.'

'So you are staying with Zack?'

'Shona is residing with her aunt, Lady Franklyn, at present,' Zack explained, sensing Shona's apprehension and coming to her rescue. 'She will move in here with me as soon as the house is ready.'

'Which shouldn't be too long by the look of things,' Harry remarked, casting an approving look about him before settling his gaze on Shona. 'If we seem surprised, that's because we are. This sea-roving brother of mine gave us no indication that he was to wed. But I see he has excellent judgement.' Harry was not about to let his brother escape without an explanation. 'I'm surprised you married without telling us.'

It was an enquiry, Zack knew, but still a request for an explanation, but the débâcle that had preceded his marriage to Shona and his own dishonesty would remain between Shona and himself. He laughed to conceal his unease. 'Shona and I came together through the efforts of her brother—who just happens to be the owner of the small island of Santamaria. He wanted Shona and I to get to know each other and threatened me with dire consequences if I refused him. He is what you would call a matchmaker of sorts. A very wilful gentleman.' His face was expressionless as he regarded Shona for a moment, then a small, one-sided smile appeared. 'Is that not so, Shona?'

Shona met his gaze. He told no lie, yet made it all seem so completely proper, saving her the pain of having them know the more embarrassing facts. She smiled at him, pleased with his answer. 'Yes,' she agreed. 'My brother can be very persuasive.'

'Now if you don't mind,' Zack said, hoping to forestall an embarrassing barrage of questions, 'I was on the point of taking her home. You are welcome to stay and see the house—Jessen will be more than happy to show you around.'

'Thank you, we'd love to,' Miranda said, unable to hide her excited curiosity at this, her brother-in-law's first house. 'But make sure you bring Shona to visit us soon, Zack. In fact, I insist that you both accompany us to the theatre tomorrow night. It will give us a chance to get to know her.'

Zack hesitated until he saw Shona's wide-eyed look of eagerness. He accepted the invitation graciously.

'I shall look forward to it,' Shona said with a gentle smile, her mind whirling with worrying doubts and hopeless questions about Zack's true relationship to Caroline Donnington as he escorted her out of the house and into the carriage.

And who was Victoria?

Seated behind the groom for the short drive to her aunt's house, Shona turned and looked at Zack, and what surprised her was the look in his eyes. He was gazing at her with the same tender light that she had seen when she had lain in his arms. It warmed her to have him looking at her so.

'Miranda was right. You really are very lovely, Shona.'

'Thank you,' she said, his husky tone vibrating through her, warming her. 'Although I hadn't expected to meet your family at this time.'

'I know and I apologise for any awkwardness you might have felt. But they genuinely like you. I have no doubt that Harry will grill me for information about how we came to wed later.'

'What will you tell him?'

'Only as much as you and I agree upon— that we met, were attracted to one another and were married. If he finds it strange that we didn't travel to England together, I shall explain there were reasons why you were unable to leave Santamaria—perhaps the imminent arrival of your brother's first offspring will suffice to satisfy their curiosity. What about your aunt? Did she question you?'

'Yes, she found the whole situation rather amusing—which is typical of her—but you can count on her discretion.' She swallowed, her voice suddenly deserting her as she gazed into his eyes. She felt herself being drawn into his gaze, into the vital, rugged aura that was so much a part of him. Being this close to him was having a strange effect on her senses once more. She was acutely aware of him as a man, of his heat, his power, his strength. 'I'm going to miss you,' she whispered. 'Do we have to be apart now?'

'I hate the thought of it as much as you do. I'll speak to Harry about you moving in with me. It won't be for long, I promise you.' He ensnared her gaze through the warm glow of the sunlight shining through the windows and carefully probed those dark green, lustrous orbs as a slow smile curved his lips. 'You've awakened emotions within me that I was sure I was incapable of feeling until we became reacquainted—some of which I'm greatly appreciative, others I'm still trying to restrain.'

Shona peered at him obliquely. 'And what are they?'

Zack's eyes narrowed and his lips curved in a smile. 'Oh, I shan't divulge that bit of knowledge just yet. I must plumb the depth of the matter more fully before I give that power over into your hands.'

'Don't tease, Zack,' she accused softly. 'I've done nothing, yet you would have me believe I've influenced you in some mysterious way. I think you're teasing me.'

A soft chuckle escaped his lips. 'I see you're

not easily taken in, Shona, but can you not understand what a man like myself experiences in the presence of such a beautiful woman? But no need to fear. As much as I'd enjoy making love to you right now, I shall have to control my lusts. However, I hope in time—when we move into our new home together, or you join me in my brother's house—that you'll prove as receptive to my attentions as you were earlier.'

Shona could feel her cheeks warming as she met those smiling silver-grey eyes. The warmth shining in those translucent depths was unmistakable. 'You seem terribly sure of yourself, Zack.'

'As sure as I can be. During the time I spent at sea, I became familiar with the skills of keeping my vessels afloat—be it battle against the weather or miscreants trying to board or sink me. There is also an art to the intimacy a man and woman can share together. I've come to realise after today that I won't be content until we are living together as man and wife.' His eyes lowered to her face as he traced the outline of her delectable mouth, still slightly swollen and soft from his kisses. 'You're like a potent wine that has gone to my head. I've never desired another woman as much as I've come to desire you since I first set eyes on you. You must know that by now.'

As the carriage came to a halt, having reached its destination, he took her hand and raised it to his lips. His expression became grave and his gaze intensified. 'Shona, I need to talk to you.'

Disturbed by his touch, Shona gazed at his hand holding hers—a strong, brown hand that had power to control a wildly plunging ship, yet could be gentle and caressing and arousing... arousing not just for herself, but for Lady Caroline Donnington...and someone named Victoria. All these glorious days they had been together there had been no mention of either of these women and she wanted desperately to know, for Zack to tell her what he was holding back.

Taking a deep breath, summoning her courage, she said, 'Is it about Lady Donnington?'

His expression was wary and oddly grim. 'Partly.'

'Zack? Tell me. What is it?' She watched him, waiting expectantly for him to say more. Instead he looked away, avoiding her gaze. The door to the house opened and her aunt appeared in the doorway and waved.

'We can't discuss it here—not now.'

'When can we discuss it?' she asked quietly.

When Augusta began walking towards the carriage, he bent his head and lightly kissed her lips. 'I'll see you tomorrow evening when I call to take you to the theatre. We'll talk after that. I promise.'

Chapter Ten

Shona was relieved when she found the opportunity to escape to her room, grateful to have some time to herself. She settled back into the steaming water of her bath with a deep sigh of appreciation. She lifted a large sponge and dribbled water over her breasts, memories of the moments spent in carnal union with Zack swimming provocatively through her mind. The impressions were so overpowering and vivid that they rekindled fires that burned her from within.

Her eyes drifted closed and she could almost feel his large body moving upon hers, his hardened chest teasing her breasts and his harsh gasps filling her mind. She remembered how he had kissed her with such leisurely expertise, how her head had spun with the intoxicating male taste of him and the passion in his kiss which had robbed her of her senses, her pulse throbbing under his deft touch.

A long, trembling sigh slipped from her lips as she luxuriated in the sensations that flooded through her, making her realise just how deeply she had been affected by their union and the bliss she had found within it. For one sinful moment she longed for him again, to have his arms around her right then. She could not believe that she had sought to proceed with the annulment of their marriage upon her arrival in London—with pride part of the equation, to be the mistress of her own destiny, never to let him have control of her—only to find her control leaking away under his seduction and that she had surrendered to him of her own free will.

She was his, whether she wanted to admit it or not.

It was a pleasant day for March, fine and mild, and the park was crowded. Shona accompanied her aunt in the carriage, finding herself involved in more than a few delightful chats with Aunt Augusta's friends and acquaintances whom they had encountered. Their discussions ranged anywhere from passing comments on the balmy March weather to light-hearted observations on the various entertainments being performed at London's theatres. With her evening with Zack to look forward to, Shona was feeling light-hearted and sublimely happy—until she looked ahead in time to see a familiar black carriage and four splendid black horses roll to a halt.

Her heart did a somersault and she was about to raise her hand and wave, until she saw he was not alone. Her eyes were drawn to the occupants of the carriage. One of the women had striking features and dark brown hair beneath a stylish lavender hat which matched her jacket. Another woman dressed in plain black sat beside a small child.

Her eyes unblinking, Shona watched as Zack alighted and held out a hand to assist his female companion in her descent and a child. The woman was Lady Caroline Donnington—she assumed she was the mother of the child, a girl, in a pretty pink-and-white dress festooned with bows. Immediately Shona was caught in the throes of acute despondency with a fair amount of jealousy thrown in.

Zack was completely unaware of his wife's presence and his teeth flashed whitely in sharp contrast to his darkly burnished skin as he threw back his head and laughed at whatever the little girl had said to him. He was exceptionally well dressed and looked every bit the nobleman he was. Indeed, no gentleman in the park could match his debonair appearance. His fine, dark green coat was set off to perfection by thinly striped grey trousers and a waistcoat in dove grey. A darker grey cravat was a stunning addition to his elegant garb. If anything, his dashing good looks were even more striking than before. His companion evidently thought so, too, for she swayed against him, brushing against his arm as she smiled up at him and lightly touched his broad chest. Taking a quiet path through the trees, they strolled leisurely along, the child scampering on ahead.

Shona watched the touching scene in ringing silence. She felt as though every drop of blood in her brain had left it, leaving her faint and sick. Something unpleasant was moving through her, making its way from her wounded heart up to her slowly thawing mind, which was frozen with disbelief. Her heart lurched into her throat, choking her, and had she not been sitting in the carriage her knees would have buckled.

'Is something wrong, Shona?' Augusta asked, noting her niece's pallor and genuinely concerned. 'Are you not feeling well?'

Heartbreakingly aware that something awe-inspiring and terrifying had happened to her in that moment, Shona forced a smile to her lips, cursing herself for allowing her distress to show so obviously. 'I am quite well, Aunt. Why ever should I not be? I just feel a little chilled, that's all.' Though her heart throbbed painfully, she felt inclined to shiver despite the tender warmth of the spring-like sunshine.

'Then we'll head back to the house. You must leave yourself plenty of time to get ready for the theatre.'

As the carriage turned for home, Shona looked back. Zack and Lady Donnington were still in sight and appeared to be absorbed deep in conversation. Their attention was constantly drawn to the antics of the child skipping ahead. Shona felt as though a knife had been plunged into her heart, damaging it irretrievably. She made a small sound in her throat, but there was so much noise about her that Aunt Augusta did not hear. As the carriage was heading out of the park, turning her head one last time, she saw her husband run after the child, his face creased in a huge grin of delight, his arms opened wide to draw her into his embrace.

Over the head of the wriggling child, who was

a small replica of her mother, Zack saw his wife watching and his eyes widened with shock, for he had not expected her to be there. For a moment or two he stood there, holding his young charge, until Shona turned away and, before he could stop her, the carriage left the park.

Zack realised that he had made a mistake in coming here. He felt like he was cheating. Suddenly it was the wrong place, the wrong time and the wrong woman. He was uncomfortable and he wanted to get away from here.

Meanwhile Shona was in agony, impatient for the quiet seclusion of her room, a space with no one in it, in which to recover her composure, though how in the name of God she could do that she could not imagine. She looked ahead, but her eyes were blinded—she could see nothing but a blur of colour before her. No matter what might happen later, though it cost her every shred of strength and willpower, and her own bloody-minded pride, she must bear the pain in silence without anyone knowing how much she suffered.

But how could he? her mind screamed wretchedly. How could Zack do this to her? How could he do something so highly indiscreet—and him a married man—as to escort another woman under society's nose when only yesterday he had paraded his wife on his arm in the park?

The shock of seeing him with Lady Donnington had triggered off some sleeping thing inside her, bringing it to life and revealing to her the true state of her heart. He had told her there was something he wanted to speak to her about—was this what it was about, that Lady Donnington was his mistress and he was not prepared to give her up? Was the rapture she, Shona, had found in his arms, a rapture he did not value as she did, to be shared with another woman?

That night Shona was breathtakingly beautiful. The pale gold silk of her dress had been chosen by Morag, after long and careful thought, to blend perfectly with the warm colour of her skin and hair.

Zack arrived on time to collect his wife for the theatre. He was dressed immaculately, fastidiously even, the cut of his expensive jacket setting off the powerful width of his shoulders, his legs smooth and shapely in the well-tailored perfection of his trousers, his dark hair smoothly brushed.

Shona swallowed convulsively. She wanted to cover her eyes for a moment, to shut out the sight of the man who stood before her. He was so stern, so oppressive and yet so breathtaking. He took her breath away. His chiselled profile was touched by the warm light of the candles and the growing ache in her bosom attested to the degree of its handsomeness. In an attempt to maintain her serenity, she let out a slow, steadying breath. His eyes were dark and intense with concern—not for her, she knew that, but because of what she had seen in the park earlier.

As she walked towards him, her heels tapping against the tiled floor, Zack surveyed her from beneath lowered eyebrows. His face was carefully blank, his eyes looking somewhere over her head as though he didn't really care to consider her face. Even as she burned with questions, her heart beat agonisingly and longingly, despairingly, wanting his arms about her, wanting his hard, protective body against hers in the way of a man who loves a woman. He did love a woman, but it wasn't her and she must find the strength to accept that.

The man who watched her approach, her dress flowing in shimmering waves about her as her mind moved like a disembodied wraith through the quandaries she faced, wanted to go to her and take her in his arms, kiss her and soothe her and tell her he would make everything all right and yet how could he after what had happened earlier. But her pale face and empty eyes told him she was evidently much distressed—and who could blame her after what she had seen?

'Shona. Allow me to compliment you. You are exquisite tonight.'

Shona stared at him. His tone was formal, almost ceremonious. Stiffened by pride, she managed with a painful effort to dominate her hurt and accept the slap that fate had dealt her. She raised her head, schooling her features to a smile and her voice to the necessary social lightness.

'Thank you.'

'Are you ready?'

'Not quite. I would like to speak to you before we leave.'

Zack studied the dark green eyes regarding him solemnly from beneath a heavy fringe of dark lashes. 'We will be late.'

'Never mind. What I have to say to you is too important to put off. Please, come into the drawing room. My aunt is making preparations to travel to Berkshire in the morning with Thomas, so we will not be interrupted.'

Shona went ahead, closing the door when he followed her inside. Clasping her hands in front of her, she turned and faced her husband squarely. 'I think you know what this is about.'

'I think so. You were in the park today.'

Shona nodded, choosing her words carefully. 'Yes. So were you. You…were not alone, I saw.'

'No.'

Shona gave him a level look, her eyes ice-cold green. 'You seemed close. Perhaps Lady Donnington is no longer inclined to wed Lord Byrne now you are back in London. What were you trying to do to me, Zack? Humiliate me with your open association with your mistress in full view of everyone? You cannot, in all conscience, expect me to accept that.'

'No, I don't—and Caroline is not my mistress.'

'No? And who is Victoria?' Shona watched him, waiting expectantly. She had difficulty reading his expression, but she could see his features were taut with some kind of emotional struggle. Zack's hesitation was beginning to alarm her. 'Just tell me. It concerns Lady Donnington, doesn't it?'

Still he hesitated. There wasn't an easy way for a man to tell his wife that he had sired a child with a married woman. The muscles worked in his cheek as his jaw tightened and he turned and strode to the fireplace. With his rigid back to her, he thrust hands into his pockets. After a moment he turned and looked at her.

'Caroline is the mother of my daughter. Victoria.'

Zack distinctly saw Shona recoil as though a knife had been thrust into some deep and agonising part of her—as though it was turning slowly, damaging her so badly she was unlikely to survive it—but her face remained impassive.

'You have a daughter—a daughter you clearly forgot to tell me about?'

'I didn't forget. In the beginning I merely preferred not to have the discussion until I was ready. Then…the closer we became and our relationship developed into something more profound—a closeness I treasure—it was…difficult. I suppose I was afraid the revelation would damage that closeness—that you might walk away.'

Shona was mortified and deeply offended that he would think she would do that. 'Then you do not know me as well as you think you do,' she said, her voice shaking with emotion. 'I had a right to be told, Zack. You should not have kept this from me. It was cruel and despicable.'

Zack wasn't trying to hurt her, she realised. The rigid muscles of his jaw showed his dismay clearly. A sudden weight fell on her heart at what he had told her. She was stunned, bewildered and a thousand thoughts raced across her brain and crashed together in confusion. She thought of Zack—her love—and all the feelings and emotions he had created were blighted and crushed, trust and confidence destroyed. It shouldn't have been so painful discovering that he had a daughter—the little girl she had seen in the park, some small part of her mind rationalised—but it was.

'You should have told me before we…before we… I can't believe you have done this. You cannot expect me to ignore your indiscretion, to overlook what you have done and how it will affect me. You lied to me.'

'I never lied to you.' Zack suddenly realised how important it was to him that she knew the truth. He wanted her to understand. Looking down at her, he felt a cruel smart of anguish and a sudden surge of shame. When she lifted her hurt eyes to meet his own, he felt an overpowering tenderness. She looked to him like a wounded deer which holds itself proud and lithe, even as it breathes hard to avoid the fatal blow.

'You deceived me. You tricked me! Kept things hidden! Again! After all the things I let you do to me—and all the time you were playing me false. I trusted you,' she said.

'You can still trust me.'

'Things have changed. I can only wonder what else you're not telling me.' She glanced away from him. Having heard the note of despair in Zack's voice, she realised how adamant he had been in his refusal to marry her. She had misunderstood his reasons then. He hadn't wanted to marry her, that was true, but it wasn't his loss of freedom that had so disturbed him. It was the loss of his daughter. And neither she nor her family had given him a way out. She was not so naïve as to believe there had been no women in his life before her—shadowed women, faceless women, the sort of women men have for a moment's pleasure—but this was different. This woman had a face. This woman had given him a child. 'Clearly you were not married to Lady Donnington, so the child is…'

'A bastard,' Zack provided quietly, watching her face closely for her reaction. He was not flippant about it, but serious and troubled. But he showed no shame or embarrassment, not even any regret, except for the pain he had caused his wife.

'Yes, although it is not a word I like.'

'Nor I.'

'How old is your daughter?'

'She will be four years old come July.'

'And does she favour you?'

Zack hadn't expected her to ask that, but he answered it honestly. 'A little—she has my eyes. But she resembles her mother in other ways.'

'And when you refused to marry me when I asked you, it was because you were planning— hoping—to give your daughter your name by marrying her mother, in the event of her elderly husband having passed away.' When he cast her a sharp, enquiring look she smiled bitterly. 'Aunt Augusta put me in the picture when I asked her about Lady Donnington. But that was the reason, wasn't it, Zack? You intended to marry her.' It was a statement.

Zack frowned, his expression grave as he considered her question. 'I confess that there was a time when I seriously contemplated returning to England and marrying Caroline when old Donnington passed on, to try to salvage something out of our relationship for Victoria's sake. The trouble was,' he murmured, his voice husky as his gaze settled lovingly on her face, 'I never expected my decision to be beset by anything as powerful and consuming as a lovely young woman called Shona McKenzie. For the first time in my life I was at the mercy of my emotions, when reason and intelligence were powerless.'

Deeply moved by his words, Shona swallowed down the emotional lump that had risen in her throat. 'You—you don't love her, do you, Zack?'

He shook his head. 'No. I have never felt love for her—and she has none for me. I don't want to marry Caroline. I was driven to it out of necessity.'

'But you would have married her all the same—had you not married me and had Lady Donnington not taken a lover.'

'To claim my daughter—that was what I intended.'

'And you have known Lady Donnington for some time?'

He nodded, his face grim. 'Yes, but not well. She was a friend of a friend. Her upbringing was stricter than most. We were never close. When I came home after a long voyage, she had married Donnington. He was an old man, a mean, arrogant, impotent man, who resented the loss of his youth. He married Caroline to feed his vanity. I found her alone one day—lonely, unhappy and weeping.'

'And you comforted her.' He nodded. 'And one thing led to another.'

'Something like that. We—'

'Please,' Shona interrupted sharply, her voice trembling with anger. 'I don't need to be given a more explicit explanation of what occurred between you. I can picture it clearly—a beautiful desperately lonely woman, an elderly husband and a strong, virile man. Oh, yes,' she scoffed, unable to conceal her bitterness, 'I understand very well. When you realised I was your wife you should have had our marriage annulled. Lady Donnington is the mother of your child. Despite any obstacles, you should have reconciled yourself with her and put your daughter first—both of you. I happen to believe that a child belongs with both its parents. I'm sorry I put you in this predicament,' she said on a calmer note. 'Do you intend for Victoria to live with us?'

Zack's eyes scrutinised her face as he wondered how to tell her that since Victoria's own mother didn't want her, this was what he intended. 'The situation is complicated.'

There was a look in his eyes that alerted Shona. 'Zack, you can't take a child from its mother.'

'I won't be. Victoria doesn't live with Caroline. Her husband refused to allow Victoria to live in his house. Rather than leave him and her assumed inheritance on his death, Caroline fostered our daughter out.'

Shona stared at him. Suddenly she glimpsed in his eyes the pain of a man deeply wounded. In their depths she saw a plea, though she was not sure what he was pleading for. She tried to conceal the shock she felt, unable to understand how a woman could abandon her child to a foster mother, but without success. 'That is quite shocking. A child belongs with its mother.'

'Normally that would be the case. Caroline doesn't see it that way. Victoria's future is something that has to be decided, but for her sake it is important that you and I are united. Since her mother doesn't want her, it is my intention that she makes her home with us in a secure and loving family environment.'

Shona was deeply saddened that Lady Donnington had put position and wealth above the happiness of her daughter. 'I see. In fact, I'm beginning to see it all now—and why you seduced me into your bed,' she uttered with a sudden burst of resentment for the hurt he had caused her, regretting her remark the moment it passed her lips when she reminded herself of Zack's own suffering.

'I took you to my bed because you are my wife and a very sensual woman. From the moment we met I was attracted to you. I wanted you—very badly, Shona. Don't deny that you felt the same. The moment I looked into your eyes I knew it. Caroline couldn't hold a candle.'

'Perhaps I did know it,' she admitted, 'but your purpose has become clear to me now. This is why you wouldn't have our marriage annulled—so that I could be a stepmother to your daughter. Is this why you took me to your bed, to make it harder for me to leave you?'

'You are mistaken if you think that. It is the future that counts, Shona. We are man and wife and we'll have to make the best of it.' Realising how insensitive he sounded, he added quickly, 'We didn't have the best beginning, I know, but we can make a fresh start.'

'I assume that because you and Lady Donnington walk with your daughter openly in the park, it is acknowledged that she is your daughter.'

Zack nodded. 'I don't care what society thinks. I am not proud of my conduct, Shona. But I have paid for my sin in my own way. I am still paying,' he remarked quietly, almost as an afterthought. 'Until now, repressing the rumours meant I could not lavish affection on my offspring, which is a father's right.'

'Perhaps you should have thought of that before you took Lady Donnington to your bed,' Shona retorted. Was it her feelings for him that made such bitter jealousy twist her heart? 'I understand the way of the world and that many ladies have doubtless met this same situation many times and shrugged it off with a smile and a witty phrase. I cannot do that and I am not ashamed of it. Everything inside me recoils from doing so.'

A shutter came down over her eyes and Zack was shocked as she turned her face away sharply. It was then that the first shivers of disquiet began to feather themselves down the length of his spine. He was concerned. He knew of stepmothers who loathed the very sight of their husband's offspring, be it to a previous wife or mistress, and would have nothing to do with them. He prayed to God that this was not the case with Shona. It had not occurred to him that she might not want Victoria, that she might see her as a burden she would be forced to endure.

In the space of a second the realisation that

this might apply to Shona stunned him. His body became taut, his face a hard, grinding mask, his hands clenching and unclenching at his sides as he tried to bring his feelings under control. Was the sweet drift of happiness he had felt on finding Shona again and becoming reconciled under threat once more? *Dear Lord,* he prayed in twisted torment, *don't let me have to choose between my wife and my daughter.*

He looked at her. His face was expressionless. His eyes were empty, a dark emptiness that told Shona nothing of what he felt. 'Whatever hardships I have suffered, I cannot wish the damage undone, for to do that would be to wish my daughter had never been born. To my regret I was not able to save her from the stigma of illegitimacy. I can't give her up, Shona,' he said with quiet anguish. 'I will not.'

Shona could feel the raw emotion in him throbbing in her own veins. His words seemed to be a warning to her, final—*Do not interfere. I protect and keep what is mine.* She thought back to seeing him in the park with Lady Donnington. The memory of them together with their daughter between them was too intimate, too painful to bear. She lifted her chin and clasped her gloved hands tightly in front of her as she always did in moments of stress.

'Do you think I am so cruel, so heartless, that I would ask you to? I would never ask that of you.' Her own voice was husky with emotion. She thought it must have reassured him, for his intense expression relaxed infinitesimally.

Zack seemed deeply troubled. Shona looked at him, ready to do, or be, whatever he wished. She was young, but despite this she knew how to deal with loss and sorrow and her heart was warm and compassionate. She longed to offer words of comfort, but Zack Fitzgerald was a man always in control of his own emotions. Even now when they had been as close as two people could be, she would hesitate to probe into his thoughts. She wanted to believe his assurances, but she was still uneasy about his relationship with Lady Donnington. She was so beautiful. But this wasn't the only issue. The woman shared something with Zack that she, Shona, couldn't. A daughter.

A picture of the little girl she had seen in the park crept into her mind. She had been so lovely, so sweet, so full of life as she had skipped about. Lowering her eyes, she tried to get hold of her emotions, ashamed because they were so unadmirable. It wasn't commendable to be jealous of a small child just because she could command Zack's affection. Nor was it commendable to envy a woman her daughter. But she couldn't deny that she would have liked to have claimed Zack's love, or that she would have liked to have his daughter as her own.

'There isn't time to discuss this properly just now,' Zack said briskly. 'It's time we left. We will talk after the theatre.'

Shona nodded. At least by then she would have had time to collect herself. 'Before we go, I have something to give you.' She took an object wrapped in fine fabric from her reticule and handed it to him. 'You left it in my chamber at Melrose Hill. I'm sorry. I should have returned it to you sooner.'

Unwrapping it carefully, holding it gently in his hand, Zack gazed down at the locket. 'Thank you.' Something moved in the depths of his eyes. Without opening it, he said, 'It's a lock of Victoria's hair.' He shoved it in his pocket, unaware how thankful Shona was to hear him say that—that it belonged to the child and not the mother as she had always believed.

Shona managed to school her facial muscles into a semblance of equanimity as she stepped out of the coach at the Covent Garden theatre. The vision of pale gowns and glittering jewels was strangely blurred. She placed her fingers, which seemed to be trembling suddenly, in the waiting hand. With his composure held tightly about him as Zack escorted her into the theatre, she was still striving to throw off the odd feeling of unreality. At all costs, she must find something to interest her, she must try at least to look as if she was enjoying the play.

On meeting Harry and Miranda in the foyer, she turned a dazzling, forced smile on them, forcing herself to make polite conversation as they passed through the throngs of people on their way to their private box.

With her eyes fixed firmly on the stage, she sat with her arms pressed to her sides, her gloved hands folded in her lap. She was glad of the play. It meant she didn't have to speak to anyone. She had married Zack in the full knowledge that he did not love her, but the magic they had spun in the privacy of his bedroom had delighted her. She had given him her heart, but she supposed he was not aware of it. She had hoped he would come to love her, to give her his whole self, that inner self a man gives to one woman, only to

find another woman had prior claim to that—
and his daughter.

Turning her head slightly to her husband
seated on her right, she noticed that his face was
taut, his expression grim. His eyes were empty,
a glacial grey emptiness that told her nothing
of what he felt. As she sensed his dejection her
throat tightened. Perhaps it would be better if
she were to ask him again to set her free, but as
soon as this thought entered her mind, she realised how bleak her future would be without
him. With misery stabbing at her heart, she continued to look at the stage through a blur of tears.

Chapter Eleven

Zack was frustrated by the shuttered look that forbade any insight into his wife's thoughts as she focused her eyes on the stage. In the simple elegance of her golden silk gown, his breath caught in his throat as he watched the irresistible curve of her lips and the brilliance of her green eyes as they gazed at the performers.

Yet there was something remote and detached in the attitude of this dazzling creature. Observing her closely, he saw there was something mechanical in the smile pinned to her face. The love, the warmth and the passion that he had roused in her and had flourished in the times they had been together over the past few days had become frozen into this beautiful effigy. But he had never seen her look so provocatively lovely, so regal, glamorous and bewitching—and she belonged to him.

But did she?

Her remoteness told him that her feelings were no different now than they had been when he had told her about Victoria. Did she really want nothing to do with him or his daughter?

Regret surged upwards within him and was so intense, he was nearly taken aback by surprise. When he'd hatched out his plan to trick Shona on Santamaria, he had never dreamed he'd come to care so deeply for her since that time, but it seemed his reluctance to have their marriage invalidated was all for naught. He realised he had been foolhardy to nurture even a slender thread of optimism that she might wish their marriage to continue and could come to feel some wifely fondness for him and come to accept and love his daughter.

His thwarted aspirations were further sundered by a wilful pride that set his jaw to snapping. Maybe he had expected too much after all.

Finding herself alone with Miranda during the interval when Zack and Harry made themselves scarce, refusing to disgrace herself by revealing any of her emotions, Shona gave her a polite smile that was neither cool nor warm.

If Miranda noticed anything different in Shona's demeanour, she didn't show it, but she had an apology to make and it was long overdue. 'I'm glad of the opportunity to speak with you alone, Shona,' she said, her eyes filled with an odd kind of regret as they searched Shona's. 'I want to apologise for my outspoken remark when we met yesterday and beg your forgiveness. I hardly slept last night for thinking of the harm I might have caused between you and Zack. I really shouldn't have mentioned Caroline Donnington.'

Momentarily confused about the social technicalities of how she ought properly to respond to an apology from a viscountess, Shona gave up worrying about protocol and did what she could to soothe her obvious unease. 'Please don't trouble yourself about it,' she said with soft sincerity. 'Zack's association with Lady Donnington is not unknown to me—although I had no idea they had a daughter together until tonight.'

Miranda nodded, unsmiling, observing a deep sadness and forlorn look in Shona's wide eyes, and her instinct told her she was looking at an extremely unhappy young woman. 'That was remiss of him.' She laid a gentle hand on Shona's arm. 'I can't imagine how you must have felt, but you must have been terribly shocked. Shona, I think I know what is troubling you. But be assured that my brother-in-law will not dishonour his marriage vows with a mistress—even if that woman does happen to be the mother of his child.'

Shona felt her lower lip begin to tremble. Despairingly she turned her face away and drew in a deep breath to keep the tears from coming. 'Oh, Miranda, she is so beautiful.' The words were dredged from her throat, as if her fears had to be spoken out loud.

'You are underestimating your appeal. She is not as beautiful as you are.'

After a long moment, Shona got hold of herself and looked at her. 'Why is it,' she said with quiet vehemence, 'that I feel such…such resentment for Lady Donnington?'

Miranda chuckled. 'Because you're human, Shona, and you see your claim on your man being threatened. If you have the sense I think you do, you will fight for him.'

Shona stared at her. 'Fight? I was just contemplating asking him for a divorce.'

'Please don't do that. I doubt he would grant you one if you did.'

'Are you usually so frank and outspoken, Miranda?'

'It's my nature. Dear Harry scolds me about it all the time. Zack doesn't love Caroline—and with good reason. She has a lover, don't forget.'

Somehow this didn't quite console Shona. 'And now Zack has reappeared on the scene, will she cast aside her present lover in favour of Zack—the father of her child?'

'As to that, you will have to speak to him. Caroline Donnington's life has not always been a happy one, Shona. She is not all she seems.'

Shona glanced at her curiously. Zack had told her that Lady Donnington had married Lord Donnington against her will. She wondered how much Miranda knew about her, but she did not press her on the matter. 'Zack loves his daughter.'

'That's not the same thing and, God willing, you'll soon have a child of your own.'

Shona felt herself flushing. 'At the moment, bearing Zack's child seems highly unlikely.'

'It will be while you occupy separate houses. It's most unsatisfactory. If you carry on in this vein, you will both be dreadfully unhappy.' She gave Shona a look of cool scepticism. 'You do want him, don't you?'

'Of course I do. But what can I do? I cannot dominate him. I do not know how—and nor do I wish to.'

'Nonsense. You're a woman, Shona—and a woman can assert an inordinate power over a man if she can find a chink in his armour and push through.'

'Unfortunately our relationship took a knock this evening. When he told me about Lady Donnington and his daughter, I'm afraid I was not favourably receptive to the news. Naturally Zack was angry—as well as shocked and surprised by my reaction.'

'That is so like him. You wounded his male ego. Zack is marked with a proud arrogance and indomitable will. When their manhood is involved, men are such weak creatures. Believe me, my dear, being several years older than you and experienced enough, I know what I say.'

'I'm sure you do. I am prepared to expend all the patience I possess on breaking down the barriers that exist between us—namely Lady Donnington.'

'Of course you are, and if you learn to dominate him by his senses there is no reason why you cannot obtain what your heart desires most. It is just a matter of determination and application, and of careful ministering to the embers that glow within Zack. A beautiful woman can always work her will on a man and her arms are a powerful weapon when they embrace him. There comes a moment when his self-defence yields to his sensual desire,' Miranda said softly, her eyes twinkling wickedly. 'A clever and experienced woman can turn that into an advantage.'

Shona grimaced wryly. 'Experienced I most certainly am not, and at this moment I have my doubts about being clever.' She sighed.

'Rubbish!' Miranda exclaimed, not unkindly. 'I do not believe that for one moment. You strike me as being an extremely clever young woman. I think you should come and stay with us until you move into your house. I'll speak to Harry and we will arrange for you to move in tomorrow.'

Shona smiled for the first time as she shook her head. Harry must love his wife dearly. It was easy to guess what any man of discernment saw in such a generous, loving woman. 'Thank you,' she said simply, with gratitude for being accepted so unquestioningly. 'You have been very kind. From the time I spent at school in Hertfordshire, I know Colonists are often regarded unflatteringly as being ill-bred barbarians and I am sure you and your husband must have wondered what could have possessed Zack to marry one of them.'

'We can see why he did, Shona, and I am so glad.'

Nothing else was said, for at that moment Zack and Harry returned to take their places for the second half of the play. As the actors came back on to the stage, Shona was determined to make a concerted effort to somehow put things right between her and Zack before the night was over. If it meant unconditional surrender on her part, then so be it. She loved Zack too much to carry on this unpleasant argument about his daughter.

The idea of being with Zack, of being a proper wife, brought a soft smile to her lips. *Wife*. The word had a wonderful ring to it. A glow warmed her as she remembered his refusal to seek a divorce. It was what she had hoped for, a chance to prove to Zack that he hadn't made a terrible mistake in marrying her. Perhaps their relationship would be different now they had both accepted their marriage.

When the time came for them to leave the theatre, pleasantries were exchanged with Miranda and Harry as they waited for their carriages to draw up. When Shona was alone at last with Zack in the coach, drawing a deep breath and sinking into the upholstery, gazing across at his handsome face cast in shadow, she realised she really had fallen in love with him. That alone explained the delightful warm glow, the excited quivery feeling.

He was a dark, brooding presence in the confines of the coach, and he wore the same grim expression he had when they had been arguing over Lady Donnington and Victoria. Uncertain of his mood after their angry and extremely bitter exchange earlier, which had opened up so many painful wounds between them, she stole a surreptitious look at him.

'Did—did you enjoy the play?' she stammered for want of something to say to break the awkward silence. She was extremely uncomfortable with the dark way he was regarding her, his gaze narrowed and assessing.

'Not particularly. Did you?'

'I—I found it difficult to concentrate,' she admitted quietly.

'And why was that?'

'Because of what happened between us before that.'

'You certainly had plenty to say. Are you sorry?'

'Of course not.'

'Then there's nothing more to be said. But I won't apologise for Victoria, Shona. She's an important part of my life.'

'I do accept that, Zack. I am not heartless. If I upset you, then I apologise, but I do not retract one word. During the interval I spoke to Miranda. She—she is of the opinion that I should move out of Aunt Augusta's house and move in with you. She is bound to raise the matter with you. I—I just want you to be prepared.'

'Harry has suggested it.'

Zack fell silent. Distracted, he raised his head and studied his wife from beneath sceptical raised brows, unable to prevent his eyes moving over her shapely form and appreciating the subtle scent of her alluring perfume, which settled over him like an invisible, unrelenting net. His gaze became riveted on her lovely face, the softness in her large eyes and the delectable curve of her soft lips.

Shona was surprised that he hadn't more to say on the subject since, after showing her his house, he'd been voluble on his determination to have her move in with him.

'From your reaction, you…don't think it a good idea, do you?' she ventured. Was it her imagination or did he stiffen?

'Since you ask, Shona, I have it in mind to suggest that we give ourselves time to think over our relationship before actually proceeding one way or the other.'

They stared at each other for a long moment. Shona's eyes began to flash quietly. She would not beg him to live with her. Nor would she back down. Finally she broke the tense silence. 'I see—in which case I will go with Aunt Augusta in the morning when she leaves with Thomas to go to his parish in Berkshire.'

'Of course, your aunt and your cousin take precedence,' Zack replied snidely.

Shona was overwhelmed by his sarcasm. Taking a deep breath, she willed herself to be calm. Lifting her gaze to the carefully hooded eyes that studied her closely in return, how, she wondered, could she tell him what she had decided, that she intended to fight for their marriage? There was a strange silence while she searched about in her mind for something to say, but he turned his head away.

'I—I had hoped…' she murmured in a feeble

attempt to find out why he didn't want her to live with him.

'What?'

She sighed. 'Nothing.'

Suddenly going to Berkshire didn't seem such a bad idea after all. How could she have imagined he might have put behind him their bitter words of earlier! He was cold and cynical and hard, and he had a vicious, unpredictable temper. No man could make love to a woman one day, only to turn cold and hateful a day later because she disagreed with him. Didn't he know that he meant more to her than her trip to Berkshire? Couldn't he understand that she was desperately, hopelessly in love with him? Or had he foolishly imagined that because she had reacted badly to his disclosure about Lady Donnington and his daughter that she wanted no part of him? If he had, then he was both blind and witless! She allowed the hurt she felt and her impatience with such a notion to be conveyed with her own practicality.

'Aunt Augusta is naturally concerned about Thomas's decision to leave the church and how he will adjust to life without it. She has been very good to me and it is important to me that she has my support.'

Zack chafed in darkening humour. 'Of course. You must go.'

Looking down at her hands, Shona replied with all the serenity she could muster, 'I don't wish to inconvenience you in any way, Zack. At least, not any more than I have already done. Please proceed as you see fit.'

'In which case, Shona, I will spend some time with my daughter and see you when you return to London.'

Shona nodded rigidly, unable to force a verbal response through the choking misery welling up in her throat. It was a long moment before she realised she was gripping her hands with a tenseness that set her fingers aching. Looking out of the window and keeping her gaze fixed on the passing scenery, she eased her hands apart by slow degrees and managed to feign indifference even when Zack escorted her inside the house and left her without another word.

As Shona watched him go she sighed with frustration, knowing she had lost a prime opportunity to sort things out between them. With hurt and disappointment searing through her, she reproached herself severely for foolishly allowing herself to think that the softening of his attitude towards her at the theatre might mean he was prepared to put behind him their earlier differences. She now realised their minds were running along different lines, that his mind was well and truly shuttered against her.

As Shona lay in bed listening to the night sounds beyond the window, sleep evaded her. Her mind was on Zack, her heart filled with the warmth of her love. He was hurting in his efforts to do right by his daughter, whom he clearly loved and had a profound need to protect, and Shona's heart constricted when she realised that she might have given him the impression that she didn't want the child to have a place in their life together. Oh, what a fool he was if he thought that. She must tell him and would do that when she had told Aunt Augusta that she wouldn't be accompanying her to Berkshire after all.

There was no sign of Harry and Miranda when Zack arrived at the house. Pouring himself a stiff brandy, he suddenly remembered that friends had invited them to a supper party after the theatre and they wouldn't be back until later. Draining the contents of the glass, he poured himself another and settled into a chair by the fire.

Propping his feet on the fender, resting his head back and closing his eyes, he began trying to straighten out the confusing array of emotions beating at him. Suddenly he felt a heavy load of self-recrimination for the manner in which he had lashed out at Shona. The words were cruelly unjust and he knew it even as they spilled from his mouth, but it was the only way he had been able to keep the terrible thought at bay that she might not accept Victoria.

She was right. He had deceived her. And he was wrong. Why had he been so cold with her, hurting her, he knew, and she had been bewildered. He had never meant to hurt her in his desire to protect himself. They had come to know each other in some way that had nothing to do with the flesh. Nothing had been spoken between them that could be construed as an understanding of love, but their hearts had told them, their very souls had answered and her bewilderment was turning to anger, her very manner icing over.

She had taken him to task about his lack of morals—what else could he have expected? Shona's protected upbringing had never prepared her for such a situation and he should have known it. He was a fool. Facing the truth his heart had hidden, he knew that he loved her. She was the dearest, sweetest, most magnificent woman he'd known and he loved her so much he ached with it.

How long had he loved her? he asked himself curiously. The truth was that he didn't know. From the first moment he had seen her, probably, and he desperately wanted her love. Nothing made sense when he thought of her, in all her audaciousness, defiant and brave, her eyes blazing as she prepared to do battle with him and those same eyes docile and brimming with contentment after making love.

So what was he doing here in the house alone? She was his wife, for God's sake! They were meant to be together, not living in separate houses and sleeping in separate beds—each of them wrapped up in hurt and anger—and alone. The whole point of showing her his house and taking her to his bed had been to cement the bond between them. He had not anticipated the effect making love to her would have on *him*. He was quite certain that he could not survive the bleakness he'd feel if she turned away from him.

Getting to his feet, he strode to the door. Unable to bear the thought of her going to Berkshire, he would go to her and persuade her to stay. Someone rang the doorbell. The butler opened the door just as he was crossing the hall. A woman stood there, a maid he recognised. She worked for Mrs Young, the woman who looked after his daughter.

Something dark began to form in his mind. He looked at her hard. Something was wrong. The suspense hovered thickly and ominously. 'What is it? Has something happened to Victoria?'

'Yes, sir. She—she became poorly this afternoon and is running a high fever. Mrs Young has sent for Dr Coleman. She says you should come at once.'

The following morning, with a new understanding of her own feelings and wishing she understood his, Shona lost no time in going to see Zack. She was disappointed that he was not at home but when Miranda told her the reason why, feeling the grief Zack must be going through and desperately wanting to be with him, she immediately ordered the driver to take her to Mrs Young's house.

Mrs Young opened the door herself and ushered her inside. She was a small woman, her neatly arranged, fading dark hair crowning a smooth, intelligent face and shrewd grey eyes. Her graceful movements, calm features and soft voice disguised a formidable efficiency and energy. She smiled a warm welcome when Shona introduced herself as Lord Harcourt's wife.

'Lord Harcourt has been here all night. Would you like me to tell him you're here?'

'No—thank you. I'll go straight in, if I may.'

In the dim light of the room Shona saw him. He had his back to her. The light shone on his strong, strikingly beautiful hands braced against the mantelpiece. He had discarded his coat, waistcoat and neckcloth and, above his breeches, his fine white linen shirt was stretched taut across his powerful shoulders. His head was bowed, his hair tousled, a heavy lock falling over his brow.

Shona might have stood there for a long time without moving if some animal instinct of Zack's had not made him sense someone's presence.

'Zack—I hope you don't mind me coming here?'

At the sound of her voice he turned his head slightly and she saw the stern pride stamped on that lean profile, his jaw as rigid as granite. In the agonised silence he looked at her for sev-

eral seconds, his face preoccupied and stony—
he looked like a man in the grip of a nightmare.

Shona moved towards him, her heart going
out to him. 'I'm so sorry about Victoria. I had
to come.'

His head came up and he peered at her.
Clothed in a dark green gown, her hair bound
with a ribbon in a single heavy fall down her
back, she was like a pale ghost haunting the
night.

'Shona?' Zack mouthed her name, his gaze
becoming fixed on her face, then he was striding across the room and she was in his arms. He
crushed her to him, his anguish so great, so tearing, that it carried him beyond all boundaries.
He was totally unprepared for the feelings and
the emotions that almost overwhelmed him. He
continued to hold her, trying to absorb her body
into his. They stayed like that for a long time.
He was feeling all the tautness slowly draining
from his muscles.

Shona was too deeply moved to speak. After
what seemed like an eternity she raised her head
and looked at him, loving him, her eyes moist
with tears. 'I would like to stay—if you don't
mind.'

'I'd like you to,' he replied, his voice hoarse

with emotion. Placing his hands on either side of her face, he gently kissed her lips. 'I'm glad you're here. Thank you for coming.'

'How could I not? How is Victoria?' She stared into his pain-filled eyes. They were bloodshot, his lids heavy, stark evidence of his tortured night as he had kept vigil over his beloved daughter.

'The doctor says she is over the worst. It was some kind of fever. There are always fevers in children—fevers with names and many without. There was nothing to be done, the doctor said, but to let it run its course. Luckily Victoria is well nourished and stronger than most children.'

Remembering the little girl she had seen in the park—a bonny-spirited, healthy child with the rounded cheeks and plump limbs of the well fed—she felt a lump come into her throat and her heart turn over with pity.

'How did you know to come here?' Zack asked.

'I called at the house, wanting to surprise you. Instead I was the one to be surprised when I arrived and found you were not there. Miranda told me what had happened and so I came here.'

'And here I was thinking you would be halfway to Berkshire by now.'

'I decided not to go. I couldn't. I couldn't leave things as they were between us.'

Seeing her concern, Zack closed his fingers around her arms. 'Shona—will you please tell me what this is all about?'

She hated having to confess, but it didn't matter any longer how she humbled herself before him. She started to explain, but her throat was so tight she found it hard to speak. 'After the theatre, when…when I got to thinking about everything—the awful things we said to each other last night—I realised I might have given you the impression that I didn't want Victoria. If I did, then I am so very sorry, Zack. The truth is that I was confused. I suppose I was jealous of Caroline. I—I thought you might still have feelings for her despite your denial—and that perhaps you are sorry you married me.' With tears not far away, Shona pulled her arms from his hands and turned from him.

Zack frowned, as though puzzled himself. Standing behind her, he put his hands gently on her shoulders and drew her to his chest. 'If you mean do I wish I'd married her, I don't,' he murmured, his mouth touching the crown of her head just where the thick golden hair parted. You're the only woman I ever *wanted* to marry—believe me, my darling. You have nothing to fear. I feel nothing for Caroline. You must believe that. Please forgive me if I gave you that impression.'

With a convulsive movement she turned and flung herself into his arms, which tightened about her once more. Her head tucked itself beneath his chin and her face pressed itself into the curve of his throat.

'You wonderful, brave, incredibly beautiful woman,' he murmured against her hair. 'How could you think that? I never wanted to hurt you. It is you I love, Shona. How could I not love you? I love you more than anything on earth.'

Shona's breath caught in her throat and, raising her head, she looked up at him, suddenly feeling happy and secure. All the doubts and fears of the past days—weeks and months, even from the first time they had met on Santamaria—were gone. 'But—you never told me.'

'That's because it took me a while to realise it,' he said tenderly. 'And then there was so much going on between us that I was afraid to mention it until I was sure I stood a chance of winning your regard. I do love you, my darling Shona. Very much.'

Shona believed him, but the thought of Caroline would not go away. 'But—what about Caroline?'

'I've told you. She means nothing to me. It is you I want by my side for the rest of my life. Not Caroline.'

Hearing the gentleness in his voice, Shona drew back to search his rugged face. Sunlight slanting in through the windows highlighted his thick hair and increased the sharp clarity of his eyes, making it impossible for her to deny the love she saw there. She took a steadying breath, daring to believe. 'I thought I had lost you,' she whispered, a break in her voice, 'and I couldn't bear it.'

His mouth curved with amusement. 'Is that why you were going to Berkshire?'

'Partly.'

'Then let me put your mind at rest. Last night when I left you I did some serious thinking. I realised that I wanted you. I was just about to leave the house to return to you when someone came with a message from Mrs Young informing me about Victoria.'

'If only I had known. Has—has Victoria's mother been to see her?'

He shook his head, combing his hair back from his forehead. 'Not yet.'

'But—she has been informed of her daughter's illness?'

'Of course, but Caroline is a selfish wretch. I never knew how much until today. Ever since Victoria was born she's never shown any maternal instincts as a mother should. I cannot fathom what goes on inside her head, what makes her like she is. Perhaps it's a result of frustration caused by her strict upbringing, followed by a forced marriage to the equally strict and formidable Lord Donnington. Or maybe it's some flaw inherited from her family that has made her like she is. But she's not a bad person and would never hurt Victoria.'

Suddenly Shona glimpsed in his eyes the pain of a man deeply wounded by what he saw as Caroline's betrayal of her daughter. She tried to conceal the shock she felt, unable to understand how a woman could disregard her child when she most needed her, but without success.

'You made me aware of what happened between the two of you, Zack. That is not my concern. My concern is for your daughter, and to my mind a small child should be with its mother.'

Zack's lips curled scornfully. 'Normally that would be the case, but nothing Caroline has done since Victoria was born has been normal.'

'I'm beginning to realise that—but to abandon one's own flesh and blood in such a callous manner is not right. Does she not realise that what she is doing is sheer wickedness?' Shona burst out, unable to conceal her anger at the woman.

'I am aware of that, Lady Harcourt,' a woman's voice rang out from across the room. 'However, you may think of me what you like, but where Victoria is concerned, regardless of how it looks, I do care about my daughter.'

Zack stiffened when he looked round and saw Caroline hovering in the doorway. Elegantly arrayed, tilting her chin in her usually proud manner, she slowly moved into the room.

'So you have finally decided to come and ask after Victoria, Caroline. I trust you slept well.'

Caroline was doing her best to remain steady in the face of what she thought would be a battle. She could see it on Zack's face and in his eyes, which were cold and as brittle as broken glass.

Shona moved away from him. 'Excuse me. I'll step outside while you talk.'

'No.' Zack gripped her arm. 'Stay, Shona. You are my wife and I would like you to hear whatever Caroline has to say.' His cold eyes settled on Caroline. 'What the hell does it take to make you love Victoria?'

'I'm sorry. I've been out of town and have only just got back. I had no idea Victoria was ill.

You must believe that. I would have come right away had I known. Mrs Young has told me she is over the worst—thank God.'

'Indeed,' Zack ground out coldly. 'When children fall ill it is dealt with reasonably and one does not evade one's responsibilities. Her illness and your lack of concern makes me all the more determined to have her with me. Unfortunately there is no legal way to adopt a child in England, but I should tell you that I am seeking to obtain legal custody as Victoria's guardian through the courts.'

Caroline looked at him, turning his words over in her mind, then she nodded. There was something new in her eyes—remorse. 'I won't contest it. You have my word. I will sign whatever papers are necessary. I know what I have done is wrong—that I have not been the best mother.'

'Too damned right you haven't,' Zack bit back, surprised to see her eyes glazed with what he thought must be tears. 'What's this, Caroline? Regret?'

Caroline paled and looked strangely meek and humble. 'It's a terrible thing—regret,' she replied with a break in her voice. 'It plagues you—never leaves you alone. I'm not proud of the way I've treated our daughter.' She looked at Shona in beseeching appeal. 'I had wondered if Zack had told you about Victoria and now I know. I hope you love her as sincerely as if she were your own. I hope you will allow me to write to her on occasion—that I can still see her. I would be grateful. You won't stop me doing that, will you? I am still her mother when all is said and done.'

Shona met her gaze. She had expected to feel a stab of painful jealousy on coming face-to-face with the woman whose child had become her stepchild, but she felt nothing other than a profound pity and a new understanding. Before her was a woman whose life had been shaped by a strict upbringing. Her parents, with their toe in the door of society and meaning to get themselves firmly inside, had forced their daughter into marriage with an austere, impotent old man she did not even like. These were not qualities to recommend him to a young girl whose heart and mind would be full of dreams and yearnings of handsome, virile young men who would sweep her off her feet.

It was easy to see how, in a moment of weakness, all the loneliness that was past and still to come had flooded up within her, bursting out of her control. And Zack had been there to take her in his arms, trying to soothe and comfort her until they had settled their wants and needs in the age-old way. She must have suffered all the torments of the damned when she had produced a child as a result of that one weakness. Her husband, refusing to acknowledge its existence to avoid scandal and shame, had made her cast the child aside.

Seeing the pain and sadness in the other woman's eyes, Shona said nothing for a moment, then she nodded. 'We are not here to indulge in the rights and wrongs of the situation and it is not my place to judge you, Lady Donnington. Victoria has to be our main concern and I give you my word that when she is well and Zack brings her to live with us, she will be loved and cared for. You will be able to see her whenever you wish.'

'Thank you,' Caroline said, meeting Shona's eyes directly. 'I think you really mean that.'

'Yes, I do.'

'I do appreciate that. I don't think I could be so generous, were I in your position.' On a sigh Caroline turned from them. 'I'll go and see Victoria.' At the door she turned and looked back, her dimples once again in evidence. 'I should tell you that Robert has asked me to marry him. I have accepted, of course. Our betrothal is to be announced in *The Times* tomorrow. Will you wish me well, Zack?'

Zack smiled sardonically. 'Your marriage is not high on my list of reasons to celebrate just now, Caroline. But, yes, I do.'

When Caroline had left them, transfixed, Zack stared down at his wife sagely, a flash of pride in his eyes. He was strangely moved by what she had just done. 'That was very noble of you, Shona. You are an extraordinary woman.'

The compliment warmed her. She couldn't mistake the approval in the tender smile Zack gave her. It was reward enough, she decided, for her efforts to quell her jealousy. 'And you are an extraordinary man.' She smiled and laid her head against his warm, strong chest. 'Most people would not have allowed me to say that to her when we had not even been introduced.'

'Well,' he said slowly, as though carefully choosing each word, 'I suppose everything happens for the best. I've been bitter ever since Victoria was born and I was unable to give her a proper home—but now I can see the good that can come out of it. I hope Caroline appreciates your generosity.'

Shona sighed, the firelight casting shades of gold across her pensive face. 'Have I really done the right thing? You are not angry with me?'

'Far from it,' he murmured, taking her hand and kissing her fingers. 'Caroline is still Victoria's mother. I would not deny her the right to see her. Although she might have to wait a while. When Victoria is well enough I'm planning to take her down to Harcourt Hall. Some country air will be good for her. It will also be a chance for the two of you to get to know each other.'

Shona smiled. 'I would like that. I look forward to meeting her. I hope we can be friends.'

'You will be. She won't be able to resist you.'

She looked up lovingly into his silver-grey eyes. His tender words inspired her. 'Might we stay there for a while? London holds no attraction for me just now and I do so love the English countryside.'

He grazed his knuckle along the curve of her cheek. 'I don't see why not. We need time together and my business can be conducted from Harcourt. Besides, it is your home now. Our home.'

Shona kissed his lips lightly. 'Thank you,

Zack. It would seem that everything has been resolved happily at last.'

'The happiest thing of all is that Victoria will recover and the situation between us has been resolved,' he answered, the scent of her perfume making his senses reel. The glow from the fire was shining on her, warming her eyes. He had never wanted her more and he longed for the moment when they could be together in the privacy of their room and he could awaken all that was sensual in her nature. 'I do not deserve you. I'm sorry, Shona. Last night I spoke in bitterness and anger, wounding you without meaning to. If I had driven you away, it was only what I deserved—especially after what I did to you on Santamaria…'

'Hush,' she whispered, putting her fingers on his lips to silence him. 'It is in the past.'

'When your brother insisted that I should marry you, I was repulsed by the very idea of having my life laid out and being forced to commit to something I had not thought of myself. Yet much as I wanted to rebel against it, I found myself wanting you, more than I have wanted anyone or anything in my life.'

Shona's heart soared and his confession brought a smile to her lips. Nothing else mattered but the fact that he wanted her, that she was his wife and she was not going to lose him. Her life was so complete and wholly absorbed in him.

Epilogue

One week later Shona looked at the pretty little girl clinging to Zack as he carried her into his brother's house. She was an extremely pretty child. Her dark brown hair fell in gentle waves about her oval face, which was pale and delicate following her illness. Her brown eyes fringed with sooty-black lashes were searching Shona's intently. Praying silently for acceptance, Shona smiled softly, gently touching her cheek, hoping to put her at ease.

'Hello, Victoria. I've been looking forward to seeing you so much. Your father's told me all about you. I do hope we can be friends.'

'This lady is my wife, Princess—your stepmother,' Zack explained gently.

Victoria looked at Shona a little uncertainly. She didn't see her own mother very much and

was unsure what a stepmother was. A little smile
began to appear at the corners of her mouth.
She seemed to be assessing her. When her eyes
ceased to regard her so seriously and her smile
gradually broadened, which was a delight to see,
Shona began to relax. It also brought a relieved
smile to Zack's features, which told Shona how
apprehensive he had been about this meeting
between herself and his daughter.

It really was a breathtaking smile that lit up
the child's face. In the dimpling creases in her
cheeks, in the lovely directness of her gaze,
Shona could clearly see Victoria's resemblance
to Zack.

Victoria looked up at her father and said very
softly, 'Can I be the lady's friend, Papa?'

'I think she would like that.' His eyes twinkled at his wife.

'What shall I call her?' Victoria asked with a
little frown creasing her pretty nose.

Sitting beside her husband and taking Victoria's hand in hers, Shona said, 'Why don't you
call me Shona? I would like that.'

'That's a pretty name,' Victoria replied.
'Shona.'

Shona sensed that Victoria hadn't known
much kindness in her short life—only that

shown to her by Zack and Mrs Young. And she was right. Victoria didn't understand the significance of this strange woman's relationship to her father. But her presence and her soft words had a comforting effect on her and she smiled, her soft pink lips opening like a tiny rosebud.

As the lowering sun was beginning to stain the sky with swirls of pink and blue, with sunset hues that lit the trees and turned the glittering river to gleaming gold, it touched upon Harcourt Hall's ancient stones with a honey-toned hue and gave the mullioned windows a fiery glow.

Zack and Shona stood on the terrace, watching Victoria indulgently as she scampered about the lawn surrounded by lovingly cared-for gardens. They could see that she was responding to the love that was being wrapped around her. Zack had presented her with a puppy that very day and the two were noisily getting to know each other.

'Which of them will tire first, do you think?' Shona asked as her husband's arms snaked about her waist and he hugged her to him.

'There's a question,' he murmured, nuzzling her neck. 'Would you care to place wager?'

Shona laughed on being reminded of the time

she had bid five hundred guineas for his pleasure. 'I don't think so. I did that once before and look where my recklessness got me.'

Brushing her hair aside, Zack chuckled softly as his lips caressed her nape. 'Into my bed, as I recall.'

'I remember it well.' Sliding her hands along his arms, she sighed with contentment as Victoria ran and skipped and attempted a cartwheel before tumbling harmlessly on to the puppy. 'Thank you for bringing me to this. There is so much peace in this world of ours.'

'It was my pleasure. What did your brother have to say?' he asked, curious as to the contents of her brother's letter which had arrived earlier.

'Not much—you know Antony—except that Carmelita has been delivered of her baby, a boy. He's to be called Colin—after our father. Naturally Antony's very happy—an heir for Melrose Hill. I also had a letter from Aunt Augusta— she's to visit very soon. She also told me that Thomas has taken ship for Virginia. At last he has what he always wanted.'

'And you, Shona—do you miss the island?'

'Sometimes, but then I look around me—at this beautiful place—and when I think of you and Victoria, I know this is where I want to be.'

'I love you,' he whispered, kissing her cheek with boyish sweetness, knowing he would wake in the morning as he had done every morning for the weeks they had been together at Harcourt, in a state of luxurious bliss. His body would be heavy and sated from loving her and he would stretch, knowing her womanly body was next to him.

A burst of joy would explode inside him when he remembered the night past and he would know that all was well with the world.

* * * * *

A sneaky peek at next month...

HISTORICAL

IGNITE YOUR IMAGINATION, STEP INTO THE PAST...

My wish list for next month's titles...

In stores from 4th April 2014:

- ❏ Unlacing Lady Thea — Louise Allen
- ❏ The Wedding Ring Quest — Carla Kelly
- ❏ London's Most Wanted Rake — Bronwyn Scott
- ❏ Scandal at Greystone Manor — Mary Nichols
- ❏ Rescued from Ruin — Georgie Lee
- ❏ Welcome to Wyoming — Kate Bridges

Available at WHSmith, Tesco, Asda, Eason, Amazon and Apple

Just can't wait?

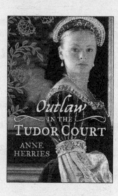
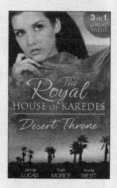